Charles Dickens, Robert Henry Newell

The Cloven Foot:

Being an Adaptation of the English Novel

Charles Dickens, Robert Henry Newell

The Cloven Foot:
Being an Adaptation of the English Novel

ISBN/EAN: 9783337001032

Printed in Europe, USA, Canada, Australia, Japan

Cover: Foto ©Andreas Hilbeck / pixelio.de

More available books at **www.hansebooks.com**

THE CLOVEN FOOT:

BEING

AN ADAPTATION OF THE ENGLISH NOVEL

"THE MYSTERY OF EDWIN DROOD,"

(By Charles Dickens,)

TO AMERICAN SCENES, CHARACTERS, CUSTOMS, AND NOMENCLATURE.

BY

ORPHEUS C. KERR,

AUTHOR OF "THE ORPHEUS C. KERR PAPERS," ETC.

NEW YORK:

Carleton, Publisher, Madison Square.

LONDON: S. LOW, SON & CO.

MDCCCLXX.

CONTENTS.*

* The titles of Chapters in "*The Mystery of Edwin Drood*" are as follows : I., The Dawn ; II., A Dean, and a Chapter also ; III., The Nuns' House ; IV., Mr. Sapsea ; V., Mr. Durdles and Friend ; VI., Philanthropy in Minor Canon Corner ; VII., More Confidences than one ; VIII., Daggers Drawn ; IX., Birds in the Bush ; X., Smoothing the Way ; XI., A Picture and a Ring ; XII., A Night with Durdles ; XIII., Both at their Best ; XIV., When shall these Three meet again? XV., Impeached ; XVI., Devoted ; XVII., Philanthropy, Professional and Unprofessional ; XVIII., A Settler in Cloisterham ; XIX., Shadow on the Sun-Dial ; XX., A Flight ; XXI., A Recognition ; XXII., A Gritty State of Things comes on ; XXIII., The Dawn again — . . . .

APOLOGY.

As the work upon which the great Master of modern English Fiction was engaged when death claimed all of him that could die, the half-finished *Mystery of Edwin Drood*, possesses a quality far beyond the estimation of literary criticism; and, by the sympathetic eloquence even of its incompleteness, is more preciously suggestive of the immortal Writer's own mortal personality than is any one of the many inimitable creations that his genius was permitted to complete. Perused with an understanding of the intimate relations existing between intellectual endeavor and physical and moral passivity, it has a positively painful interest, as a revelation of the tired Worker in the Work never to be finished; nobly striving to compass the round fulness of a living reality from a dying dream, and, in the occasional unconscious despair of prophetic instinct, involuntarily showing fate-struck Nature upon the page as the evening shadow, and the prayer, of faltering Art.

The Story, opening with an elaboration of masterly purpose in which the strength of intense concentration for a moment counterfeits the strength of spontaneity, soon

halts with the halting power of the Story-teller so near his
rest; then turns intractable and prone to break beneath
the relaxing hand uncertain of its former cunning; a little
later, shows the indomitable mind, constrained almost convulsively to a greater light because of the approaching
shadow of the body's dissolution, and in its darkening premo-
nitions throwing a shadow of that shade, and even a defined portion of the physical struggle against it,* upon the
wavering mimic scene; and, at last, breaks off, half told,
to remain the tenderest of all its Master's stories — the story
of his Death!

If as *that*, alone, the *Mystery of Edwin Drood* could be
accepted and 'estimated by the critic, its completeness in
incompleteness would be questioned by none; but, as an
effort of art, in which the artist still lives, it has, and must
have, another aspect; and in the latter is the justification of
such exacting commentary, as unprejudiced literary judgment may properly award, to any published work challeng-
ing its verdict. The half of the novel which we have, is
unmistakable evidence that another half could not possibly
have formed a whole in any way equal to the standard
which the author's previous triumphs had erected for himself.
To read it critically, is to believe readily the current report,
that its writer regarded it with peculiar uneasiness, as a

---

* It is well known that Mr. Dickens passed so many hours daily in the open air, to
keep down that inherited sanguine tendency to the brain, of which he ultimately
died. See opening of Chapter XII. and note to Chapter XIV.

task in which he was anything but confident of artistic success, and that, after committing its first monthly numbers to the press, he expressed to several friends a fear that it might injure his literary reputation. The art of Dickens, like that of all great genius, comes by the immediate inspiration of his unpremeditated sympathy with what, to others, might seem the most unlikely of human subjects ; and it becomes a mere forced and lifeless imitation of itself, when, as in this case, anticipated and pledged for a deliberately complicated plot and what is called a psychological study of abnormal character. *Mr. Jasper*, the central personage of the *Mystery*, is an unwholesome monstrosity, of which the writer of " David Copperfield," even in the fullest flush of his matchless powers, could never have made happy imaginative use ; and, from his first appearance in the narrative, there is an overwrought laboriousness of mystification about him which, in illustration of extremes meeting, has very soon the awkward effect of making him no mystery at all. The design of representing a man with a dual existence, in one phase of which he intends to, and thinks he does, commit murder, while in the other he confounds the deed and doer with a personality distinct from his own, is kept so nervously apparent at the beginning, as a justification of the plotted *dénoûment*, that any reader fairly skilled in the necessary artistic relations of one part of a story to another, must derive therefrom a premature knowledge of what the designer supposably wishes to conceal for the time being. The

1*

author could scarcely have been without some presentiment of this likelihood, while striving to manipulate an artificial type of character so wholly unnatural to his wholesome, straightforward genius; and the depressing effect upon himself is plainly to be seen, not more in furthers pasmodic excesses of shade, than in the falsity of his unequalled Humor to itself, in such a mechanical " side light" as *Mr. Sapsea.*

It is because his Adaptation of *The Mystery of Edwin Drood* serves, in unavoidable proportion to its fidelity, to make prominent the artistic infelicities of the latter, that the adapter has ventured such a preface as the foregoing to his apology for turning the serious work of an illustrious foreign writer to ludicrous native use.

As one not without some studious knowledge of the scope and various approved methods of art in Fiction, and practice in the difficulties of American novel-writing, the present scribe has more than once employed the sober print of literary journalism to assert his belief, that the notorious lack of the higher order of imaginative writing in this Country is due rather to the physical, social, and artistic crudity of the Country itself, than to its deficiency in that order of genius which has given to older lands their greater poets, artists, and novelists. Commenting, not long ago, upon Mr. Disraeli's " Lothair," as a striking social and artistic study, he wrote :

" The American literary student has in this elegant work of fiction a most useful hint respecting the practicabilities of an American novel. It has scarcely any mechanical plot; yet its interest as a narrative never flags for an instant. It abounds in dialogue upon trite subjects; yet that dialogue always possesses a marked intellectual value for its evidence of a high mental class-cultivation. In short, 'Lothair' is such a novel as could not be written of a country like ours with the smallest chance of being anything but drearily commonplace. We have our mercantile palaces on Fifth Avenue, our gorgeous assemblies of fashion, our men of score millions, our expensive churches and proselyting clergy; but they are all of yesterday, they are without tradition or history, and the wonders of swift creation that they give to fact would furnish but prosaic monstrosities to the graceful hand of Disraelitish fiction. Journalists who prate about the lack of first-class imaginative writing here at home, and pretend to designate materials for the native romancer, commit a great mistake in presuming that a novel of society is the work offering choicest matter and opportunity to the coming master of home fiction. Your figures and their action in the foreground will make but a cheap photograph, if there is no suggestive background; and it is lack of *permanent romantic background* for his picture that places the novelist of American higher society in the position either of a didactic social essayist, or of a satirist of the caprices of shopkeeping fortune. In former days, the South, with its patriarchal and feudal usages, offered a background upon which our only American novels proper were drawn. What artistic possibilities there still may be in that section are only to be ascertained by future experiment ; but there can be little doubt that the general American field of opportunities for the writer of fiction lies rather in the picturesquery of Western adventure, or the dramatic contrast of the extremes of wealth and poverty in the great cities, than in the lives and abodes of the native social class superficially corresponding with the foreign social strata celebrated by ' Lothair.' The first rightly-directed step toward effective novel-writing in America must be inspired by a determination to discard all existing foreign models as thoroughly impracticable, and a courage to treat what there is of the genuinely picturesque and dramatic in American life with an originality of style and method suited especially to American subjects. Wholesome strength, rather than poetical daintiness, must be the great characteristic of the romancer ; and his characters must be made to think and act and talk like Americans only."

To the above, after quoting it, a literary publication of high character * replied :

" There is, doubtless, a large share of truth in all this ; but we must still hope that a competent artistic skill would be able to make of our social pictures something more than a ' cheap photograph.' The absolute mastership of fictitious writing, as an art, is the great need. Washington Irving succeeded in giving to the Hudson a series of legends that attach a classic interest to its shores, such as no other locality

* " Appleton's Journal."

in America possesses; Hawthorne could give to the rudest incidents of colonial life every quality of picturesque mellowness. But these men had the superior artistic touch, and this is a gift or attainment that always seems to us peculiarly lacking in American literature. When the accomplished master shall appear, we hope he will show us how ordinary American life may be photographed in blending, contrasted, and vivid groups, without that rawness that marks the ordinary attempts to portray us."

An accomplished theatrical critic* also attacked the proposition, in its implied bearing upon the drama, and said :

" I am of opinion that men in America have the same inscrutable hearts, prone to love and hate and lie and venerate, that beat in the jungles of Africa or the saloons of London : they are swayed by pretty much the same vices and animated by the same virtues; swollen with vanity or collapsed with humiliation; roaring, defying, praying, suffering, achieving, and dying — everywhere with the same desperation or devoutness. Our women, too, are they not as vain, as self-sacrificing, as tender, as trivial, as any in Bath or Baden? Are they not everywhere the same, if we come to look at them narrowly; with immortal souls under their caprices and carmine, drawn by the same mysterious destiny this way and that ?

"Society, then, even in America, is, first of all, flesh and blood, with souls in it, and plays its own intense and multi-

* Mr. A. C. Wheeler, in the *World* newspaper,

form comedy of life in our homes and hovels with as much meaning as if it felt the pressure of all the ages since Adam, and were lifted occasionally by the promise of as great a hereafter as exists for communities whose art is older. Are they not the fit subjects for that elder art which seeks the remote and ideal beauty that is universal? Or are they, with all their kinship of flesh and immortality, to be weighed only for their manners in this balance ?"

To both of whom the answer, in part, was : "Mastery of art may enable the American novelist to plot a symmetrical fable, devise varied incidents, plan effective alternations of incidental light and shadow, and observe the various other mechanical requisites of fabulous construction ; yet, after all this, it is upon the specific social genius of the grade of life to be reflected that his own intellectual genius must depend for the yielding of *a defined Romantic interest* to the fiction. If that social genius is incorrigibly prosaic and crude, without stability from one day to another, and involving no single permanent principle of class prestige and distinction, the fabulating genius can make it romantically interesting only at the expense of fidelity to nature. Our American higher society, originating almost wholly as it does from the tendency of fluctuating wealth to spasmodic sensational luxury, and not from hereditary privilege or æsthetical aspiration, is informed much more by the logic of trade and the pride of financial energy than by the obligations of illustrious ancestry and the fine egotism of conscious superiority in class

cultivation. It is without normal body, it has no distinctive
manner, and its saliencies are better calculated to surprise
than interest. While such characteristics may be republican,
and creditable enough for reality, they are inexorable draw-
backs to the *romantic* interest of fictitious presentment ; and
no charm of literary style, nor *vraisemblant* effort of the imagination, can make them poetic."

It was after thus arguing the question seriously, and being
rather vexed at the apparent failure of his critics to appreciate his exact meaning — they talking about legends, and
figures in the foreground, while he, conceding those, con-
tended for present social coloring, permanent romantic background, and an atmosphere and a middle distance to give artistic body to the picture — that the present writer conceived
the idea of serio-comically demonstrating the assumed accuracy of his views by deliberately reducing the current work of
some great foreign novelist to American equivalents. Hence
the CLOVEN FOOT.

In the latter, the adapter has aimed to Americanize his
original as conscientiously as possible, while imitating, to
the best of his ability, the style and idiosyncrasies of the
English author. Mr. *John Jasper*, the English opium-smoker,
would, if transferred to this country, be scarcely other than
Mr. John Bumstead, the American clove-eater. For the
ancient city of Cloisterham, with its venerable Cathedral and
Nun's House, the nearest transatlantic match, in a majority
of respects, is the suburban Bumsteadville, with its Ritualistic

Church and Alms-House. The English *"Rosebud's"* equivalent by adaptation is the American " Flowerpot. " *Edwin Drood,* the not very brilliant young man of London, would be the mere boy in New York, — and so on through all the characters, scenes, and incidents of the Original and its Adaptation, as varied by the social genius, usages, and characteristics of either country.

To give the Adaptation all possible romantic illusion, an illustrated "Sketch of the Author" is also "adapted": and if, after this preliminary exposition, and the elucidation of the numerous foot-notes, the intelligent reader can still see no more than an indifferent joke in the ensuing pages, it may be as well for him to ask himself if he is so very intelligent, after all ?

O. C. K.

1870.

Dickens.

The homage of our world to thee,
  O Matchless Scribe! when thou wert here,
Was all that's loving in a Laugh,
  And all that's tender in a Tear.

So, if with quiv'ring lip we name
  The fellow Mortal who Departs,
A Smile shall call him back again,
  To live Immortal in our Hearts.

SKETCH OF THE ADAPTER.

It is now nearly a twelfth of a century since the veracious Historian of the imperishable Mackerel Brigade first man-œuvred that incomparably strategical military organization in public, and caused it to illustrate the fine art of waging heroic war upon a life-insurance principle. Equally re-nowned in arms for its feats and legs, and for being always on hand when any peculiarly daring retrograde movement was on foot, this limber martial body continually fell back

upon victory throughout the war, and has been coming forward with hand-organs ever since. Its complete History,
by the gentleman now adapting the literary struggles of Mr.
E. Drood to American minds and matters, was subsequently issued from the press of Carleton, in more or less
volumes, and at once attracted profound attention from the
author's creditors. One great American journal said of it :
"We find the paper upon which this production is printed
of a most amusing quality." Another observed : "The bind-
ing of this tedious military work is the most humorous we
ever saw. " A third added : "In typographical details, the
volumes now under consideration are facetious beyond compare."

The present residence of the successful Historian is Begad's Hill, New Jersey, and, if not existing in Shakspeare's
time, it certainly looks old enough to have been built at
about that period. Its architecture is of the no-capital Co-
rinthian order ; there are mortgages both front and back,
and hot and cold water at the nearest hotel. From the central front window, which belongs to the author's library, in
which he keeps his Patent Office Reports, there is a fine
view of the top of the porch ; while from the rear casements
you get a glimpse of blind-shutters which won't open. It is
reported of this fine old place, that the present proprietor
wished to own it even when a child ; never dreaming the
mortgaged halls would yet be his without a hope of re-sell-
ing.

Although fully thirty years of age, the owner of Begad's Hill Place still writes with a pen ; and, perhaps, with a finer thoughtfulness as to not suffusing his fingers with ink than in his more youthful moments of composition. He is sound and kind in both single and double harness ; would undoubtedly be good to the Pole if he could get there ; and, although living many miles from the city, walks into his breakfast every morning in the year.

THE CLOVEN FOOT.

[*The American Press's Young Gentlemen, when taking their shady literary walks among the Columns of Interesting Matter, have been known to remark — with a glibness and grace, by Jove, greatly in excess of their salaries — that the reason why we don't produce great works of imagination in this country, as they do in other countries, is because we haven't the genius, you know. They think — do they? — that the bran-new localities, post-office addresses, and official titles, characteristic of the United States of America, are rife with all the grand old traditional suggestions so useful in helping along the romantic interest of fiction. They think — do they? — that if an American writer could write a Novel in the exact style of Collins, or Trollope, or Dickens, only laying its scenes and having its characters in this country, the work would be as romantically effective as one by Collins, or Trollope, or Dickens; and that the possibly necessary incidental mention of such native places as Schermerhorn Street, Dobb's Ferry, or Chicago, wouldn't disturb the nicest dramatic illusion of the imaginative tale. Very well, then! All right! Just look here! — Oh! A. P's. Young Gentlemen, just look here —]*

CHAPTER I.

DAYLIGHT IN THE MORN.

A MODERN American Ritualistic Spire!* How can the modern American Ritualistic Spire be here? The well-known tapering brown Spire, like a closed umbrella on end! How can that be here? There is no rusty rim of a shocking bad hat between the eye and that Spire in the real pros-

* In the original, "an ancient English Cathedral Tower."

pect. What is the rusty rim that now intervenes, and confuses the vision of at least one eye ?   It must be an intoxicated hat that wants to see, too.   It *is* so, for ritualistic
choirs strike up, acolytes swing censers dispensing the heavy
odor of punch, and the ritualistic rector and his gaudily
robed assistants in alb, chasuble, maniple and tunicle, intone
a *Nux Vomica* in gorgeous procession.   Then come twenty
young clergymen in stoles and bivettas, running after twenty
marriageable young ladies of the congregation who have
sent them worked slippers.   Then followed ten thousand
black monkies swarming all over everybody and up and
down everything, chattering like fiends.   Still the Ritualistic
Spire keeps turning up in impossible places, and still the
intervening rusty rim of a hat inexplicably clouds one eye.
There dawns a sensation as of writhing grim figures of
snakes in one's boots, and the intervening rusty rim of the
hat that was not in the original prospect takes a snake-like
— but stay ! Is this the rim of my own hat tumbled all
awry? I' mushbe! A few reflective moments, not un-
relieved by hiccups, mush be d'voted to co-shid-ERATION of
th' posh'bil'ty.   .

Nodding excessively to himself with unspeakable gravity,
the gentleman whose diluted mind has thus played the
Dickens with him, slowly arises to an upright position by a
series of complicated manœuvres with both hands and feet ;
and, having carefully balanced himself on one leg, and shaking his aggressive old hat still further down over his left

eye, proceeds to take a cloudy view of his surroundings. He is in a room giving on one side to a bar, and on the other side to a pair of glass doors and a window, through the broken panes of which various musty cloth substitutes for glass ejaculate toward the outer Mulberry Street. Tilted back in chairs against the wall, in various attitudes of dislocation of the spine and compound fracture of the neck, are an Alderman of the ward, an Assistant-Assessor, and the lady who keeps the hotel.* The first two are shapeless with a slumber defying every law of comfortable anatomy ; the last is dreamily attempting to light a stumpy pipe with the wrong end of a match, and shedding tears, in the dim morning ghastliness, at her repeated failures.

"Thry another," says this woman, rather thickly, to the gentleman balanced on one leg, who is gazing at her, and winking very much. "Have another, wid some bitters."

He straightens himself extremely, to an imminent peril of falling over backward, sways slightly to and fro, and becomes as severe in expression of countenance as his one uncovered eye will allow.

The woman falls back in her chair again asleep, and he, walking with one shoulder depressed, and a species of sidewise, running gait, approaches and poises himself over her.

"What vision can *she* have?" the man muses, with his hat now fully upon the bridge of his nose. He smiles unexpectedly ; as suddenly frowns with great intensity ; and

* In the original, a low haunt of opium-smokers, in London.

involuntarily walks backward against the sleeping Alderman.
Him he abstractedly sits down upon, and then listens intently for any casual remark he may make.   But one word
comes — "Wairzernat'chal'zationc'tif'kits."

"Unintelligent !" mutters the man, wearily ; and, rising
dejectedly from the Alderman, lurches, with a crash, upon
the Assistant-Assessor.   Him he shakes fiercely for being so
bony to fall on, and then hearkens for a suitable apology.

"Warzwaz-yourwifesincome-lash' — lash'-year ? "

A thoughtful pause, partaking of a doze.

"Unintelligent ! "

Complicatedly arising from the Assessor, with his hat now
almost hanging by an ear, the gentleman, after various futile
but ingenious efforts to face toward the door by turning his
head alone that way, finally succeeds by walking in a circle
until the door is before him.   Then, with his whole countenance charged with almost scowling intensity of purpose,
though finding it difficult to keep his eyes very far open, he
balances himself with the utmost care, throws his shoulders
back, steps out daringly, and goes off at an acute slant
toward the Alderman again.   Recovering himself by a
tremendous effort of will and a few wild backward movements, he steps out jauntily once more, and cannot stop
himself until he has gone twice around a chair on his extreme left and reached almost exactly the point from which
he started the first time.   He pauses, panting, but with the
scowl of determination still more intense, and concentrated

chiefly in his right eye. Very cautiously extending his dexter hand, that he may not destroy the nicety of his perpendicular balance, he points with a finger at the knob of the door, and suffers his stronger eye to fasten firmly upon the same object. A moment's balancing, to make sure, and then, in three irresistible, rushing strides, he goes through the glass doors with a burst, without stopping to turn the latch, strikes an ash-box on the edge of the sidewalk, rebounds to a lamp-post, and then, with the irresistible rush still on him, describes a hasty wavy line, marked by irregular heel-strokes, up the street.

That same afternoon, the modern American Ritualistic Spire rises in duplicate illusion before the multiplying vision of a traveller recently off the ferry-boat, who, as though not satisfied with the length of his journey, makes frequent and unexpected trials of its width. The bells are ringing for vesper service; and, having fairly made the right door at last, after repeatedly shooting past and falling short of it, he reaches his place in the choir and performs voluntaries and involuntaries upon the organ, in a manner not distinguishable from almost any fashionable church-music of the period.

CHAPTER II.

A DEAN, AND A CHAP OR TWO ALSO.

WHOSOEVER has noticed a party of those sedate and Germanesquely philosophical animals, the pigs, scrambling precipitately under a gate from out a cabbage-patch toward nightfall, may, perhaps, have observed, that, immediately upon emerging from the sacred vegetable preserve, a couple of the more elderly and designing of them assumed a sudden air of abstracted musing, and reduced their progress to a most dignified and leisurely walk, as though to convince the human beholder that their recent proximity to the cabbages had been but the trivial accident of a meditative stroll.

Similarly, service in the church being over, and divers persons of piggish' solemnity of aspect dispersing, two of the latter detach themselves from the rest, and try an easy lounge around toward a side door of the building, as though willing to be taken by the outer world for a couple of unimpeachable low-church gentlemen, who merely happened to be in that neighborhood at that hour for an airing.

The day and year are waning, and the setting sun casts a ruddy but not warming light upon two figures under the arch of the side door ; while one of these figures locks the

door, the other, who seems to have a music-book under his
arm, comes out, with a strange, screwy motion, as though
through an opening much too narrow for him, and, having
poised a moment to nervously pull some imaginary object
from his right boot and hurl it madly from him, goes unexpectedly off with the precipitancy and equilibriously con-
centric manner of a gentleman in his first private essay on a
tight-rope.

"Was that Mr. Bumstead, Smythe?"*

"It wasn't anybody else, your Reverence."

"Say 'his identity with the person mentioned scarcely
comes within the legitimate domain of doubt,' Smythe — to
Father Dean," the younger of the piggish persons softly interposes.

"Is Mr. Bumstead unwell, Smythe?"

"He's pretty bad to-night."

"Say 'incipient cerebral effusion marks him especially
for its prey at this vesper hour,' Smythe — to Father Dean,"
again softly interposes Mr. Simpson, the Gospeller.†

"Mr. Simpson," pursues Father Dean,‡ whose name has
been modified, by various theological stages, from its original
form of Paudean, to Père Dean — Father Dean, "I regret
to hear that Mr. Bumstead is so delicate in health; you

---

* In the original, Mr. *John Jasper*, Chorister of the Cathedral; and *Tope*, a
Verger.

† In the original, *Mr. Crisparkle*, Minor Canon.

‡ In the original, "*the Dean.*"

may stop at his boarding-house on your way home, and ask
him how he is, with my compliments. *Pax vobiscum.*"

Shining so with a sense of his own benignity that the
retiring sun gives up all rivalry at once and instantly sets in
despair, Father Dean departs to his dinner, and Mr. Simpson, the Gospeller, betakes himself cheerily to the second-
floor-back, where Mr. Bumstead lives.   Mr. Bumstead is a
shady-looking man of about six-and-twenty, with black hair
and whiskers of the window-brush school, and a face reminding you of the Bourbons.   As, although lighting his lamp, he
has, abstractedly, almost covered it with his hat, his room is
but imperfectly illuminated, and you can just detect the
accordeon on the window-sill, and, above the mantel, an
unfinished sketch of a school-girl.   (There is no artistic
merit in this picture; in which, indeed, a simple triangle
on end represents the waist, another and slightly larger
triangle the skirts, and straight-lines with rake-like termina-
tions the arms and hands.)

"Called to ask how you are, and offer Father Dean's
compliments," says the Gospeller.

"I'm allright, shir!" says Mr. Bumstead, rising from the
rug where he has been temporarily reposing, and dropping
his umbrella.   He speaks almost with ferocity.

"You are awaiting your nephew, Edwin Drood?"

"Yeshir."   As he answers, Mr. Bumstead leans languidly
far across the table, and seems vaguely amazed at the aspect
of the lamp with his hat upon it.

Mr. Simpson retires softly, stops to greet some one at the foot of the stairs, and, in another moment, a young man fourteen years old enters the room with his carpet-bag.

" My dear boys !   My dear Edwins !"

Thus speaking, Mr. Bumstead sidles eagerly at the new-comer, with open arms, and, in falling upon his neck, does so too heavily, and bears him with a crash to the floor.

" Oh, see here ! this is played out, you know," ejaculates the nephew, almost suffocated with travelling-shawl and Bumstead.

Mr. Bumstead rises from him slowly and with dignity.

" Excuse me, dear Edwin ; I thought there were two of you."

Edwin Drood regains his feet with alacrity and casts aside his shawl.

" Whatever you thought, uncle, I am still a single man, although your way of coming down on a chap was enough to make me beside myself.   Any grub, Jack ?"

With a check upon his enthusiasm and a sudden gloom of expression amounting almost to a squint, Mr. Bumstead motions with his whole right side toward an adjacent room in which a table is spread, and leads the way thither in a half-circle.

" Ah, this is prime !" cries the young fellow, rubbing his hands ; the while he realizes that Mr. Bumstead's squint is an attempt to include both himself and the picture over the mantel in the next room in one incredibly complicated look.

Not much is said during dinner, as the strength of the boarding-house butter requires all the nephew's energies for single combat with it, and the uncle is so absorbed in a dreamy effort to make a salad with his hash and all the contents of the castor, that he can attend to nothing else. At length the cloth is drawn, Edwin produces some peanuts from his pocket, and passes some to Mr. Bumstead, and the latter, with a wet towel pinned about his head, drinks a great deal of water.

" This is Sissy's birthday, you know, Jack," says the nephew, with a squint through the door and around the corner of the adjoining apartment toward the crude picture over the mantel, " and, if our respective respected parents hadn't bound us by will to marry, I'd be mad after her."

Crack.   On Edwin Drood's part.

Hic.   On Mr. Bumstead's part.

" Nobody's dictated a marriage for you, Jack. *You* can choose for yourself.   Life for *you* is still fraught with free-dom's intoxicating —"

Mr. Bumstead has suddenly become very pale, and perspires heavily on the forehead.

" Good Heavens, Jack ! I haven't hurt your feelings ? "

Mr. Bumstead makes a feeble pass at him with the water-decanter, and smiles in a very ghastly manner.

" Lem me be a mis'able warning to you, Edwin," says Mr. Bumstead, shedding tears.

The scared face of the younger recalls him to himself, and he adds :

" Don't mind me, my dear boys. It's cloves ; you may notice them on my breath. I take them for my nerv'shness." Here he rises in a series of trembles to his feet, and balances, still very pale, on one leg.

" You want cheering up," says Edwin Drood, kindly.

" Yesh — cheering up. Let's go and walk in the grave-yard," says Mr. Bumstead.

" By all means. You won't mind my slipping out for half a minute to the Alms House* to leave a few gum-drops for Sissy? Rather spoony, Jack."

Mr. Bumstead almost loses his balance in an imprudent attempt to wink archly, and says, " Norring-half-sh'-shweet-'n-life." He is very thick with Edwin Drood, for he loves him.

" Well, let's skedaddle, then."

Mr. Bumstead very carefully poises himself on both feet, puts on his hat over the wet towel, gives a sudden horrified glance downward toward one of his boots, and leaps frantically over an object.

" Why, that was only my cane," says Edwin.

Mr. Bumstead breathes hard, and leans heavily on his nephew as they go out together.

* In the original, " *the Nun's House.*"

2*

CHAPTER III.

THE ALMS-HOUSE.

FOR the purpose of preventing an inconvenient rush of literary tuft-hunters and sight-seers thither next summer, a fictitious name must be bestowed upon the town of the Ritualistic church. Let it stand in these pages as Bumsteadville.* Possibly it was not known to the Romans, the Saxons, nor the Normans by that name, if by any name at all; but a name more or less weird and full of damp syllables can be of little monent to a place not owned by any advertising Suburban-Residence benefactors.

A disagreeable and healthy suburb, Bumsteadville, with a strange odor of dried bones from its ancient pauper burial-ground, and many quaint old ruins in the shapes of elderly men engaged as contributors to the monthly magazines of the day. Antiquity pervades Bumsteadville; nothing is new; the very Rye is old; also the Jamaica, Santa Cruz, and a number of the native maids. A drowsy place, with all its changes lying far behind it; or, at least, the sun-browned mendicants passing through say they never saw a place offering so little present change.

* In the original, *Cloisterham.*

In the midst of Bumsteadville stands the Alms-House ; a building of an antic order of architecture ; still known by its original title to the paynobility and indigentry of the surrounding country, several of whose ancestors abode there in the days before voting was a certain livelihood; although now bearing a door-plate inscribed, "Macassar Female College, Miss Carowthers."* Whether any of the country editors, projectors of American Comic papers, and other inmates of the edifice in times of yore, ever come back in spirit to be astonished by the manner in which modern serious and humorous print can be made productive of anything but penury by publishing True Stories of Lord Byron and the autobiographies of detached wives, may be of interest to philosophers, but is of no account to Miss Carowthers. Every day, during school-hours, does Miss Carowthers, in spectacles and high-necked alpaca, preside over her Young Ladies of Fashion, with an austerity and elderliness before which every mental image of Man, even as the most poetical of abstractions, withers and dies. Every night, after the young ladies have retired, does Miss Carowthers put on a freshening aspect, don a more youthful low-necked dress—

> As though a rose
> Should leave its clothes
> And be a bud again, —

and become a sprightlier Miss Carowthers. Every night at the same hour, does Miss Carowthers discuss with her First

* In the original, *Miss Twinkleton,*

Assistant, Mrs. Pillsbury, * the Inalienable Rights of
Women ; always making certain casual reference to a gentleman in the dim past, whom she was obliged to sue for
breach of promise, and to whom, for that reason, Miss Carowthers airily refers, with a toleration bred of the lapse of
time, as, "Breachy Mr. Blodgett."

The pet pupil of the Alms-House is Flora Potts,† of
course called the Flowerpot ; for whom a husband has been
chosen by the will and bequest of her departed papa, and at
whom none of the other Macassar young ladies can look
without wondering how it must feel. On the afternoon after
the day of the dinner at the boarding-house, the Macassar
front-door bell rings, and Mr. Edwin Drood is announced as
waiting to see Miss Flora. Having first rubbed her lips and
cheeks, alternately, with her fingers, to make them red ;
held her hands above her head to turn back the circulation
and make them white ; and added a little lead-pencilling to
her eyebrows to make them black ; the Flowerpot trips in-
nocently down to the parlor, and stops short at some distance from the visitor in a curious sort of angular deflection
from the perpendicular.

"O, you absurd creature !" she says, placing a finger in
her mouth and slightly wriggling at him. "To go and have
to be married to me whether we want to or not! It's perfectly disgusting."

---

* In the original, *Mrs. Tisher.*
† In the original, *Rosa Bud*, "of course called 'Rosebud.'"

"Our parents *did* rather come a little load on us," says Edwin Drood, not rendered enthusiastic by his reception.

"Can't we get a *habeas corpus*, or some other ridiculous thing, and ask some perfectly absurd Judge to serve an injunction on somebody?" she asks, with pretty earnestness.

"Don't, Eddy — do-o-n't."

"Don't what, Flora?"

"Don't try to kiss me, please."

"Why not, Flora?"

"Because I'm enamelled."

"Well, I do think," says Edwin Drood, "that you put on the Grecian Bend rather heavily with me. Perhaps I'd better go."

"I wouldn't be so exquisitely hateful, Eddy. I got the gum-drops last night, and they were perfectly splendid."

"Well, that's a confort, at any rate," says her affianced, dimly conscious of a dawning civility in her last remark. "If it's really possible for you to walk on those high heels of yours, Flora, let's try a promenade out-doors."

Here Miss Carowthers glides into the room to look for her scissors, is reminded by the scene before her of Breachy Mr. Blodgett; whispers, "Don't trifle with her young affections, Mr. Drood, unless you want to be sued, besides being interviewed by all the papers;" and glides out again with a sigh.

Flora then puts upon her head a fig-leaf trimmed with lace and ribbon, and gets her hoop and stick from behind the hall-door. Edwin Drood takes from one of his pockets an india-rubber ball, to practice fly-catches with as he walks ; and driving the hoop and throwing and catching the ball, the two go down the ancient turnpike of Bumsteadville together.

"Oh, please, Eddy, scrape yourself close to the fences, so that the girls can't see you out of the windows," pleads Flora. "It's so utterly absurd to be walking with one that one's got to marry whether one likes it or not ; and you do look so perfectly ridiculous in that short coat, and all your other things so tight."

He gloomily scrapes against the fences, dropping his ball and catching it on the rebound at every step. "Which way shall we go ? "

"Up by the store, Eddy, dear."

They go to the all-sorts country store in question, where Edwin Drood buys her some sassafras bull's-eye candy, and then they turn toward home again.

"Now be a good-tempered Eddy," she says, trundling her hoop beside him, "and pretend that you aren't going to be my husband."

"Not if I can help it," he says, catching the ball almost spitefully.

"Then you're going to have somebody else ? "

"You make my head ache, so you do," whimpers Edwin Drood. "I don't want to marry anybody at all ! "

She tickles him under the arm with her hoop-stick, and turns eyes that are all serious upon his.

" I wish, Eddy, that we could be perfectly absurd friends to each other, instead of utterly ridiculous engaged people. It's exquisitely awful, you know, to have a husband picked out for you by dead folks, and I'm so sick about it sometimes that I hardly have the heart to fix my back-hair. Let each of us forbear, and stop teazing the other."

Greatly pleased by this perfectly intelligent and forgiving arrangement, Edwin Drood says : " You're right, Flora. Teazing is played out ; " and drives his ball into a perfect frenzy of bounces.

They have arrived near the Ritualistic church, through the windows of which come the organ-notes of one practising within. Something familiar in the grand air rolling out to them causes Edwin Drood to repeat, abstractedly, " I feel — I feel — I feel — "

Flora, simultaneously affected in the same way, unconsciously murmurs,— " I feel like a morning star."

They then join hands, under the same irresistible spell, and take dancing steps, humming, in unison, " Shoo, fly ! don't bodder me."

" That's Jack Bumstead's playing," whispers Edwin Drood ; "and he must be breathing this way, too, for I can smell the cloves."

" O, take me home," cries Flora, suddenly throwing her hoop over the young man's neck, and dragging him violently after her. " I think cloves are perfectly disgusting."

At the door of the Alms-House the pretty Flowerpot blows a kiss to Edwin, and goes in.   He makes one trial of his ball against the door, and goes off.   She is an in-fant, he is an off-'un.

CHAPTER IV.

MR. SWEENEY.

Accepting the New American Cyclopædia as a fair stand-ard of stupidity — although the prejudice, perhaps, may arise rather from the irascibility of the few using it as a ref-erence, than from the calm judgment of the many employ-ing it to fill-out a showy book-case — then the newest and most American Cyclopædist in Bumsteadville is Judge Sweeney.*

It is Judge Sweeney's pleasure to found himself upon Father Dean, whom he greatly resembles in the intellectual details of much forehead, stomach, and shirt-collar. When upon the bench in the city, even, granting an injunction in favor of some railroad company in which he owns a little stock, he frequently intones his accompanying remarks with an eccle-siastical solemnity eminently calculated to suppress every possible tendency to levity in the assembled lawyers; and his discharge from arrest of any foreign gentleman brought

---

* *Mr. Sapsea* the original of this character in Mr. Dickens' romance, is an auc-tioneer. The present Adapter can think of no nearer American equivalent, in the way of a person at once resident in a suburb and who sells to the highest bidder, than a supposable member of the New York judiciary.

before him for illegal voting, has often been found strikingly similar in sound to a pastoral Benediction.

That Judge Sweeney has many admirers, is proved by the immense local majority electing him to judicial eninence ; and that the admiration is mutual is likewise proved by his subsequent appreciative dismissal of certain frivolous complaints against a majority of that majority for trifling misapprehensions of the Registry law. He is a portly, double-chinned man of about fifty, with a moral cough, eye-glasses making even his red nose seem ministerial, and little gold ballot-boxes, locomotives, and five-dollar pieces, hanging as " charms" from the chain of his Repeater.

Judge Sweeney's villa is on the turnpike, opposite the Alms-House, with doors and shutters giving in whichever direction they are opened; and he is sitting near a table, with a sheet of paper in his hands, and a bowl of warm lemon tea before him, when his servant-girl announces " Mr. Bumstead."

"Happy to see you, sir, in my house, for the first time," is Judge Sweeney's hospitable greeting.

"You honor me, sir," says Mr. Bumstead, whose eyes are set, as though he were in some kind of a fit, and who shakes hands excessively. "You are a good man, sir. How do you do, sir? Shake hands again, sir. I am very well, sir, I thank you. Your hand, sir. I'll stand by you, sir — though I never spoke t' you b'fore in my life. Let us shake hands, sir."

But instead of waiting for this last shake, Mr. Bumstead abruptly turns away to the nearest chair, deposits his hat in the very middle of the seat with great care, and recklessly sits down upon it.

The lemon tea in the bowl upon the table is a fruity compound, consisting of two very thin slices of lemon, which are maintained in horizontal positions, for the free action of the air upon their upper surfaces, by a pint of whiskey procured for that purpose. About half a pint of hot water has been added to help soften the rind of the lemon, and a portion of sugar to correct its acidity.

With a wave of the hand toward this tropical preserve, Judge Sweeney says : " You have a reputation, sir, as a man of taste. Try some lemon tea."

Energetically, if not frantically, his guest holds out a tumbler to be filled, immediately after which he insists upon shaking hands again. " You're a man of insight, sir," he says, working Judge Sweeney back and forth in his chair. " I *am* a man of taste, sir, and you know the world, sir."

" The *World?* " says Judge Sweeney, complacently. " If you mean the religious female daily paper of that name, I certainly do know it. I used to take it for my late wife when she was trying to learn Latin."

" I mean the terrestrial globe, sir," says Mr. Bumstead, irritably. " The great spherical foundation, sir, upon which Boston has since been built."

" Ah, I see," says Judge Sweeney, genially. " I believe,

though, that I know that world, also, pretty well ; for, if I have not exactly been to foreign countries, foreign countries have come to me. They have come to me on — hem ! — business, and I have improved my opportunities. A man comes to me from a vessel and I say 'Cork,' and give him Naturalization Certificates for himself and his friends. Another comes, and I say 'Dublin ;' another, and I say 'Belfast.' If I want to travel still further, I take them all together and say 'the Polls.' "

"You'll do to travel, sir," responds Mr. Bumstead, abstractedly helping himself to some more lemon tea ; " but I thought we were to talk about the late Mrs. Sweeney."

"We were, sir," says Judge Sweeney, abstractedly removing the bowl to a sideboard on his farther side. " My late wife, young man, as you may be aware, was a Miss Haggerty, and was imbued with homage to Shape. It was rumored, sir, that she admired me for my Manly Shape. When I offered to make her my bride, the only words she could articulate were, "O, my! *I?*" — meaning that she could scarcely believe that I really meant *her.* After which she fell into strong hysterics. We were married, despite certain objections on the score of temperance by that corrupt Radical, her father. From looking up to me too much she contracted an affection of the spine, and died about nine months ago. Now, sir, be good enough to run your eye over this Epitaph, which I have composed for the monument row erecting to her memory."

Mr. Bumstead, rousing from a doze for the purpose, fixes glassy eyes upon the slip of paper held out to him, and reads as follows :

MARY ANN,

Unlitigating and Unliterary Wife of

HIS HONOR, JUDGE SWEENEY.

In the darkest hours of

Her Husband's fortunes

She was never once tempted to Write for

THE TRIBUNE, OR THE INDEPENDENT ; *

Nor did even a disappointment about a

new bonnet ever induce her to

threaten her husband with

AN INDIANA DIVORCE.

STRANGER, PAUSE,

and consider if thou canst say

- the same about

THINE OWN WIFE !

if not,

WITH A RUSH RETIRE. †

Mr. Bumstead, affected to tears, interspersed with nods, by his reading, has barely time to mutter that such a wife was too good to live long· in these days, when the servant announces that " McLaughlin has come, sir."

John McLaughlin,‡ who now enters, is a stone-cutter and

---

* Two journals notoriously rich in strong-minded female contributors.

† In the original : "Ethelinda, Reverential wife of Mr. Thomas Sapsea, Auctioneer, Valuer, Estate Agent, etc. of this city. Whose knowledge of the world, though some-what extensive, never brought him acquainted with a Spirit more capable of looking up to Him. Stranger, pause and ask thyself the question : canst thou do likewise? If not, with a Blush Retire."

‡ In the original, *Durdles*, a stone mason.

mason, much employed in patching dilapidated graves and cutting inscriptions, and popularly known in Bumsteadville, on account of the dried mortar perpetually hanging about him, as "Old Mortarity." He is a rickètty man, with a chronic disease called bar-roomatism, and so very grave-yardy in his very '*Hic*' that one almost expects a *jacet* to follow it as a matter of course.

"John McLaughlin," says Judge Sweeney, handing him the paper with the Epitaph, "there is the inscription for the stone."

"I guess I can get it all on, sir," says McLaughlin. "Your servant, Mr. Bumstead."

"Ah, John McLaughlin, how are you?" says Mr. Bumstead, his hand with the tumbler vaguely wandering toward where the bowl formerly stood. "By the way, John Mc-Laughlin, how came you to be called 'Old Mortarity?' It has a drunken sound, John McLaughlin, like one of Sir Walter Scott's characters disguised in liquor."

"Never you mind about that," says McLaughlin. "I carry the keys of the Bumsteadville churchyard vaults, and can tell to an atom, by a tap of my trowel, how fast a skeleton is dropping to dust in the pauper burial-ground. That's more than they can do who call me names." With which ghastly speech John McLaughlin retires unceremoniously from the room.

Judge Sweeney now attempts a game of backgammon with the man of taste, but becomes discouraged after Mr.

Bumstead has landed the dice in his vest-opening three times
running and fallen heavily asleep in the middle of a move.
An ensuing potato salad is made equally discouraging by Mr.
Bumstead's persistent attempts to cut up his handkerchief in
it. Finally, Mr. Bumstead wildly finds his way to his feet,
is plunged into profound gloom at discovering the condition
of his hat, attempts to leave the room by each of the windows and closets in succession, and at last goes tempestu-
ously through the door by accident.

CHAPTER V.

MR. MCLAUGHLIN AND FRIEND.

JOHN BUMSTEAD, on his way home along the unsteady turnpike — upon which he is sure there will be a dreadful accident some day, for want of railings — is suddenly brought to an unsettled pause in his career by the spectacle of Old Mortarity leaning against the low fence of the pauper burial-ground, with a shapeless boy· throwing stones at him in the moonlight. The stones seem never to hit the venerable John McLaughlin, and at each miss the spry monkey of the moonlight sings "sold again,", and casts another missile still further from the mark. One of these give violently to the nose of Mr. Bumstead, who, after a momentary enjoyment of the evening fireworks thus lighted off, makes a wrathful rush at the playful child, and lifts him from the ground by his ragged collar, like a diminished suit of Mr. · Greeley's customary habiliments.

"Miserable snipe," demands Bumstead, eying his trophy gloomily, and giving him a turn or two as though he were a mackerel under inspection, "what are you doing to that gooroleman ?"

"Oh, come now !" says the lad sparring at him in the air,

"you just lemme be, or I'll fetch you a wipe in the jaw. I ain't doing nothink ; and he's werry good to me, he is."

Mr. Bumstead drops the presumptuous viper, but immediately seizes him by an ear and leads him to McLaughlin, whom he asks : "Do you know this insect ? "

"Smalley," * says McLaughlin with a nod.

"Is that the name of the sardine ? "

"Blagyerboots," adds McLaughlin.

"Shine 'em up, red hot," explains the boy. "I'm one of them fellers." Here he breaks away and hops out again into the road, singing :

> "Aina, maina, mona, Mike,
> Bassalona, bona, strike !
> Hay, way, crown, rack,
> Hallico, ballico, we — wo — wack ! "

— which he evidently intends as a kind of Hitalian ; for simultaneously, he aims a stone at John McLaughlin, grazes Mr. Bumstead's whiskers instead, and in another instant a sound of breaking glass is heard in the distance.

"Peace, young scorpion !" says Mr. Bumstead, with a commanding gesture. "John McLaughlin, let me see you home. The road is too unsteady to-night for an old man like you. Let me see you home, as far as my house, at least."

"Thank you, sir, I'd make better time alone. When you

---

* In the original, "'*Deputy*,' man-servant up at the Travellers' two-penny in Gas Works Garding."

came up, sir, Old Mortarity was meditating on this bone-
farm," says Mr. McLaughlin, pointing with a trowel, which
he had drawn from his pocket, into the pauper burial-ground.
" He was thinking of the many laid here when the Alms-
House over yonder used to be open *as* a Alms-House. I've
patched up all these graves, as well as them in the Ritual
churchyard, and know 'em all, sir. Over there, Editor of
Country Journal ; next, Stockholder in Erie ; next, Gentleman who Undertook to be Guided in His Agriculture by
Mr. Greeley's ' What I Know about Farming ; ' next,
Original Projector of American *Punch ;* next, Pro-
prietor of Rural Newspaper ; next, another Projector
of American *Punch ;* — indeed, all the rest of that
row is American *Punches ;* next, Conductor of Rustic
Daily ; next, Manager of Italian Opera ; next, Stockholder in
Morris and Essex ; next, American Novelist ; next, Husband
of Literary Woman ; next, Pastor of Southern Church ; next,
Conductor of Provincial Press.— I know 'em ALL, sir," says
Old Mortarity, with exquisite pathos, " and if a flower could
spring up for every tear a friendless old man has dropped
upon their neglected graves, you couldn't see the wooden
head-boards for the roses."

" Tharsverytrue," says Mr. Bumstead, much affected —
" Not see 'em for your noses — beaut'ful idea ! You're a
gooroleman, sir. Here comes Smalley again."

" I ain't doing nothink, and you're all the time wanting
me to move on, and he's werry good to me, he is," whimpers

Smalley, throwing a stone at Mr. Bumstead and hitting Old Mortarity.

" Didn't I tell you to always aim at *me* /" cries the latter, angrily rubbing the place. " Don't I give you a penny a night to aim right at me ?"

" I only chucked once at him," says the youth penitently.

" You see, Mr. Bumstead," explains John McLaughlin, " I give him an Object in life. I am that Object, and it pays me. If you've ever noticed these boys, sir, they never hit what they aim at. If they throw at a pigeon on a tree, the stone goes through a garret winder. If they throw at a dog, it hits some passer-by on the leg. If they throw at each other, it takes you in the back as you're turnin' a corner. I used to be getting hit all over every night from Smalley's aiming at dogs, and pigeons, and boys, like himself; but now I hire him to aim at me, exclusively, and I'm all safe. — There he goes, now, misses me, and breaks another winder."

" Here, Smalley," says Mr. Bumstead, as another stone, aimed at McLaughlin, strikes himself, " take this other penny, and aim at *both* of us."

Thus perfectly protected from painful contusion, although the air continues full of stones, Mr. Bumstead takes John McLaughlin's arm, as they move onward, to protect the old man from harm, and is so careful to pick out the choice parts of the road for him that their progress is digressive in the extreme.

" I have heard," says Mr. Bumstead, " that at one end of
the pauper burial-ground there still remains the cellar of a
former chapel to the Alms-House, and that you have
broken through into it, and got a step-ladder to go down.
Isthashso ? "

" Yes ; and there's coffins down there."

" Yours is a hic-stremely strange life, John McLaughlin."

" It's certainly a very damp one," says McLaughlin,
silently urging his strange conpanion to support a little more
of his own weight in walking. " But it has its science.
Over in the Ritualistic burial-yard, I tap the wall of a vault
with my trowel-handle, and if the sound is hollow I say to
myself: ' Not full yet.' Say it's the First of May, and I tap
a coffin, and don't hear anything move in it, I say : ' Either
you're not a woman in there, or, if you are, you never kept
house.'— Because, you see, if it was a woman that ever kept
house, it would take but the least thing in the world to make
her insist upon ' moving ' on the First of May."

" Won'rful ! " says Mr. Bumstead. " Sometime when
you're sober, John McLaughlin, I'll do a grave or two with
you."

On their way they reach a bar-room, into which Mr. Bumstead is anxious to take Old Mortarity, for the purpose of
getting something to make the latter stronger for his remaining walk. Failing in his ardent entreaties to this end —
even after desperately offering to eat a few cloves himself
for the sake of company — he coldly bids the stone-cutter

good-night, and starts haughtily in a series of spirals for his own home. Suddenly catching sight of Smalley in the distance, he furiously grasps a stone to throw at him; but allowing his hand to describe too much of a circle before parting with the stone, the latter strikes the back of his own head, and he goes on, much confused.

Arriving in his own room, and arising from the all-fours attitude in which, from eccentricity, he has ascended the stairs, Mr. Bumstead takes from a cupboard a curious antique flask, and nearly fills a tumbler from its amber-hued contents. He drinks the potion with something like frenzy; then softly steals to the door of a room opening into his own, and looks in upon Edwin Drood. Calm and untroubled lies his nephew there, in pleasant dreams. "They are both asleep," whispers Mr. Bumstead to himself. He goes back to his own bed, accompanied unconsciously by a chair caught in his coat-tail; puts on his hat, opens an umbrella over his head, and lies down to dread serpentine visions.

CHAPTER VI.

INSURANCE IN GOSPELLER'S GULCH.

THE Reverend Octavius Simpson (Octavius, because there had been seven other little Simpsons, who all took after their father when he died of mumps, like seven kittens after the parental tail,) having thrown himself all over the room with a pair of dumb-bells much too strong for him, and taken a seidlitz powder to oblige his dyspepsia, was now parting his back hair before a looking-glass. An unimpeachably consumptive style of clerical beauty did the mirror reflect; the countenance contracting to an expression of almost malevolent piety when the comb went over a bump, and relaxing to an open-mouthed charity for all mankind, amounting nearly to imbecility, when the more complex requirements of the parting process compelled twists of the head scarcely compatible with even so much as a squint at the glass.

It being breakfast time, Mrs. Simpson — mother of Octavius — was just down for the meal, and surveyed the operation with a look of undisguised anxiety.

"You'll break one of them yet, some morning, Octave," said the old lady.

" Do what, Oldy ? " asked the writhing Gospeller, apparently speaking out of his right ear.

" You'll break either the comb, or your neck, some morning."

Rendered momentarily irritable by this aggravating remark, the Reverend Octavius made a jab with the comb at the old lady's false-front, pulling it down quite askew over her left eye ; but, upon the sudden entrance of a servant with the tea-pot, he made precipitate pretence that his hand was upon his mother's head to give her a morning blessing.

They were a striking pair to sit at breakfast together in Gospeller's Gulch,* Bumsteadville : she with her superb old nut-cracker countenance, and he with the dyspepsia of more than thirty summers causing him to deal gently with the fish-balls. They sat within sound of the bell of the Ritualistic Church, the ringing of which was forever deluding the peasantry of the surrounding country into the idea that they could certainly hear their missing cows at last (hence the name of the church — Saint Cow's) ; while the sonorous hee-hawing of an occasional Nature's Congressman in some distant field reminded them of the outer political world.

"Here is Mr. Schenck's letter," said Mrs. Simpson, handing an open epistle across the table, as she spoke, to her son, "and you might read it aloud, my Octave."

Taking the tea-cup off his face, the Reverend Octavius accepted the missive, which was written from "A Perfect

* In the original, *Minor Canon Corner.*

Stranger's Parlor, New York," and began reading thus:
" Dear Ma-a-dam —

> I wri-i-te in the-e
> Chai-ai-ai-air — "

" Dear me, Octave," interrupted the old lady, " can't you read even a letter without Intoning — and to the tune of 'Old Hundredth,' too ? "

" I'm afraid not, dear Oldy," responded the Gospeller. " I'm so much in the habit of it. You're not so ritualistic yourself, and may be able to do better."

" Give it back to me, my sing-sing-sonny," said the old lady ; who at once read as follows : " Dear Madam, I write from the chair which I have now occupied for six hours, in the house of a man whom I never saw before in my life, but who comes next in the Directory to the obstinate but finally conquered being under whose roof I resolutely passed the greater part of yesterday. He sits near me in another chair, so much weakened that he can just reply to me in whispers, and I believe that a few hours more of my talk will leave him no choice between dying of exhaustion at my feet and taking a Policy in the Boreal Life Insurance Company, of which I am Agent. I have spoken to my wards, Montgomery and Magnolia Pendragon,* concerning Magnolia's being placed at school in the Macassar,' and Montgomery's acceptance of your son, Octavius, as his tutor, and shall take them with me to Bumsteadville to-morrow, for

---

* In the original, *Neville* and *Helena Landless*, from Celyon.

such disposition. Hoping, Madam, that neither you nor your son will much longer fly into the face of Providence by declining to insure your lives, through me, in the Boreal, I have the honor to be Yours, for two Premiums, Melancthon Schenck."*

"Well, Oldy," said Octavius, with dismal countenance, "do you think we'll have to do it?"

"Do what?" asked the old lady.

"Let him insure us."

"I'm afraid it will come to that yet, Octave. I've known persons to die under him."

"Well, well, Heaven's will be done," muttered the patient Gospeller.

"And now, mother, we must do something to make the first coming of these young strangers seem cheerful to them. We must give a little dinner-party here, and invite Miss Carowthers, and Bumstead and his nephew, and the Flowerpot. Don't you think the codfish will go round?"

"Yes, dear: that is, if you and I take the spine," replied the old lady.

So the party of reception was arranged, and the invitations hurried out.

At about half an hour before dinner there was a sound in the air of Bumsteadville as of a powerful stump-speaker addressing a mass-meeting in the distance; rapidly intensifying to stentorian phrases, such as — "provide for your

* In the original, *Luke Honeythunder*, professional Philanthropist.

3*

miserable surviving offspring" — "lower rates than any other company" — "full amount cheerfully paid upon hearing of your death" — until a hack appeared coming down the cross-road descending into Gospeller's Gulch, and stopped at the Gospeller's door. As the faint driver, trembling with nervous debility from great excess of deathly admonition addressed to him, through the front window of his hack, all the way from the ferry, checked his horses in one feeble gasp of remaining strength, the Reverend Octavius stepped forth from the doorway to greet Mr. Schenck and the dark-complexioned, sharp-eyed young brother and sister who came with him.

"Now remember, fellow," said Mr. Schenck to the driver, after he had come out of the vehicle, shaking his cane menacingly at him as he spoke, "I've warned you in time, to prepare for death, and given you a Schedule of our rates to read to your family. If you should die of apoplexy in a week, as you probably will, your wife must pick rags, and your children play a harp and fiddle. Dream of it, think of it, dissolute man, and take a Policy in the Boreal."

As the worn-out hackman, too despondent at thought of his impending decease and family-bankruptcy to make any other answer than a groan, drove wretchedly away, the genial Mr. Schenck hoarsely introduced the young Pendragons to the Gospeller, and went with them after the latter into the house.

The Reverend Octavius Simpson, with dire forebodings of

the discomfiture of his dear old nut-cracker of a mother, did the honors of a general introduction with a perfect failure of a smile ; and, thenceforth, until dinner was over, Mr. Schenck was the Egyptian festal skeleton that continually reminded the banqueters of their latter ends.

"Great Heavens! what signs of the seeds of the tomb do I not see all around me here," observed Mr Schenck, in a deep base voice, as he helped himself to more codfish. "Here is my friend, Mr. Simpson, withering under our very eyes with Dyspepsia. In Mr. Bumstead's manly eye you can perceive Congestion of the Brain. General Debility has marked the venerable Mrs. Simpson for its own. Miss Potts and Magnolia can bloom and eat caramels now ; but what will be their anguish when malignant Small Pox rages, as it surely must, next month! Mr. Drood and Montgomery are rejoicing in the health and thin legs of youth ; but how many lobster salads are there between them and fatal Cholera Morbus? As for Miss Elizabeth Cady Carowthers, there, her Skeleton is already coming through at the shoulders. — Oh, my friends!" exclaimed the ghastly Mr. Schenck, with beautiful enthusiasm, "insure while yet there is time ; that the kindred, or friends, whom you will all leave behind, probably, within the next three months, may have something to keep them from the Poor-House, or, its dread alternative — Crime !" He considerately paused until the shuddering was over, and then added with melting softness — "I'll leave a few of our Schedules with you."

When, at last, this boon-companion said that he must go, it was surprising to see with what passionate cordiality everybody helped him off. Mr. Bumstead frenziedly crammed his hat upon his beaming head, and, with one eager blow on the top, drove it far down over his ears; Flora Potts and Magnolia thrust each a buckskin glove far up either sleeve; Miss Carowthers frantically stuck one of his overshoes under each arm; Mr. Drood wildly dragged his coat over his form, without troubling him at all about the sleeves, and breathlessly buttoned it to the neck; and the Reverend Octavius and Montgomery hurried him forth by the shoulders, as though the house were on fire and he the very last to be snatched from the falling beams.

These latter two then almost ran with him to the livery stable where he was to obtain a hack for the ferry; leaving him in charge of the liveryman — who, by the way, he at once frightened into a Boreal Policy, by a few felicitous remarks (while the hack was preparing) upon the curious recent fatality of Heart-Disease amongst middle-aged podgy men with bulbous noses.

CHAPTER VII.

MORE CONFIDENCES THAN ONE.

"You and your sister have been insured, of course," said the Gospeller to Montgomery Pendragon, as they returned from escorting Mr. Schenck.

"Of course," echoed Montgomery, with a suppressed moan. "He is our guardian, and has trampled us into a couple of policies. We had to yield, or excess of Boreal conversation would have made us maniacs."

"You speak bitterly for one so young," observed the Reverend Octavius Simpson. "Is it derangement of the stomach, or have you known sorrow?"

"Heaps of sorrow," answered the young man. "You may be aware, sir, that my sister and I belong to a fine old heavily mortgaged Southern family — the Penrutherses and Munchausens of Chipmunk Court House, Virginia, are our relatives — and that Sherman marched through us during the late southward projection of certain of your Northern military scorpions. After our father's felo-desease, ensuing remotely from an overstrain in attempting to lift a large mortgage, our mother gave us a step-father of Northern birth, who tried to amend our constitutions and reconstruct us."

" Dreadful ! " murmured the Gospeller.

" We hated him ! Magnolia threw her scissors at him several times.   My sister, sir, does not know what fear is.   She would fight a lion ; inheriting the spirit from our father, who, I have heard said, frequently fought a tiger.   She can fire a gun and pick off a State Senator as well as any man in all the South.   Our mother died.   A few mornings thereafter our step-father was found dead in his bed, and the doctors said he died of a pair of scissors which he must have swallowed accidentally in his youth, and which were found, after his death, to have worked themselves several inches out of his side, near the heart."

" Swallowed a pair of scissors ! " exclaimed the Reverend Octavius.

" He might have had a stitch in his side at the time, you know, and wanted to cut it," explained Montgomery. . " At any rate, after that we became wards of Mr. Schenck, up North here.   And now let me ask you, sir, is this Mr. Edwin Drood a student with you ? "

" No.   He is visiting his uncle, Mr. Bumstead," answered the Gospeller, who could not free his mind from the horrible thought that his young companion's fearless sister might have been in some way acscissory to the sudden cutting off of her step-father's career.

" Is Miss Flora Potts his sister ? "

Mr. Simpson told the story of the betrothal of the young couple by their respective departed parents.

"Oh, *that's* the game, eh?" said Montgomery. "I understand now his whispering to me that he wished he was dead." In a moment afterwards they re-entered the house in Gospeller's Gulch.

The air was slightly laden with the odor of cloves as they went into the parlor, and Mr. Bumstead was at the piano, accompanying the Flowerpot while she sang. Executing without notes, and with his stony gaze fixed intently between the nose and chin of the singer, Mr. Bumstead had a certain mesmeric appearance of controlling the words coming out of the rosy mouth. Standing beside Miss Potts was Magnolia Pendragon, seemingly fascinated, as it were, by the Bumstead method of playing, in which the performer's fingers performed almost as frequently upon the woodwork of the instrument as upon the keys. Mr. Pendragon surveyed the group with an arm resting on the mantel; Mr. Simpson took a chair by his maternal nut-cracker, and Mr. Drood stealthily practised with his ball on a chair behind the sofa.

The Flowerpot was singing a neat thing by Longfellow about the Evening Star, and seemed to experience the most remarkable psychological effects from Mr. Bumstead's wooden variations and extraordinary stare at the lower part of her countenance. Thus, she twitched her plump shoulders strangely, and sang —

"Just a-bove yon sandy bar,
As the day grows faint — (te-hee-he-he !)
Lonely and lovely a single — (now do-o-n't !)
Lights the air with" — (sto-o-op ! It tickles —)

Convulsively giggling and exclaiming, alternately, Miss Potts abruptly ended her beautiful bronchial noise with violent distortion of countenance, as though there were a spider in her mouth, and sank upon a chair in a condition almost hysterical.

"Your playing has made Sissy nervous, Jack," said Edwin Drood, hastily concealing his ball and coming forward. "I noticed, myself, that you played more than half the notes in the air, or on the music-rack, without touching the keys at all."

"That is because I am not accustomed to playing upon two pianos at once," answered Bumstead, who, at that very moment, was industriously playing the rest of the air some inches from the nearest key.

"He couldn't make *me* nervous!" exclaimed Miss Pendragon, decidedly.

They bore the excited Flowerpot (who still tittered a little, and was nervously feeling her throat) to the window, for air; and when they came back Mr. Bumstead was gone. "There, Sissy," said Edwin Drood, "you've driven him away; and I'm half afraid he feels unpleasantly confused about it; for he's got out of the rear door of the house by mistake, and I can hear him trying to find his way home in the back-yard."

The two young men escorted Miss Carowthers and the two young ladies to the door of the Alms-House, and there bade them good-night; but, at a yet later hour, Flora Potts and the new pupil still conversed in the chamber which they were to occupy conjointly.

After discussing the fashions with great excitement; asking each other just exactly what each gave for every article she wore; and successively practising male-discouraging, male-encouraging and chronically-indifferent expressions of face in the mirror (as all good young ladies always do preparatory to their evening prayers), the lovely twain made solemn nightcap-oath of eternal friendship to each other, and then, of course, began picking the men to pieces.

"Who is this Mr. Bumstead?" asked Magnolia, who was now looking much like a ghost.

"He's that absurd Eddy's ridiculous uncle, and my music-teacher," answered the Flowerpot, also presenting an emaciated appearance.

"You do not love him?" queried Magnolia.

"Now go'wa-a-ay! How perfectly disgusting!" protested Flora.

"You know that he loves you!"

"Do-o-n't!" pleaded Miss Potts, nervously. "You'll make me fidgetty again, just thinking of to-night. It was too perfectly absurd."

"What was?"

"Why, *he* was, — Mr. Bumstead. It gave me the funniest feeling! It was as though some one was trying to see through you, you know."

"My child!" exclaimed Miss Pendragon, dropping her

cheek-distenders upon the bureau, "you speak strangely. Has that man gained any power over you?"

"No, dear," returned Flora, wiping off a part of her left eyebrow with cold cream. "But didn't you see? He was looking right down my throat all the time I was singing, until it actually tickled me!"

"Does he always do so?"

"Oh, I don't know what he always does!" whimpered the nervous Flowerpot. "Oh, he's such an utterly ridiculous creature! Sometimes when we're in company together, and I smell cloves, and look at him, I think that I see the lid of his right eye drop over the ball and tremble at me in the strangest manner. And sometimes his eyes seem fixed motionless in his head, as they did to-night, and he'll appear to wander off into a kind of a dream, and feel about in the air with his right arm as though he wanted to hug somebody. Oh! my throat begins to tickle again! Oh, stay with me, and be my absurdly ridiculous friend!"

The dark-featured Southern linen spectre leaned soothingly above the other linen spectre, with a bottle of camphor in her hand, near the bureau upon which the back-hair of both was piled; and in the flash of her black eyes, and the defiant flirt of the kid-gloves dipped in glycerine which she was drawing on her hands, lurked death by lightning and other harsh usage, for whomsoever of the male sex should ever be caught looking down in the mouth again.

CHAPTER VIII.

A DAGGERY TYPE OF FOETALKRAPHY.

THE two young gentlemen, having seen their blooming charges safely within the door of the Alms-House, and vainly endeavored to look through the keyhole at them going upstairs, scuffle away together with that sensation of blended imbecility and irascibility which is equally characteristic of callow youth and inexperienced Thomas Cats when retiring together from the society of female friends who seem to be still on the fence as regards their ultimate preferences.

"Do you bore your friends here long, Mr. Drood?" inquires Montgomery; as who should say : Maouiw-ow-ooo — sp't ! sp't !

"Not this time, Secesh," is the answer ; as though it were observed, ooo-ooo — sp't ! "I leave for New York again to-morrow ; but shall be off and on again in Bumsteadville until midsummer, when I go to Egypt, Illinois, to be an engineer on a railroad. The stamps left me by my father are all in the stock of that road, and the Mr. Bumstead whom you saw to-night is my uncle and guardian."

"Mr. Simpson informs me that you are destined to assume the expenses of Miss Potts, when you're old enough," remarks Montgomery, his eyes shining quite greenly in the moonlight.

"Well, perhaps you'd like to make something out of it," says Edwin, whose orbs have assumed a yellowish glitter. "Perhaps you Southern Confederacies didn't get quite enough of it at Gettysburg and Five Forks."

"We had the exquisite pleasure of killing a few thousand Yankee free-lovers," intimates Montgomery, with a hollow laugh.

"Ah, yes, I remember — at Andersonville," suggests Edwin Drood, beginning to roll back his sleeves.

"This is your magnanimity to the conquered, is it!" exclaims Montgomery, scornfully. "I don't pretend to have your advantages, Mr. Drood, and I've scarcely had any more education than an American Humorist; but where I came from, if a carpet-bagger should talk as you do, the cost of his funeral would be but a trifle."

"I can prepare you, at shortest notice, for something very neat and tasteful in the silver-trimmed rosewood line, with plated handles, my dark-complexioned Ku-klux," returns Mr. Drood, preparing to pull off his coat.

"Who would have believed," soliloquizes Montgomery Pendragon, "that even a scalawag Northern spoon-thief, like our scurrilous contemporary, would get so mad at being reminded that he must be married some day!"

"Whoever says that I'm mad," is the answer, "lies deliberately, wilfully, wickedly, with naked intent to defame and malign."

But here a heavy hand suddenly smites Edwin on the back, almost snapping his head off, and there stands spectrally between them Mr. Bumstead, who has but recently found his way out of the back-yard in Gospeller's Gulch, by removing at least two yards of picket fence from the wrong place, and wears upon his head a gingham sun-bonnet, which, in his hurried departure through the hall of the Gospeller's house, he has mistaken for his own hat. Sustaining himself against the fierce evening breeze by holding firmly to both shoulders of his nephew, this striking apparition regards the two young men with as much austerity as is consistent with the flapping of the cape of his sun-bonnet.

"Gentlelemons," he says, with painful syllabic distinctness, "can I believe my ears? Are you already making journalists of yourselves?"

They hang their heads in shame under the merciless but just accusation. "Here you are," continues Bumstead, "a quartette of young fellows who should all be friends. Neds, Neds! I am ashamed of you! Montgomeries, you should not let your angry passions rise; for your little hands were never made to bark and bite." After this, Mr. Bumstead seems lost for a moment, and reclines upon his nephew, with his eyes closed in meditation. "But let's all five of us go up to my room," he finally adds, and restore friendship with lemon tea. It is time for the North and South to be reconciled over something hot. Come."

Leaning upon both of them now, and pushing them into a walk, he exquisitely turns the refrain of the rejected National Hymn —

> "'Twas by a mistake that we lost Bull Run,
> When we all skedaddled to Washington,
> And we'll all drink stone blind,
> Johnny fill up the bowl ! "

Thus he artfully employs music to soothe their sectional animosities, and only skips into the air once as they walk, with a "Whoop! That was something *like* a snake ! "

Arriving in his room, the door of which he had some trouble in opening, on account of the knob having wandered in his absence to the wrong side, Mr. Bumstead indicates a bottle of lemon tea, with some glasses, on the table, accidentally places the lamp so that it shines directly upon Edwin's triangular sketch of Flora over the mantel, and taking his umbrella under his arm, smiles horribly at his young guests from out of his sun-bonnet.

"Do you recognize that picture, Pendragons?" he asks, after the two have drunk fierily at each other. "Do you notice its stereoscopic effect of being double?"

"Ah," says Montgomery, critically, "a good deal in the style of Hennessy, or Winslow Homer, I should say. Something in the school-slate method."

"It's by Edwins, there!" explains Mr. Bumstead, triumphantly. "Just look at him as he sits there both together, with all his happiness cut out for him, and his dislike of Southerners his only fault."

"If I could only draw Miss Pendragon, now," says Edwin Drood, rather flattered, "I might do better. A good sharp nose and Southern complexion help wonderfully in the expression of a picture."

"Perhaps my sister would prefer to choose her own artist," remarks Montgomery, to whom Mr. Bumstead has just poured out some more lemon tea.

"Say a Southern one, for instance, who might use some of the flying colors that were always warranted to run when our boys got after yours in the late war," responds Edwin, to whom his attentive uncle has also poured out some more lemon tea for his cold.

"For instance — at Fredericksburg," observes Montgomery.

"I was thinking of Fort Donelson," returns Edwin.

The conservative Bumstead strives anxiously to allay the irritation of his young guests by prodding first one and then the other with his umbrella; and, in an attempt to hold both of them and the picture behind him in one commanding glance under his sun-bonnet, presents a phase of strabismus seldom attained by human eyes.

"If I only had you down where I come from, Mr. Drood," cries Montgomery, tickled into ungovernable wrath by the

ferule of the umbrella, I'd tar and feather you like a Yankee
teacher, and then burn you like a freedman's church."

" Oh ! — if you only had me *there*, you'd do so," cries Edwin Drood, springing to his feet as the umbrella tortures his
ribs. "*If*, eh ? Pooh, pooh, my young fellow, I perceive
that you are a mere Cincinnati Editor."

The degrading epithet goads Pendragon to fury, and, after
throwing his remaining lemon tea about equally upon Edwin
and the sun-bonnet, he extracts the sugar from the bottom
of the glass with his fingers, and uses the goblet to ward off
a last approach of the umbrella.

" Edwins ! Montgomeries !" exclaims Mr. Bumstead,
opening the umbrella between them so suddenly that each is
grazed on the nose by a whalebone rib, " I command you to
end this Congressional debate at once.   I never saw four
such young men before !   Montgomeries, put up your penknife thizinstant ? "

Pushing aside the barrier of alpaca and whalebone from
under his chin, Montgomery dashes wildly from the house,
tears madly back to Gospeller's Gulch, and astounds the
Gospeller by his appearance.

" Oh, Mr. Simpson," he cries, as he is conducted to the
door of his own room, "I believe that I, too, inherit some
tigerish qualities from that tiger my father is said to have
fought so often.   I've had a political discussion with Mr.
Drood in Mr. Bumstead's apartments, and, if I'd stayed

there a moment longer, I reckon I should have murdered somebody in a moment of Emotional Insanity."

The Reverend Octavius Simpson makes him unclose his clenched fist, in which there appears to be one or two cloves, and then says : " I am shocked to hear this, Mr. Pendragon. As you have no political influence, and have never shot a *Tribune* man,* neither New York law nor society would allow you to commit murder with impunity. I regret, too, to see that you have been drinking, and would advise you to try a chapter from one of Professor De Mille's novels, as a mild emetic, before retiring. After that, two or three sentences from one of Mr. George Ticknor Curtis's Constitutional essays will ensure sleep to you for the remainder of the night."

Returning the unspeakably thankful pressure of the grateful young man's hand, the Gospeller goes thoughtfully down stairs, where he is just in time to answer the excited ring of Mr. Bumstead.

" Dear me, Mr. Bumstead !" is his first exclamation, "what's that you've got on your head ? "

" Perspiration, sir," cries Bumstead, who, in his agitation, is still ringing the bell. " We've nearly had a murder tonight, and I've come around to offer you my umbrella for your own protection."

---

* A "*Tribune* man" had been slain, recently, by a lady's husband, and the slayer pronounced "Not Guilty" by a jury of his fellow-countrymen.

4

"Umbrella!" echoes Mr. Simpson, "why, really, I don't see how —"

"Open it on him suddenly when he makes a pass at you," interrupts Mr. Bumstead, thrusting the alpaca weapon upon him. "I'll send for it in the morning."

The Gospeller stands confounded in his own doorway, with the defence thus strangely secured in his hand ; and, looking up the moonlighted road, sees Mr. Bumstead, in the sunbonnet, leaping high, at short intervals, over the numerous adders and cobras on his homeward way, like a thoroughbred hurdle-racer.

CHAPTER IX.

BALKS IN A BRUSH.

FLORA, having no relations in the world that she knew of, had, ever since her seventh new bonnet, known no other home than Macassar Female College, in the Alms-House, and regarded Miss Carowthers as her mother-in-lore. Her memory of her own mother was of a lady-like person who had swiftly waisted away in the effort to be always taken for her own daughter, and was, one day, brought down-stairs, by her husband, in two pieces, from tight lacing. The sad separation (taking place just before a party of pleasure), had driven Flora's father into a frenzy of grief for his better halves ; which was augmented to brain fever by Mr. Schenck, who, having given a Boreal policy to deceased, felt it his duty to talk gloomily about wives who sometimes died apart after receiving unmerited cuts from their husbands, and to suggest a compromise of ten per cent. upon the amount of the policy, as a much more cheerful settlement than a coroner's inquest. Flora's betrothal had grown out of the soothing of Mr. Potts's last year of mental disorder by Mr. Drood, an old partner in the grocery business, who, too, was a widower from his wife's use of arsenic and lead for her complexion. The two bereaved friends, after comparing tears and looking mournfully at each other's tongues, had talked themselves to death over the fluctuations in sugar ; willing their respective children to marry in future for the sake of keeping up the controversy.

From the Flowerpot's first arrival at the Alms-House, her new things, engagement to be married, and stock of chocolate caramels, had won the deepest affections of her teachers and schoolmates ; and, on the morning after the sectional dispute between Edwin and Montgomery, when one of the young ladies had heard of it as a profound secret, no pains were spared by the whole tender-hearted school to make her believe that neither of the young men was entirely given up yet by the consulting physicians. It was whispered, indeed, that a knife or two might have passed, and two or three guns been exchanged ; but she was not to be at all worried, for persons had been known to get well with the tops of their heads off.

At an early hour, however, Miss Pendragon had paid a visit to her brother, in Gospeller's Gulch ; and, coming back with the intelligence, that, while he had been stabbed to the heart, it was chiefly by cruel insinuations and an umbrella, was enabled to assure Miss Carowthers, in confidence, that nothing eligible for publication in the New York *Sun* had really occurred. Thus, when the legal conqueror of Breachy Mr. Blodgett entered that principal recitation-room of the

Macassar, formally known as the Cackleorium, she had no difficulty in explaining away the panic.

She said that "Unfounded Rumor, Ladies, is, we all know, a descriptive phrase applied by the Associated Press to all important foreign news procured a week or two in advance of its own similar European advices, by the Press Association. We perceive then, Ladies (Miss Jenkins will be good enough to stop scratching her nose while I am talking), that Unfounded Rumor sometimes means — hem! —

> 'The Associated Press
> In bitter distress.'

In Bumsteadville, however, it has a signification more like what we should give it in relation to a statement that Senator Sumner had delivered a Latin quotation without a speech selected for it. In this sense, Ladies (Miss Parkinson can scarcely be aware of how much cotton stocking can be seen when she lolls so), the Unfounded Rumor concerning two gentlemen of different political views in this county was not correct (Miss Babcock will learn four chapters in Chronicles by heart to-night, for making a handkerchief into a baby), as proper inquiries have assured us that no more blood was shed than if the parties to the strife had been a Canadian and a Fenian. We will, therefore, drop the subject, and enter at once upon the flowery path of the first lesson in algebra."

This explanation destroyed all the interest of a majority of the young ladies, who had anticipated a horridly delight-

ful duel, at least ; but Flora was slightly hysterical about it,
even late in the afternoon, when it was announced that her
guardian had come to see her.

Mr. Dibble,* of Gowanus, had been selected for his trust
on account of his pre-eminent goodness, which, as seems to
be invariably the case, was associated with an absence of
personal beauty trenching upon the scarecrow. Possibly an
excess of strong and disproportionate carving in nose, mouth,
and chin, accompanied by weak eyes and unexpectedness
of forehead, may tend to make the Evil One but languid in
his desire for the capture of its human exemplar. This may
help account for the otherwise rather curious coincidence of
frightful physiognomy and preternatural goodness in this
world of sinful beauties. Under such a theory, Mr. Dibble's
easy means of frightening the Arch-Tempter into immediate
flight, and keeping himself free from all possible incitement
to be anything but good, were a face, head and neck shaped
not unlike an old-fashioned water-pitcher, and a form suggestive of an obese lobster balancing on an upright horse-
shoe. His nose was too high up ; his mouth and chin bulged
too tremendously ; his neck inside a whole mainsail of shirt-
collar was too much fluted, and his eyes were as much too
small and oyster-like as his ears were too large and horny.

Mr. Dibble found his ward in Miss Carowthers' own private room, from which even the government mails were generally excluded; and, after saluting both ladies, and politely

---

* In the original, *Mr. Grewgious,* a lawyer, of London.

desiring the elder to remain present, in order to be sure that his conversation was strictly moral, the monstrous old gentleman pulled a memorandum book from his pocket and addressed himself to Flora.

"I am a square man myself, dear kissling," he said, with much double chin in his manner, "and like to do everything on the square. I am now 'interviewing' you, and shall make notes of your answers, though not necessarily for publication. First: is your health satisfactory?"

Miss Potts admitted that, excepting occasional attacks of insatiable longing for True Sympathy, chiefly produced by over-eating of pickles and slate-pencils to avert excessive plumpness, she could generally take pie twice without experiencing a subsequent reactionary tendency to piety and gloomy presentiments.

"Second: is your allowance of pin-money sufficient to keep you in cold cream, Berlin wool, and other necessaries of life?"

The Flowerpot confessed that she had now and then wished herself able to buy a church and a velvet dressing-gown, (lined with cherry,) for a young clergyman with the consumption and side-whiskers; but, under common circumstances, her allowance was enough to procure all absolutely requisite Edging without running her into debt, and still leave sufficient to buy materials for any reasonable altar-cloth.

"And now, my dear," said Mr. Dibble, evidently glad

that all the more important and serious part of the interview was over, "we come to the subject of your marriage. Mr. Edwin has seen you here, occasionally, I suppose, and you may possibly like him well enough to accept him as a husband, if not as a friend!"

" He's such a perfectly absurd creature that I can't help liking him," returned Flora, gravely; " but I am not certain that my utterly ridiculous deeper woman's love is entirely satisfied with the shape of his nose."

" That'll be mostly hidden by his whiskers, when they grow," observed her guardian.

" I hope they'll be bushy, with a frizzle at the ends and a bald place for his chin," said the young girl, reflectively; then suddenly asked : " If we *shouldn't* be married, would either of us have to pay anything ?"

"I should say not," answered Mr. Dibble, "unless you sued him for breach." (Here Miss Carowthers was heard to murmur "Blodgett," and hastily took an anti-nervous pill.) "I should say that your respective parents wished you to marry only in case you should see no other persons whose noses you liked better. As on this coming Christmas you will be within a few months of your marriage, I have brought your father's will with me, with the intention of depositing it in the hands of Mr. Edwin's trustee, Mr. Bumstead —"

" Oh, leave it with Eddy, if you'll please to be so ridiculously kind," interrupted Flora. " Mr. Bumstead would

certainly insist upon it that there were *two* wills instead of
. one : and that would be so absurd."

"Well, well," assented Mr. Dibble, rising to go, "I'm a
perfectly square man, even when I'm looking round, and
will do as you wish. As a slight memento of my really
charming visit here, might I humbly petition yonder lady to
remit any little penalty that may happen to be in force just
now against any lovely student of the College for eating
preserves in bed, or writing notes to the Italian music teacher, who is already married, or anything of that kind?"

"Flora," said Miss Carowthers, graciously, "you may tell
Miss Babcock, that, in consequence of your guardian's request, she will be excused from studying her Bible as a punishment."

After due acknowledgment of this favor, the good Mr.
Dibble made his farewell bow, and went forth to the turnpike. Following that high road, he presently found himself
near the side-door of the Ritualistic Church of Saint Cow's,
and, while curiously watching the minor canons who were
carrying in some fireworks to be used in the next day's service, was confronted by Mr. Bumstead just coming out.

"Let me see you home," said Mr. Bumstead, hastily holding out an arm. "I'll tell the family it's only vertigo."

"Why; nothing is the matter with me," pleaded Mr. Dibble. "I've only been having a talk with my ward."

"I'll bet cloves for two that she didn't say she preferred

4*

me to Ned," insinuated Mr. Bumstead, breathing audibly through his nose.

" Then you'll not lose," was the answer ; "for she did not tell me whom she preferred to the one she wishes to marry. They never do ; and sometimes it is only discovered in Indiana. You and I surrender our respective guardianships on Christmas, Mr. Bumstead ; until when good-bye ; and be early marriage their lot ! "

" Be early Divorce their lot !" said Bumstead, thrusting his book of organ-music so far under his coat-flap that it stuck out at the back like a curvature of the spine.

" I said marriage," cried Mr. Dibble, looking back.

" I said Divorce," retorted Mr. Bumstead, thoughtfully eating a clove. " Don't one generally involve the other ? "

CHAPTER X.

OILING THE WHEELS.

No husband who has ever properly studied his mother-in-law can fail to be aware, that woman's perception of heartless villany and evidences of intoxication in man is often of that curiously fine order of vision which rather exceeds the best efforts of ordinary microscopes, and subjects the average human mind to considerable astonishment. The perfect ease with which she can detect murderous proclivities, Mormon instincts, and addiction to maddening liquors, in a daughter's husband — who, to the most searching inspection of everybody else, appears the most watery, hen-pecked, and generally intimidated young man of his age — is one of those common illustrations of the infallible acuteness of feminine judgment which are doing more and more, every day, to establish the positive necessity of woman's superior insight and natural dispassionate fairness of mind, for the future wisest exercise of the elective franchise and most just administration of the highest judicial office. It may be said that the mother-in-law is the highest development of the supernaturally perceptive and positive woman, since she usually has superior opportunities to study man in all the stages from marriage to madness; but with her whole sex, particularly after certain sour turns in life, inheres an alertness of observation as to the incredible viciousness of masculine character, which nothing less than a bit of flattery or a happily equivocal reflection upon some rival sister can either divert or mislead for a moment.

"Now don't you really think, Oldy," said Gospeller Simpson to his mother, as he sat watching her fabrication of an immense stocking for the poor, "that Hopeless Inebriate and Midnight Assassin are a rather too severe characterization of my pupil, Mr. Montgomery Pendragon?"

"No, I do not, Octave," replied the excellent old nut-cracker of a lady, who was making the charity stocking as nearly in the shape of a hatchet as possible. "When a young man of rebel sentiments spends all his nights in drinking lemon teas, and trying to spoil other young men's clothes in throwing such teas at them, and is only to be put down by umbrellas, and comes to his homes with cloves in his clenched fists, and has headaches on the following days, he's on his way either to political office or the gallows."

"But he hasn't done so at all with s's to it," exclaimed the Reverend Octavius, exasperated by so many plurals. "He did it but once, and then he was strongly provoked. Edwin mentioned the sharpness of his sister's nose to him, and reflected casually upon the late well-known Southern Confederacy."

"Don't tell me!" reasoned the fine old lady, holding up

the stocking by its handle to see how much longer it must be to reach the wearer's waist. "I'm afraid you're a copperhead, Octave."

"How you do cackle, Oldy!" said her son, who was very proud of her when she kept still. "You can't see anything good in Montgomery, because, after the first seven or eight breakfasts with us, he said he was afraid that so many fishballs would make his head swim."

"My child," returned the old lady, thrusting an arm so far into the charity stocking that she seemed to have the wrong kind of blue worsted limb growing from one of her shoulders, "I have judged this dissipated young man exactly as though he were my own son-in-law, and know that he possesses an incendiary disposition. After the fireworks at Saint Cow's Church, on Saint Vitus's Day, that devoted Ritualistic Christian, Mr. Bumstead, came up to me in the porch, with his eyes nearly closed, on account of the solemnity of the occasion, and began feeling around my neck with both his hands. When I asked him to explain, he said that he only wanted to see whether my throat was cut yet, as he had heard that we kept a Southern murderer at home. He was still very pale at what had taken place in his room over night, when he finally said 'Good-day, ladies,' to me."

"Montgomery is certainly attached to me, at any rate," murmured the Gospeller, reflectively, "and has made no attempt upon my life."

"That's because his sister restrains him," asserted the

mother, with a fond look. "I overheard her telling. him, when she was at dinner here one day, that you might be taken for a Southerner, if you only wore a dress-coat all the time and were heavily mortgaged. Withdraw her influence, and the desperate young man would tar and feather us all in our beds some night."

Falling silent after this unanswerable proof of Mr. Pendragon's guilt, Mr. Simpson mused upon as much of the dear old nut-cracker as was not hidden by the vast charity stocking. In her ruffled cap, false front, and spectacles, she was so exactly the figure one might picture Mr. John Stuart Mill to be, after reading his latest literary knitting on the Revolting Injustice of Masculine Society, that the Gospeller of Saint Cow's could not help feeling how perfectly useless it was to expect her to think herself capable of error.

As, whenever the Reverend Octavius gave indication of a capacity for speechless thoughtfulness, his benignant mother at once concluded that he needed an anti-bilious pill, she now made all haste to the cupboard to procure that imitation-vegetable and a glass of water. It was the neatest, best-stored Ritualistic cupboard in Bumsteadville. Above it hung a portrait of the Pope, from which the grand old Apostolic son of an infallible dogma looked knowingly down, as though with the contents of that cupboard he could get-up such a *schema* as would be palatable to the most sceptical Bishop in all the Œcumenical Council, and of which he might justly say : Whosoever dare think that he ever tasted

a better *schema*, or ever dreamed in his deepest conscious-
ness that a better could be made, let him be anathema maranatha! A most rakish looking wooden button, noiselessly
stealthy and sly, gave entrance to this treasury of dainties ;
and then what a rare array of disintegrated meals intoxicated
the vision ! There was the Athlete of the Dairy, commonly
called Fresh Butter, in his gay yellow jacket, looking wore
to the knife. There was turgid old Brown Sugar, who had
evidently heard the advice, go to the ant, thou sluggard !
and, mistaking the last word for Sugared, was going as
deliberately as possible. There was the vivacious Cheese,
in the hour of its mite, clad in deep, creamy, golden hue,
with delicate traceries of mould, like fairy cobwebs. The
Smoked Beef, and Doughnuts, as being more sober and un-
emotional features of the pageant, appeared on either side
the remains of a Cold Chicken, as rendering pathetic tribute
to hoary age ; while sturdy, reliable Hash and Fishballs re-
posed right and left in their mottled and rich brown coats,
with a kind of complacent consciousness of having been
created according to Mrs. Glass's standard dictum, First
catch your Hair.

Gospeller Simpson, by natural law, alternated from this
wonderful cupboard, very regularly, to another, or sister cupboard, also presided over by the good old maternal nut-
cracker, wherein the energetic pill lived in its little pasteboard house next door to the crystal palace of smooth, insinuating castor oil ; and passionate fiery essence of pepper-

mint grew hot with indignation at the proximity of plebeian rhubarb and squills.   In the present case he quietly took his anti-bilious globule : which, besides being a step in the direction of removing a pimple from his chin, was also intended as a kind of medical preparation for his coming services in the Ritualistic Church, where at a certain part of the ceremonies, he was to stand on his head before the Banner of St. Alban and balance Roman candles on his uplifted feet.   When the day had nearly passed, and the Vesper hour for those services arrived, he performed them with all the less rush of blood to the head for being thus prepared ; yet there was still a slight sensation of congestion, and, to get rid of this, when he stepped forth from Saint Cow's in the twilight, it was to take an evening stroll along the shore of Bumsteadville pond.

The Pond at Bumsteadville is sufficiently near the turn-pike to be readily reached from the latter, and, if mentioned in the advertisement of a summer boarding-house, would be called Lake Duckingham, on account of the fashionable ducks resorting thither for bathing and flirtation in the season.   When July's sun turns its tranquil mirror to hues of amber and gold, the slender mosquito sings Hum, sweet Hum, along its margin ; and when Autumn hangs his livery of motley on the trees, the glassy surface breathes out a mist wherefrom arises a spectre, with one hand of ice and the other of flame, to scatter Chills and Fever.   Strolling beside this picturesque watering-place in the dusk, the Gospeller suddenly caught the clatter of a female voice, and, in a moment, came face to face with Montgomery and Magnolia Pendragon.

"A cold and frog-like place, this, for a lady's walk, Miss Pendragon," he said, hastily swallowing a bronchial troche to neutralize the damp air admitted in speaking. "I hope you have on your overshoes."

"My sister brings me here," explained the brother, "so that her constant talking to me may not cause other people's heads to pain them."

"I believe," continued the Reverend Octavius, walking slowly on with them, "I believe, Mr. Pendragon, your sister finds out from you everything that you learn, or say, or do?"

"Everything," assented the young man, who seemed greatly exhausted. "She averages one question a minute."

"Consequently," went on Mr. Simpson, "she knows that I have advised you to make some kind of apology to Edwin Drood, for the editorial remarks passing between you on a certain important occasion?" He looked at the sister as he spoke, and took that opportunity to quickly swallow a quinine powder as a protection from the chills.

"My brother, sir," said Magnolia, "because, like the Lesbian Alcæus, fighting for the liberty of his native Mitylene, he has sympathized with his native South, finds himself treated by Mr. Drood with a lack of magnanimity of which even the renegade Pittacus would have been ashamed."

" But even at that," returned the Gospeller, much educated by her remark, "would it not be better for us all, to have this hapless misunderstanding manfully explained away, and are conciliation achieved ? "

" Did Æschylus explain to the Areopagus, after he had been unjustly abused?" asked the young female student, eagerly. " Or did he, rather, nobly prefer to remain silent, even until Ameinias reminded his prejudiced Yankee judges that he had fought at Salamis ? "

" Dear me," ejaculated the Gospeller, gasping, " I only meant —"

" I defend my brother," continued Magnolia, passionately, " as in the Antigone of Sophocles, Electra defends Orestes ; and even if he has no Pylades, he shall still be not without a friend in the habitation of the Pylopidæ."

" Upon my soul!" murmured the Reverend Mr. Simpson, " this is a dreadful state of things."

" I may as well confess to you, sir," said Montgomery, temporarily removing his fingers from his ears, ".that I admire Miss Potts as much as I'm down on Drood."

" He admires her," struck in his sister, " as Alcman, of Sardis, admired Megalostrata ; and, in her betrothal to a Yankee, sees another Sappho matrimonially sacrificed to another Cercolas of Andros."

" Mr. Pendragon," panted the Gospeller, "you must give

up this infatuation. The Flowerpot is engaged to another, and you have no business to express such sentiments for another's bride until after she is married. Eloquently as your sister —"

"I pretend to be no Myrtis, in genius," continued Magnolia, humbly. "I am not an Erinna, an Amite, a Praxilla, or a Nossis ; but all that is intellectually repugnant within me is stirred by this treatment of my brother, who is no Philodemus to find in Mr. Drood his Piso ; and sometimes I feel as though, like another Simonides, I could fly with him from this inhospitable Northern house of Scopas, to the refuge of some more generous Dioscuri. In the present macrocosm, to which we have come from our former home's microcosm, my brother is persistently maligned, even by Mr. Bumstead, who may yet, if I am any judge, meet the fate of Anacreon, as recorded by Suidas ; though, in his case, the choking will not be accompanied by a grape-stone, but by a clove."

"Well, well," said the Reverend Octavius, in a faint voice, "I shall expect you to at least meet Edwin Drood half-way in a reconciliation, Mr. Pendragon, for your own sake. I will see that he makes the first advance."

"Generous and dear tutor !" exclaimed Montgomery, "I will do anything, with you for my guide."

"Follow your guide penitently, brother," cried his sister, pathetically, "and you will find in him a relenting Polynices. Whatever we may feel towards others," she added, catching and kissing the overpowered Gospeller's hand, as they parted company, "you shall ever be our chosen, trusted, and only Psychopompos." *

Holding his throbbing head with both his hands, as he walked feebly homeward, the worn-out Gospeller noticed a light streaming from Mr. Bumstead's window ; and, inspired by a sudden impulse, entered the boarding-house and ascended straightway to the Ritualistic organist's rooms. Bumstead was asleep upon the rug before the fire, with his faithful umbrella under his arm, when Mr. Simpson, after vainly knocking, opened the door ; and never could the Gospeller forget how, upon being addressed, the sleeper started wildly up, made a futile pass at him with the umbrella, took a prolonged and staring drink from a pitcher of water on the table, and hurriedly ate a number of cloves from a saucer near an empty lemon-tea goblet over the mantel.

"Why, it's only I," explained the Reverend Octavius, rather alarmed by the glare with which he was regarded.

"Sit down, my friends," said Mr. Bumstead, huskily ; himself taking a seat upon a coal-scuttle near at hand, with considerable violence. "I'm glad you aroused me from a dreadful dream of reptiles. I sh'pose you want me to see you home, sir ?"

"Not at all," was the Gospeller's answer. "In fact, Mr.

---

* The Adapter refers confidently to any Southern female novel of the period for proof, that sentimental Magnolian school-girls always talk, or write, everything educational, except good English, when conferring with their deafened masculine friends.

Bumstead, I am anxious to bring about a reconciliation between these two young men. Let us have peace."

"If you want to let's have peash," observed the other, rather vaguely, "why don't you go fishing whenever there's any fighting talk, shir! Such a course is not, you'll Grant, unpresidented."

"I believe," said Mr. Simpson, waiving the suggestion, "that you entertain no favorable opinion of young Pendragon!"

Reaching to a book on the table, and, after various airy failures, laying hold upon it, Mr. Bumstead answered: "This is my diary, gentlemen; to be presented to Mrs. Stowe, when I'm no more, for a memoir. You, being two clergymen, wouldn't care to read it. Here's my entry on the night of the caucus in this room. Lish'n now: 'Half-pash Ten.— Considering the Democratic sentiments of the Montgomeries Pendragons, and their evident disinclination to vote the Republican Ticket, I b'lieve them capable of any crime. If they should kill my two nephews, it would be no hic-straordinary sh'prise. Have just been in to look at my nephews asleep, to make sure that the Pendragons have put no snakes in their bed.' Thash is *one* entry," continued Mr. Bumstead, momentarily pausing to make a blow with the fire-shovel at some imaginary creature crawling across the rug. "Here's another, written next morning after cloves: 'My nephews have gone to New York together this A. M. They laughed when I cautioned them against the

Montgomeries, and said they didn't see it. I am still very
uneasy, however, and have hurriedly pulled off my boots to
kill the reptiles in them. How's this for high?'" Mr.
Bumstead fell into a doze for an instant, and then added:
"I see the name 'J. Bumstead' signed to this. Who'sh
he ? — Oh ! i'mushbe myself."

"Well, well," commented the slightly astonished Gospeller, "whatever may be your private opinions, I ask you,
as a matter of evident public propriety, and for the good of
everybody, to soften Mr. Drood toward Mr. Pendragon, as
I have already softened Mr. Pendragon toward Mr. Drood.
You and I must put an end to this foolish quarrel."

"Thashis so," said Mr. Bumstead, with sudden assent,
laboriously gaining his feet to bid his guest good-bye, and
rather absent-mindedly opening the umbrella over his head
as he fumbled for the knob of the door. "You and I
musht reconcile these four young men. Gooright, shir.
Take a little soda-water in the morning and you'll be
awright, shir."

On the third day after this interview, Mr. Bumstead
waited upon Mr. Simpson with the following note, which,
after searching agitatedly for it in his hat and all his pockets,
he finally found up one of his sleeves : "*My dear* JACK : — I
am much pleased to hear of your conversation about me
with that good man whom you call 'the Reverends Mes-
sieurs Simpson,' and shall gladly comply with his wish for a
make-up between Pendragon and myself. Invite Pendragon

to dinner on Christmas Eve, when only we three shall be together, and we'll shake hands. Ever, dear clove-y Jack, yours truly, Edwin Drood."

"You think Mr. Pendragon will accept, then?" said the Gospeller.

Mr. Bumstead nodded darkly, shook hands, bowed to a large arm-chair for Mrs. Simpson, and retired with much stateliness.

CHAPTER XI.

A PICTURE AND A PARCEL.

BEHIND the most sample-room-y, fire-insuranceish, and express-wagonized part of Broadway, New York, yawns a venerable street called Nassau ; wherein architecture is a monster of such hideous mien that to be hated needs but to be rented, and more full-grown men stare into shoe-stores and shirt-emporiums without buying anything than in any other part of the world. Near the lower end of this quaint avenue rises the Post-Office, sending aloft a wooden steeple which is the coffin of a dead clock, and looking, altogether, like some good old-fashioned country church, which, having come to town many years ago to see its city cousins, and been discouraged by their brown-stone airs, retired, much demoralized, into a shady by-way, and there fell from grace into a kind of dissipated cross between Poor-House and railroad depot. To reach this amazing edifice with too much haste for more than a momentary glimpse of its harrowing exterior, and to get away from it, with a speed as little complimentary to the charms of its shadow, are, apparently, the two great and exclusive objects of the thousands swarming down and up the narrow street all through a day.

Some twenty odd boot-shops, all next-door-but-one to each other, startlingly alike in their despondent outer appearances, and uniformly conducted by embittered elderly men of savage aspect — seem to sue in vain from year to year for at least one customer ; and as many other melancholy dens for the sale of exactly the things no one but a madman would want to buy while on his way to a Post-Office, or from it, appear to wait as hopelessly for the first purchaser. There are, too, no end of open-air dealers in such curious postal incidentals as ghastly apples, insulting neck-ties, and impracticable pocket-combs; to whom, possibly, an unwholesome errand boy may be seen applying for a bargain about once in the life-time of an ordinary *habitué* of the street, but whose general wares were never seen selling to the extent of four shillings by any living observer. Still, with an affront to human credulity of which only newspapers are capable, it has been declared, in print, that there are bootmakers and apple-women of Nassau who continually buy choice up-town corner lots with their profits ; and, if it may be therefrom inferred that the other trades of the street do as incredibly well, it were wise, perhaps, to be further convinced that people have a well-established habit of stealthily laying in their new raiment, fruit, and toilet articles while going for their business-mails, and at once relinquish all earthly confidence in the senses obstinately refuting the theory.

About half-way between end and end of Nassau street

5

stands a row of what were modest dwelling-houses in the remote days when the city was under the rule of the Americans, but are now only so many floors of law offices. Who
owns them is not known ; for proprietors of real-estate in
this extraordinary highway of antiquity are never mentioned
in public like owners in any other street ; but they are
shabby, dreary, hopeless-looking old piles, suggestive of having, perhaps, been hurried and tumbled through musty law-
suits scores of times, and occupied at last by the robber Law
itself for costs. On a certain dark, foggy afternoon in December, one of the seediest of the fallen brick brotherhood
presented a particularly dingy appearance, as the gas-lights
necessitated by the premature gloom of the hour gleamed
dimly through a blearing window-pane here and there. The
house still retained the narrow street-door, hall-way, and abrupt immediate stairway of its earlier days ; and had, too, the
old-style goodly single brown stone for a " stoop," along the
front fall of which, in faded white block letters, as though
originally done with a stencil-plate, appeared the strange device :

$$S - T - 1860 - X.*$$

Whether this curious legend referred to the sweets or bitters
of the tenement's various experiences : whether it meant
Subjected To 1860 'Xecutions, or Sacrificed To 1860 'Xecu-
tors, or Sentenced To Wait-e'en-Sixty 'Xigencies, did not

* In the original "J. P. T. 1747."

bother the head of Mr. Dibble, who came in from Gowanus every morning to occupy his law-office upstairs, and was sitting thoughtfully therein, before a grate fire, on the dull, wintry afternoon in question.

Severely unostentatious was that office, with its two ink-stained desks, shelves of lettered deed-boxes, glass case of law-books in sheep, and vellum-covered reading-table in the centre of the room. Its prompt lesson for the visitor was: You are now in the office of an old-school Constitutional Lawyer, Sir; and if you want an Absolute Divorce, Obtained for No Cause, in Any State; No Publicity; No Charges; you must step around to a certain newspaper sanctum for your witnesses, and apply to some other legal practitioner. In this establishment, sir, after you have left your measure in the shape of a retaining fee, we fit you with a suit warranted to last as long as you do. We cut your pockets to suit ourselves, but furnish you as much choler as you can stand. If you are a pursey man the suit will have no lack of sighs for you ; if you are thin, it will make your waste the greater.

Mr. Dibble's usual companion in this office was his clerk, Bladams,* who generally wrote at the second desk, and, consequently, was a person of another deskscription. A politician in former days — when he was known as Mr. William Adams — this clerk had aspired to office in New York, and freely spent his means to attain the same. His name,

* In the original, *Bazzard.*

however, was too much for his fortune. Public credulity re-
volted from the pretence that a William Adams had come
from Ireland some years before, on purpose to found the
family of which the later candidate of the same name claimed
to be a descendant; and, after an election in which he had
spent the last of his money, he was "counted out" in favor
of a rather hod character named O'Glooral. Thus practi-
cally taught to understand the political genius of a Republic,
which, as gloriously contrasted with any effete monarchy
ruled by a Peerage, looks for its own governing class to the
Steerage, Mr. William Adams subsided impecuniously into
plain Bill Adams and a book-keepership in-dry goods; and
was ultimately blurred into Bladams and employment as a
copyist by Mr. Dibble, to whom his experience of spending
every cent' he had in the world, and getting nothing in the
world for it but wrinkles, seemed felicitously legal and almost
supernaturally qualifying for law-writing. Bladams was about
forty years old, though appearing much older: with a slight
cast in his left eye, a pimply pink countenance, and a cir-
cular piece of unimproved property on top of his head.

"Any news?" inquired Mr. Dibble, as this member of
the once powerful American race entered the office and still
grasped the edge of the door.

"I saw Mr. Drood across the street just now," was the
answer. .

"And what did he say, Bladams?"

"'That in turn he'd see *me* across the street; and here he is," returned the clerk, advancing into the room.

"Ah, my dear Mr. Edwin, glad to see you !" exclaimed Mr. Dibble, rising to his feet and turning about to greet the new comer. " Sit down by the fire ; and don't mind the presence of Mr. Bladams, who was once a gentleman."

"Thank you, old man, I don't know but I *will* take a glow with you," said Edwin, accepting a chair and throwing aside hat and overcoat.

"You're just in time to dine with me," continued the lawyer. "I'll send across to a restaurant for three stews and as many mugs of ale. We must ask Mr. Bladams to join us, you see ; for he was once a decent man, and might not like to be sent out for oysters unless asked to take some."

" If they're the small black ones you generally treat on, I'd rather be excused," grumbled Mr. Bladams, involuntarily placing a hand upon his stomach, as though already paying the penalty of such bivalvular hospitality.

" Order saddle-rocks this time," was the reckless response of his employer. "Mr. Edwin is so rarely our guest that we must do the princely. You'll tell them, Bladams, to send plenty of crackers, and request the waiters to keep their fingers out of the stews while bringing the latter over. I've known waiters to have their finger-nails boiled off in time, by a habit of carrying soup and stews with the ends of their digits in them."

The clerk departing to order the feast, Mr. Dibble renewed his attention to Mr. E. Drood, who had already taken his ball from his pocket and was practising against the mantel.

"I suppose you are on your way to Bumsteadville, again, Mr. Edwin, and have called to see if I have any message for my pretty ward over there."

"That's the ticket," assented Edwin, making a neat fly-catch.

"You're impatient to be there, of course?" asserted Mr. Dibble, with what might have passed for an attempt at archness, if he had not been so wholly devoted to squareness.

"I believe the Flowerpot is expecting me," yawned the young man.

"Do you keep plants there, Mr. Edwin?"

"The whole thing is a regular plant, Mr. Dibble."

"But you spoke about a flowerpot."

Edwin stretched his feet further toward the fire, and explained that he meant Miss Potts. "Did she say anything to you about the Pendragons, when you saw her?" he inquired.

"What *are* Pendragons?" asked the lawyer, wonderingly.

"One of them is a schoolmate of hers. A girl with some style about her."

"No," said Mr. Dibble, "she did not. — But here comes Bladams."

Bladams ushered in two waiters — one Irish and one German — who wore that look of blended long-suffering and ex-

treme weariness of everything eatable, which, in this country, seems inevitably characteristic of the least personal
agency in the serving of meals. (There may be lands in
which the not essentially revolting art of cookery can
be practised without engendering irritable gloom in the
bosoms of its practitioners, and the spreading of tables does
not necessarily entail upon the actors therein a despon-
dency almost sinister; but the American kitchen is the home
of beings who never laugh, save in that sardonic bitterness of
spirit which grimly mocks the climax of human endurance
in the burning of the soup ; and the waiter of the American
dining-room can scarcely place a dish upon the board without making it eloquent of a blighted existence.) Having
dashed the stews upon the reading-table before the fire, and
rescued a drowning fly* from one of them with his least ap-
petizing thumb-nail, the melancholy Irish attendant polished
the spoons with his pocket-handkerchief and hurled them on
either side of the plates. Perceiving that his German associate, in listlessly throwing the mugs of ale upon the table,
had spilled some of the liquid, he hurriedly wiped the stain
away with Edwin Drood's worsted muffler, and dried the
sides of the glasses upon the napkin intended for Mr. Dibble's
use. There was something of the wild resources of de-

---

* In anticipation of any critical objection to the introduction of a living *fly* in *December*, the Adapter begs leave to assert that an anachronism is always legitimate in a
work of fiction when a point is to be made. Thus in Chapter VIII. of the inimitable
"Nicholas Nickleby," Mr. Squeers tells Nicholas that morning has come, "and *ready
iced*, too;" and that "the pump's *froze;*" while only a few pages later, in the same
chapter, one of Mr. Squeers' scholars is spoken of as "*weeding the garden.*"

spair, too, in this man's frequent ghostly dispatch of the
German after articles forgotten in the first trip, such as
another cracker, the cover of the pepper-cruet, the salt, and
one more pinch of butter; and so greatly did his apparent
dejection of soul increase as each supplementary luxury arrived and was recklessly slammed into its place, that, upon
finally retiring from the room with his associate, his utter
hopelessness of aspect gave little suggestion of the future
proud political preferment to which, by virtue of his low
estate and foreign birth, he was assuredly destined.

The whole scene had been a reproachful commentary
upon the stiff American system of discouraging waiters from
making remarks upon the weather, inquiring the cost of
one's new coat, conferring with one upon the general prospects of his business for the season, or from indulging in any
of the various light conversational diversions whereby bar-
bers, Fulton-street tailors, and other depressed gymnasts,
are occasionally and wholesomely relieved from the misery
of brooding over *their* equally dispiriting avocations.

After the departure of the future aldermen, or sheriffs, of
the city, the good old lawyer accompanied his young guest in
an expeditious assimilation of the stews; saying little, but
silently regretting, for the sake of good manners, that Mr.
Bladams could not eat oysters without making a noise as
though they were alive in his mouth.   At last, mug of ale
in hand, he turned to his clerk :

" Bladams ! "

"Sir to you!" responded Mr. Bladams, hastily putting down the plate from which he had been drinking his last drop of stew, and grasping his own mug.

"Your health, Bladams. — Mr. Edwin joins me, I'm sure. — And may the — may our — that is, may your — suppose we call it bump of Happiness — may your bump of. Happiness increase."

Staring thoughtfully, Mr. Bladams felt for the Bump upon his head, and having scratched what he seemed to take for it, replied : "It's a go, sir. The Bump has increased some since Kent's Commentaries fell on it from that top-shelf the other day."

"I am going to toast my lovely ward," whispered Mr. Dibble to Edwin ; "but I put Bladams first, because he was once a person to be respected, and I treat him with politeness in place of a good salary."

"Success to the Bump," said Edwin Drood, rather struck by this piece of practical economy, and newly impressed with the standard fact that politeness costs nothing.

"And now," continued Mr. Dibble, with a wink in which his very ear joined, "I give you the peerless Miss Flora Potts. Bladams, please remember that there are others here to eat crackers besides yourself, and join us in a health to Miss Potts."

"Let the toast pass — drink to the lass!" cried Mr. Bladams, husky with crackers. "All ale to her!"

"Count me in too," assented Edwin.

5*

"Dear me!" said the old lawyer, breaking a momentary spell of terror occasioned by Mr. Bladams having turned blue and nearly choked to death in a surreptitious attempt to swallow a cracker which he had previously concealed in one of his cheeks. "Dear me! although I *am* a square, practical man, I do believe that I could draw a picture of a true lover's state of mind to-night."

"A regular chromo," wheezed Mr. Bladams, encouragingly; pretending not to notice that his employer was reaching an ineffectual arm after the crackers at his own elbow.

"Subject to the approving, or correcting, judgment of Mr. E. Drood, I make bold to guess that the modern true lover's mind, such as it is, is rendered jerky by contemplation of the lady who has made him the object of her virgin affections," proceeded Mr. Dibble, looking intently at Edwin, but still making farther and farther reaches toward the distant crackers, even to the increased tilting of his chair. "I venture the conjecture, that if he has any darling pet name for her, such as 'Pinky-winky,' 'Little Fooly,' 'Chignonentity,' or 'Waxy Wobbles,' he feels horribly ashamed if any one overhears it, and coughs violently to make believe that he never said it."

It was curious to see Edwin listening with changing color to this truthful exposure of his young mind; the while, influenced unconsciously, probably, by the speaker's example, he, too, had begun reaching and chair-tilting toward the

crackers across the table. What time Mr. Bladams, at
the opposite side of the board, had apparently sunk into a
sudden and deep slumber; although from beneath one of his
folded arms a finger dreamily rested upon the rim of the
cracker-plate, and occasionally gave it a little pull farther
away from the approaching hands.

"My picture," continued Mr. Dibble, now quite hoarse,
and almost horizontal in his reaching, to Edwin Drood, also
nearly horizontal in the same way — "my picture goes on
to represent the true lover as ever eager to be with his dear
one, for the purpose of addressing implacable glares at the
Other Young Man with More Property, whom She says she
always loved as a Brother when they were Children Together; and of smiling bitterly and biting off the ends of his
new gloves (which is more than he can really afford, at his
salary), when She softly tells him that he is making a perfect
fool of himself. My picture further represents him to be
continually permeated by a consciousness of such tight boots
as he ought not to wear, even for the Beloved Object, and
of such readiness to have new cloth coats spoiled, by getting
hair-oil on the left shoulder, as shall yet bring him to a
scene of violence with his distracted tailor. It shows him,
likewise, as filled with exciting doubts of his own relative
worth : that is, with self-questionings as to whether he shall
ever be worth enough to buy that cantering imported saddle-
horse which he has already promised; to spend every summer in a private cottage at Newport; to fight off Western

divorces, and to pay an eloquent lawyer a few thousands for getting him clear, on the plea of insanity, after he shall have shot the Other Young Man with More Property for wanting his wife to be a Sister to him, again, as she was, you know, when they were Children Together."

Edwin, despite the coldness of the season, had perspired freely during the latter part of the Picture, and sought to disguise his uneasiness at its beautiful, yet severe truth, by a last push of his extended arm toward the crackers. Qnickly observing this, Mr. Dibble also made a final desperate reach after the same object; so that both old man and young, while pretending to heed each other's words only, were two-thirds across the table, with their feet in the air and their chairs poised on one leg each. At that very moment, by some unhappy chance, while nearly the whole weight of the two was pressing upon their edge of the board, Mr. Bladams abruptly awoke, and raised his elbows from *his* edge, to relieve his arms by stretching. Released from his pressure, the table flew up upon two legs with remarkable swiftness, and then turned over upon Mr. Dibble and Mr. E. Drood; bringing the two latter and their chairs to the floor under a shower of plates and crackers, and resting invertedly upon their prostrate forms, like some species of four-pillared monumental temple without a roof.

A person less amiable than the good Mr. Dibble would have borrowed the name of an appurtenance of a mill, at least once, as a suitable expression of his feelings upon such a trying occasion; but, instead of this, when Mr. Bladams, excitedly crying " Fire ! " lifted the overturned table from off himself and the young guest, he merely arose to a sitting position on the littered carpet, and said to Edwin, with a smile and a rub: " Pray, am I at all near the mark in my picture ? "

" I should say, sir," responded Edwin, with a very strange expression of countenance, also rubbing the back of his head, " that you are rather hard upon the feelings of the un- lucky lover. He may not show *all* that he feels— "

There he paused so long to feel his nose and ascertain about its being broken, that Mr. Dibble limped to his feet and ended that part of the discussion by hobbling to an open iron safe across the office.

Taking from a private drawer in this repository a small paper parcel, containing a pasteboard box, and opening the latter, the old lawyer produced what looked like a long, flat white cord, with shining tips at either end.

" This, Mr. Edwin," said he, with marked emotion, " is a stay-lace, with golden tags, which belonged to Miss Flora's mother. It was handed to me, in the abstraction of his grief, by Miss Flora's father, on the day of the funeral ; he saying that he could never bear to look upon it again. To you, as Miss Flora's future husband, I now give it."

" A stay-lace ! " echoed Edwin, coming forward as quickly as his lameness would allow, and staunching his swollen upper lip with a handkerchief.

"Yes," was the grave response. "You have undoubt-edly noticed, Mr. Edwin, that in every fashionable romance, the noble and grenadine heroine has a habit of ' drawing herself up proudly' whenever any gentleman tries to shake hands with her, or asks her how she can possibly be so ma-jestic with him. This lace was used by Miss Flora's mother to draw herself up proudly with; and she drew herself up so much with it, that it finally reached her heart and killed her. I here place it in your hands, that you may ultimately give it to your young wife as a memento of a mother who did nothing by halves but die. If you, by any chance, should not marry the daughter, I solemnly charge you, by the mem-ory of the living and the dead, to bring it back to me."

Receiving the parcel with some awe, Edwin placed it in one of his pockets.

"Bladams," said Mr. Dibble, solemnly, "you are witness of the transfer."

"Deponent, being duly sworn, does swear and cuss that he saw it, to the best of his knowledge and belief," returned the clerk, helping Mr. Drood to resume his overcoat.

When in his own room, at Gowanus, that night, Mr. Dibble, in his nightcap, paused a moment before extinguish-ing his light, to murmur to himself: "I wonder, now, whether poor Potts confided his orphan child to me because he knew that I might have been the successful suitor to the mother if I had been worth a little more money just about then?"

What time, in the law-office in town, Mr. Bladams was upon his knees on the floor, tossing crackers from all directions on the carpet into his month, like a farinaceous goblin, and nearly suffocating whenever he glanced at the disordered table.

•

CHAPTER XII.

A NIGHT OF IT WITH MCLAUGHLIN.

JUDGE SWEENEY, with a certain supercilious consciousness that he is figuring in a novel, and that it will not do
for him to thwart the eccentricities of mysterious fiction by
any commonplace deference to the mere meteorological
weakness of ordinary human nature, does not allow the fact
that late December is a rather bleak and cold time of year to
deter him from taking daily airings in the neighborhood of
the Ritualistic churchyard. Since the inscription of his epitaph on his late wife upon her monument therein, the
churchyard is to him a kind of ponderous work of imagination with marble leaves, to which he has contributed the
most brilliant chapter ; and when he sees any stranger hov-
ering about a part of the outer railings from whence the inscription may be read, it is with all the swelling pride of an
author who, having procured the publication of some trans-
cendental article in a Boston magazine, is thrown into an
ecstasy of vanity if he sees but one person glance at that
number of the periodical on a news-stand.

Since his first meeting with Mr. Bumstead, on the evening of the epitaph-reading, Judge Sweeney has cultivated

that gentleman's acquaintance, and been received at his lodgings several times with considerable cordiality and lemon-tea. On such occasions, Mr. Bumstead, in his musical capacity, has sung so closely in Judge Sweeney's ear as to tickle him, a wild and slightly incoherent Ritualistic stave, to the effect that Saint Peter's of Rome, with pontifical dome, would by ballot Infallible be; but for making Call sure, and Election secure, Saint Repeater's of Rum beats the See. With finger in ear to allay the tickling sensation, Judge Sweeney declares that this young man smelling of cloves is a person of great intellectual attainments, and understands the political genius of his country well enough to make an excellent Judge of Election.

Walking slowly near the churchyard on this particular freezing December evening, with his hands behind his back, and his eyes intent for any envious husband who may be "with a rush retiring," monumentally counselled, after reading the epitaph, Judge Sweeney suddenly comes upon Father Dean conversing with Smythe, the sexton, and Mr. Bumstead. Bowing to these three, who, like himself, seem to find real luxury in open-air strolling on a bitter night in midwinter, he notices that his model, the Ritual Rector, is wearing a new hat, like a Cardinal's, only black, and is immediately lost in wondering where he can obtain one like it short of Rome.

"You look so much like an author, Mr. Bumstead, in having no overcoat, wearing your paper collar upside down,

and carrying a pen behind your ear," Father Dean is saying, "that I can almost fancy you are about to write a
book about us. Well, Bumsteadville is just the place to furnish a nice, dry, inoffensive domestic novel in the sedative
Bayard Taylor vein."

After two or three ineffectual efforts to seize the end of
it, which he seems to think is an inch or two higher than its
actual position, Mr. Bumstead finally withdraws from between his right ear and head a long and neatly cut hollow
straw.

"This is not a pen, Holy Father," he answers, after a momentary glance of majestic severity at Mr. Smythe, who has
laughed. "It is only a simple instrument which I use, as
a species of syphon, in certain chemical experiments with
sliced tropical fruit and glass-ware. In the precipitation of
lemon-slices into cut crystal, it is necessary for the liquid
medium to be exhausted gradually; and, after using this cyl-
inder of straw for the purpose about an hour ago, I must
have placed it behind my ear in a moment of absent-minded-
ness."

"Ah, I see," said Father Dean, although he didn't. "But
what is this, Judge Sweeney, respecting your introduction of
McLaughlin to Mr. Bumstead, which I have heard about?"

"Why, your Reverence, I consider John McLaughlin a
character," responds the Judge, "and thought our young
friend of the organ-loft might like to study him."

"The truth is," explains Mr. Bumstead, "that Judge

Sweeney put it into my head to do a few pauper graves with John McLaughlin, some moonlight night, for the mere oddity and dampness of the thing.— And I should regret to believe," adds Mr. Bumstead, raising his voice as he saw that the judiciary was about to interrupt — "And I should really be loathe to believe that Judge Sweeney was not perfectly sober when he did so."

"Oh, yes — certainly — I remember — to be sure," exclaims the Judge in great haste ; alarmed into speedy assent by the construction which he perceives would be put upon a denial. "I remember it very distinctly. I remember putting it into your head — by the tumblerful, if I remember rightly."

"Profiting by your advice," continues Mr. Bumstead, oblivious to the last sentence, "I am going out to-night, in search of the moist and picturesque, with John McLaughlin —"

"Who is here," says Father Dean.

Old Mortarity, dinner-kettle in hand and more mortary than ever, is indeed seen approaching them with shuffling gait. Bowing to the Holy Father, he is about to pass on, when Judge Sweeney stops him with —

"You must be very careful with your friend Bumstead, this evening, John McLaughlin, and see that he don't fall and break his neck."

"Never you worry about Mr. Bumstead, Judge," growls

Old Mortarity. " He can walk further off the perpendick-
lar without tumbling than any gentleman I ever see."

"Of course I can, John McLaughlin," says Mr. Bumstead, checking another unseemly laugh of Mr. Smythe's
with a dreadful frown. " I often practise walking sideways,
for the purpose of developing the muscles *on* that side.
The left side is always the weaker, and the hip a trifle lower,
if one does not counteract the difference by walking sideways occasionally."

A great deal of unnecessary coughing, which follows this
physiological exposition, causes Mr. Bumstead to breathe
hard at them all for a moment, and tread with great malig-
nity upon Mr. Smythe's nearest corn.

While yet the sexton is groaning, Old Mortarity whispers
to the Ritualistic organist that he will be ready for him at
the appointed hour to-night, and shuffles away. After which
Mr. Bumstead, with the hollow straw sticking out fiercely from
behind his ear, privately offers to see Father Dean home if
he feels at all dizzy ; and, being courteously refused, retires
down the turnpike toward his own lodgings with military precision of step.

When night falls upon the earth like a drop of ink upon
the word Sun, and the stars glitter like the points of so
many poised gold pens all ready to write the softer word
Moon above the blot, the organist of St. Cow's sits in his
own room, where his fire keeps-up a kind of aspenish twilight, and executes upon his accordeon a series of wild and

mutilated airs. The moistened towel which he often wears when at home is turbaned upon his head, causing him to present a somewhat Turkish appearance ; and as, when turning a particularly complicated corner in an air, it is his artistic habit to hold his tongue between his teeth, twist his head in sympathy with the elaborate fingering, and involuntarily lift one foot higher and higher from the floor as some skittish note frantically dodges to evade him, his general musical aspect at his own hearth, is that of a partially Oriental gentleman, agonizingly laboring to cast from him some furious animal full of strange sounds. Thus engaging in desperate single combat with what, for making a ferocious fight before any recognizable tune can be rescued from it, is, perhaps, the most exhausting instrument known to evening amateurs and maddened neighborhoods, Mr. Bumstead passes three athletic hours. At the end of that time, after repeatedly tripping-up the exasperated organist over wrong keys in the last bar, the accordeon finally relinquishes the concluding note with a dismal whine of despair, and retires in complete collapse to its customary place of waiting. Then the conquering performer changes his towel for a hat which would look better if it had not been so often worn in bed, places an antique black bottle in one pocket of his coat and a few cloves in the other; hangs an unlighted lantern before him by a cord passing about his neck, and, with his umbrella under his arm, goes softly down stairs and out of the house.

Repairing to the marble-yard and home of Old Mortarity, which are on the outskirts of Bumsteadville, he wanders through mortar-heaps, monuments brought for repair, and piles of bricks, toward a whitewashed residence of small dimensions with a light at the window.

"John McLaughlin, ahoy!"

In response, the master of the mansion promptly opens the door, and it is then perceptible that his basement, parlor, spare-bedroom, and attic are all on one floor, and that a couple of pigs are spending the season with him. Showing his visitor into this ingeniously condensed establishment, he induces the pigs to retire to a corner, and then dons his hat.

"Are you ready, John McLaughlin?"

"Please the pigs, I am, Mr. Bumstead," answers Mc-Laughlin, taking down from a hook a lantern, which, like his companion's, he hangs from his neck by a cord. "My spirits is equal to any number of ghosts to-night, sir, if we meet 'em."

"Spirits!" ejaculates the Ritualistic organist, shifting his umbrella for a moment while he hurriedly draws the antique bottle from his pocket. "You're nervous to-night, J. Mc-Laughlin, and need a little of the venerable James Aker's West Indian Restorative. — I'll try it first, to make sure that I haven't mistaken the phial."

He rests the elongated orifice of the diaphanous flask upon his lips for a brief interval of critical inspection, and then applies it thoughtfully to the mouth of Old Mortarity.

"Some more! Some more!" pleads the aged McLaughlin, when the Jamaican nervine is abruptly jerked from his lips.

"Silence! Come on," is the stern response of the other, who, as he moves from the house, and restores the crystal antiquity to its proper pocket, eats a few cloves by stealth. His manner plainly shows that he is offended at the quantity the old man has managed to swallow already.

Strange indeed is the ghastly expedition to the place of skulls, upon which these two go thus by night. Not strange, perhaps, for Mr. McLaughlin, whose very youth in New York, where he was an active politician, found him a frequent nightly familiar of the Tombs; but strange for the organist, who, although often grave in his manner, sepulchral in his tones, and occasionally addicted to coughin', must be curiously eccentric to wish to pass into concert that evening with the dead heads.

Transfixed by his umbrella, which makes him look like a walking cross between a pair of boots and a hat, Mr. Bumstead leads the way athwart the turnpike and several fields, until they have arrived at a low wall skirting the foot of Gospeller's Gulch. Here they catch sight of the Reverend Octavius Simpson and Montgomery Pendragon walking together, near the former's house, in the moonlight, and, instantaneously, Mr. Bumstead opens his umbrella over the head of Old Mortarity, and drags him down beside himself under it behind the wall.

"Hallo! What's all this?" gasps Mr. McLaughlin, struggling affrightedly in his suffocating cage of whalebone and alpaca. "What's this here old lady's hoop-skirt doing on me?"

"Peace, wriggling dotard!" hisses Bumstead, jamming the umbrella tighter over him. "If they see us they'll want some of the West Indian Restorative."

Mr. Simpson and Montgomery have already heard a sound; for they pause abruptly in their conversation, and the latter asks: "Could it have been a ghost."

"Ask it if it's a ghost," whispers the Gospeller, involuntarily crossing himself.

"Are you there, Mr. G.?" quavers the raised voice of the young Southerner, respectfully addressing the inquiry to the stone wall.

No answer.

"Well," mutters the Gospeller, "it couldn't have been a ghost, after all; but I certainly thought I saw an umbrella. To conclude what I was saying, then,—I have the confidence in you, Mr. Montgomery, to believe that you will attend the dinner of Reconciliation on Christmas eve, as you have promised."

"Depend on me, sir."

"I shall; and have become surety for your punctuality to that excellent and unselfish healer of youthful wounds, Mr. Bumstead."

More is said after this; but the speakers have strolled to

the other side of the Gospeller's house, and their words can not be distinguished. Mr. Bumstead closes his umbrella with such suddenness and violence as to nearly pull off the· head of McLaughlin ; drives his own hat further upon his nose with a sounding blow; takes several wild swallows from his antique flask ; eats two cloves, and chuckles hoarsely to himself for some minutes. " Here, John McLaughlin, he says at last, " try a little more West Indian Restorative, and then we'll go and do a few skeletons."

The pauper burial-ground toward which they now progress in a rather high-stepping manner, or — to vary the phrase — toward which their steps are now very much bent, is not a favorite resort of the more cheerful village-people after nightfall. Ask any resident of Bumsteadville if he believed in ghosts, and, if the time were mid-day and the place a crowded grocery store, he would fearlessly answer in the negative ; (just the same as a Positive philosopher in cast-iron health and with no thunder shower approaching would undauntedly deny a Deity ;) but if any resident of Bumsteadville should happen to be caught near the country editor's last home after dark, he would get over that part of his road in a curiously agile and flighty manner ; — (just the same as a Positive philosopher with a sore throat, or at an uncommonly showy bit of lightning, would repeat " Now I lay me down to sleep," with surprising devotion.) So, although no one in all Bumsteadville was in the least afraid of the pauper burial-ground at any hour, it was not invaria-'

6

bly selected by the great mass of the populace as a peerless place to go home by at midnight; and the two intellectual explorers find no sentimental young couples rambling arm-in-arm among the ghastly head-boards, nor so much as one loiterer smoking his segar on a suicide's tomb.

"John McLaughlin, you're getting nervous again," says Mr. Bumstead, catching him in the coat collar with the handle of his umbrella and drawing the other toward him hand-over-hand. "It's about time that you should revert again to the hoary James Aker's excellent preparation for the human family. — I'll try it first, myself, to see if it tastes at all of the cork."

"Ah-h," sighs Old Mortarity, after his turn has come and been enjoyed at last, "that's the kind of Spirits I don't mind being a wrapper to. I could wrap *them* up all night."

Reflectively chewing a clove, the Ritualistic organist reclines on the pauper grave of a former writer for the daily press, and cogitates upon his companion's leaning to Spiritualism; while the other produces matches and lights their lanterns.

"Mr. McLaughlin," he solemnly remarks, waving his umbrella at the graves around, "in this scene you behold the very last of man's individual being. In this entombment he ends forever. Tremble, J. McLaughlin! — forever. Soul and Spirit are but unmeaning words, according to the latest big things in science. The departed Dr. Davis Slavonski, of St. Petersburg, before setting out for the Asylum, proved,

by his Atomic Theory, that men are neatly manufactured
of Atoms of matter, which are continually combining together until they form Man; and then going through the
process of Life, which is but the mechanical effect of their
combination; and then wearing apart again by attrition
into the exhaustion of cohesion called ᴿ·ath; and then
crumbling into separate Atoms of native matter, or dust
again; and then gradually combining again, as before, and
evolving another Man; and Living, and Dying, again; and
so on forever. Thus, and thus only, is Man immortal.
You are made exclusively of Atoms of matter, yourself,
John McLaughlin. So am I."

"I can understand a man's believing that *he, himself,* is
all Atoms of matter, and nothing else," responds Old Mortarity, sceptically.

"As how, John McLaughlin, — as how?"

"When he knows that, at any rate, he hasn't got one
atom of common sense," is the answer.

Suddenly Mr. Bumstead arises from the grave and frantically shakes hands with him.

"You're right, sir!" he says, emotionally. "You're a
gooroleman, sir, The Atom of common sense was one of
the Atoms that Slavonski forgot all about. Let's do some
skeletons now."

At the further end of the pauper burial-ground, and in
the rear of the former Alms-House, once stood a building
used successively as a cider-mill, a barn, and a kind of

chapel for paupers. Long ago, from neglect and bad weather, the frail wooden superstructure had fallen into pieces and been gradually carted off; but a sturdy stone foundation remained underground; and, although the flooring over it had for many years been covered with debris and rank growth, so as to be undistinguishable to common eyes from the general earth around it, the great cellar still extended beneath, and, according to weird rumor, had some secret access for Old Mortarity, who used it as a charnel store-house for such spoils of the grave as he found in his prowlings.

To the spot thus historied the two moralists of the moonlight come now, and, with many tumbles, Mr. McLaughlin removes certain artfully placed stones and rubbish, and lifts a clumsy extemporized trap-door. Below appears a ricketty old step-ladder leading into darkness.

"I heard such cries and groans down there, last Christmas-Eve, as sounded worse than the Latin singing in the Ritualistic church," observes McLaughlin.

"Cries and groans!" echoes Mr. Bumstead, turning quite pale, and momentarily forgetting the snakes which he is just beginning to discover among the stones. "You're getting nervous again, poor wreck, and need some more West Indian cough mixture. — Wait until I see for myself whether it's got enough sugar in it."

In due time the great nervous antidote is passed and replaced, and then, with the lighted lanterns worked around under their arms, they go down the tottering ladder. Down they go into a great damp, musty cavern, to which their lights give a pallid illumination.

"See here," says Old Mortarity, raising a long, curved bone from the floor. "Look at that: shoulder-blade of unmarried Episcopal lady, aged thirty-nine."

"How do you know she was so old, and unmarried?" asks the organist.

"Because the shoulder-blade's so sharp."

Mr. Bumstead is surprised at this specimen of an Agassie and Waterhouse Hawkins in such a mortary old man, and his intellectual pride causes him to resolve at once upon a rival display.

"Look at this skull, John McLaughlin," he says, referring to an object that he has found behind the ladder. "See thish fine, retreating brow, bulging chin, projecting occipital bone, and these orifices of ears that musht've been stupen'sly long. It's the skull, John McLaughlin, of a twin-brother of the man who really wished — really wished, John McLaughlin — that he could be sat'shfied, sir, in his own mind, that Charles Dickens was a Christian writer."

"Why, thash's skull of a hog," explains Mr. McLaughlin, with some contempt.

"Twin-brother — all th'shame," says Mr. Bumstead, as though that made no earthly difference.

Once more, what a strange expedition is this! How strangely the eyes of the two men look, after two or three more applications to the antique flask; and how·curiously Mr. Bumstead walks on tip-toe at times and takes short leaps now and then.

"Lesh go now," says Bumstead, after both have been asleep upon their feet several times; "I think th's snakes down here, John McBumstead."

"Wh'st! monkies, you mean,—dozens of black monkies, Mr. Bumplin," whispers Old Mortarity, clutching his arm as he sinks against him.

. "Noshir! Serp'nts!" insists Mr. Bumstead, making futile attempts to open his umbrella with one hand. "Warzesmarrer with th' light?—ansh'r me, t' once Mac Johnbuncklin!"

In their swayings under the confusions and delusions of the vault, their lanterns have worked around to the neighborhoods of their spines, so that, whichever way they turn, the light is all behind them. Greatly agitated, as men are apt to be when surrounded by supernatural influences, they do not perceive the cause of this apparently unnatural illumination; and, upon turning round and round in irregular circles, and still finding the light in the wrong place, they exhibit signs of great trepidation.

"Warzermarrer, wirra*light?*" repeats Mr. Bumstead, spinning wildly until he brings up against the wall.

"Ishgotb'witched, I b'lieve," pants Mr. McLaughlin, whirling as.frenziedly with his own lantern dangling behind him, and coming to an abrupt pause against the opposite wall.

Thus, each supported against the stones by a shoulder, they breathe hard for a moment, and then sink into a slumber in which they both slide down to the ground. Aroused by the shock, they sit up quite dazed, brush away the swarming snakes and monkies, are freshly alarmed by discovering that they are now actually sitting upon that perverse light behind them, and by a simultaneous impulse, begin crawling about in search of the ladder.

Unable to see anything with all the light behind him, but fancying that he discerns a gleam beyond a dark object near at hand, Mr. Bumstead rises to a standing attitude by a series of complex manœuvres, and plants a foot on something.

" I'morth'larrer ! " he cries, spiritedly.

" Th'larrer's on me ! " answers Mr. McLaughlin, in evidently great bewilderment.

Then ensue a momentary wild struggle and muffled crash ; for each gentleman, coming blindly upon the other, has taken the light glimmering at the other's back for the light at the top of the ladder, and, further mistaking the other in the dark for the ladder itself, has attempted to climb him. Mr. Bumstead, however, has got the first step ; whereupon, Mr. McLaughlin, in resenting what he takes for the ladder's inexcusable familiarity, has twisted both himself and his equally deluded companion into a pretty hard fall.

Another interval of hard breathing, and then the organist of Saint Cow's asks : " Di'youhear anything drop ? "

" Yeshir, th'larrer, got throwed, f'rimpudence to a gen-

'l'm'n," is the peevish return of Old Mortarity, who immediately falls asleep as he lies, with his lantern under his spine.

In his sleep, he dreams that Bumstead examines him closely, with a view to gaining some clue to the mystery of the light behind both their backs; and, on finding the lantern under him, and studying it profoundly for some time, is suddenly moved to feel along his own back. He dreams that Bumstead thereupon finds his own lantern, and exclaims, after half an hour's analytical reflection, " It must'ave slid round while John McLaughlin was intosh'cated." Then, or soon after, the dreamer awakes, and can discern two Mr. Bumsteads seated upon the step-ladders, with a lantern, baby-like, on each knee.

" You two men are awake at last, eh ? " say the organists, with peculiar smiles.

"Yes, gentlemen," return the McLaughlins, with yawns.

They ascend silently from the cellar, each believing that he is accompanied by two companions, and rendered moodily distrustful thereby.

> " Aina maina mona — Mike,
> Bassalona, bona — Strike ! "

sings a small, familiar voice, when they stand again above ground, and a stone whizzes between their heads.

In another moment Bumstead has the fell Smalley by the collar, and is shaking him like a yard of carpet.

"You wretched little tarrier ! " he cries in a fury, " you've .

been spying around to-night, to find out something about my Spiritualism that may be distorted to injure my Ritualistic standing."

"I ain't done nothing; and you jest drop me, or I'll knock spots out of yer!" carols the stony young child. "I jest come to have my aim at that old Beat there."

"Attend to his case, then — his and his friend's, for he seems to have some one with him — and never let me see you two boys again."

Thus Mr. Bumstead, as he releases the excited lad, and turns from the pauper burial-ground for a curious kind of pitching and running walk homeward. The strange expedition is at an end : — but *which* end he is unable just then to decide.

8*

CHAPTER XIII.

FOR THE BEST.

Miss Carowthers's educational hotbed of female innocence was about to undergo desolation by the temporary
dispersal of its intellectual buds and blossoms to their native
soils, therefrom to fill home-atmospheres with the mental
fragrance of " all the branches." Holiday Week drew near,
when, as Miss Carowthers Ritually expressed it, " all who
were true believers of the American Church of England in
their hearts would softly celebrate the devout Yearly Festival of Apostolic Christianity, by decking the Only True
Church with symbolical evergreens over places where the
paint was scratched off, and receiving New Year's Calls
without intoxicating liquors." In honor of this approaching
solemn season of peace on earth, good will to young men,
the discipline of Macassar Female College was slightly re-
laxed : Bible-studies were no longer rigorously inflicted as
a punishment for criminal absence of all punctuation from
English Composition, and any Young Lady whose father
was good pay could actually sneeze in her teacup without
being locked into her own room on bread-and-water until
she was truly penitent for her sin and wished she was a

Christian. Consequently, an air of unusual license pervaded the Alms-House ; woman's rights meetings were held at the heads of stairways to declare, that, *whereas* Mary Amanda Parkinson's male second-cousin has promised to meet her at the railroad station, and thereby made her pretend to us that the letter was from her father, when all the time Ann Louisa Baker accidentally caught sight of the words " My Precious Molly" while looking for her scissors in the wrong drawer ; therefore, *be it Resolved*, that we wish he knew about one shoulder being a little higher than the other, (as she *knows* the dressmaker told her,) and about that one red whisker under the left hand corner of her chin which she might as well stop trying to keep cut off; dark assemblages resembling walking bolsters were convened in special dormitories at night, to compare brothers and tell how they Byronically said that they never should care for women again after what they had sacrificed for them in the horse-cars without so much as a " Thank you, sir," but if they ever *could* be brought to liking a girl now, it would be on account of her not pretending to care for anything but money and a husband's early grave ; and very white parties of pleasure were organized in the halls, at ghostly hours, to go down to the cupboard for a mince-pie under pretence of hearing burglars, and subsequently to drink the mince-pie from curl-papers, accompanied by whispers of " H'sh ! don't eat the crust so loud, or Miss Carowthers 'll think it's a man."

In addition to these signs of impending freedom, trunks were packed in the rooms, with an adeptness of getting in things with springs twice as wide as any trunk, and of laying cologne-bottles, fans, and brushes, between objects with ruffles so as to perfectly protect the latter, that would have put the most conceited old bachelor to shame. Affected tenderly by thoughts of a separation which, so ridiculously uncertain is human life, might be forever, the young ladies who couldn't bear each other, and had been quite sorry for each other because she couldn't help it with such a natural disposition and rough forehead as hers, poor thing ! — graciously made-up with each other, in case they should not meet again until in heaven.

— You will not think any more, Henrietta Tomlinson, of what I told you about Augustus Smith's remarks to me that Sunday coming out of chapel. I *didn't* let you know before, my dear, but when he had the impudence to say that one of your eyebrows was longer than the other, and that you had a sleepy look as though a little more in the upper-story wouldn't hurt you, I stood up for you, and told him he ought to be ashamed to talk so on Sunday about you, after you'd taken such pains to please him. That's just all there was about that whole thing, Henrietta, dear, and now I hope we may part friends.

— Why *shouldn't* we, Martha Jenkins ? I'm sure *I've* never been the one to be unfriendly, and when Mr. Smith told *me*, that he guessed my friend Miss Jenkins didn't know how much she walked like a camel, I was as sarcastic as I could be, and said I didn't know before that *gentlemen* ever made *fun* of natural deformities.

— Yes, Henrietta, my love, I know how you've *always*, te-he ! spoken well of *everybody* behind their backs. Gentlemen give *you* their confidence as soon as they see you, without a *bit* of fishing for it on *your* part, and then you have a chance to befriend your poor friends.

— Oh, well, Martha, darling, there's no need of your getting provoked because I wouldn't hear you called a camel — he ! he ! — after you'd been *so* angelic with him about stepping on the middle back-breadth of your poplin.

* * * Oh, *never* mind it at *all-l*, Mayistah Sa-mith ; it's of *No-o* consequence ! — Te-he-he-he !

— When *is* it to come off, Miss Tomlinson ? When does your Augustus finally reward your *perseverance* with his big red hand ?

— I haven't asked him yet, Precious ! out of regard for your feelings. He's *so* sensitive about having any one think he's *jilted* her ; quite ridiculous, I tell him.

— Henrietta Tomlinson ! you — you'd get on your *knees* to make a man look at you : EVERYbody says *that !*

— But then, you know, Martha Jenkins, there *are* persons who wouldn't be looked at much, even if they *did* go on their knees for it, *lovey.*

— M'm'm ! Ph'h'h ! Please keep by your *own* trunk, Henrietta. I don't want anything *stolen*, Miss !

— He! he! Of course I'll go, Martha. There's so *much* danger of my stealing your old rags!

— *Don't* provoke me to slap you, Miss!

— Who are *you* pushing against, *Camel?* Aow-aouw-k!
— Ah-h-h! — R-r-r-r'p, sl'p, p'l-'l — Miss Carowthers' coming!! — * *

— And thus to usher in the merry, merry Christmas time of peace on earth, good will to young men.

At noon on the Saturday preceding Holiday-Week, Miss Carowthers, assisted by her adjutant, Mrs. Pillsbury, had a Reception in the Cackleorium, when emaciated lemonade and tenacious gingerbread were passed around, and the serene conqueror of Breachy Mr. Blodgett, addressed the assembled sweetness. Ladies, the wheel of Time, who, you know, is usually represented as a venerable man of Jewish aspect with a scythe, had brought around once more a festival appealing to all the finer feelings of our imperfect nature. Throbbed there a heart in any of our bos — hem! — in any of the superstructures of our waists, that did not respond with joy and gladness to the sentiment of such a season? In view of Christmas, Ladies, did we say, in the words of — an acceptable Ritualistic translation from the Breviary —

> " Day of vengeance, without morrow,
> Earth shall end in flame and sorrow,
> As from saint and seer we borrow?"

No ; that was not our style. We saw in Christmas a happy

time to forgive all our friends, to forget all our enemies at
the groaning board, and to keep on remembering the poor.
Might we find all our relatives well in the homes we were
about to revisit, and ready to liquidate our little semi-annual
expenses of tuition. Might we find neighborhoods willing
to take the resumption of piano-practicing in the forgiving
spirit of the Christmas-time, and to accept the singing of
Italian airs, at late hours, with the tops of windows down,
as occurrences not to be profanely criticized in sleepless·
beds at a time of year when all animosities should be re-
pressed. With love for all mankind, Ladies, where it was
strictly proper, we would now separate until after the Holidays, wishing each other a Merry Christmas and a Happy
New Year. Then ensued leave-takings all around; termin-
ating with a delicate consciousness on the part of each
young lady present that she was not to be entirely without
escort on her way to her home, inasmuch as there was
a Bill prepared to go with her and be presented to her
parents.

A number of times had Flora Potts witnessed this usual
breaking up, without any other sensation at herself being
left behind in the Alms-House than one of relief from incessant attempts of dearest friends to find out what Mr. E.
Drood wrote about longing to clasp her again, in his last;
and on this occasion she came near being really happy in
having her dear Magnolia Pendragon to remain with her.
Magnolia had never mentioned Edwin's name since the

virtual compact between herself, and her brother, and Mr.
Simpson, on the Pond shore ; which was, perhaps, carrying
woman's friendship rather too far to the other extreme : —
she might at least have said, "Are you thinking of something commencing with a D. ? " once in a while : — but the
Flowerpot, while slightly wondering, of course, found a
pleasant change in a companion of her own sex and age
who was not always raising the D. in conversation.

A lovely scene was it, and maddening to masculine imagination, when so many of Miss Potts's blooming young
schoolmates kissed her good-by in the porch, and gave her
a last chance to tell them what he *had* written, then.   It
was charming to see that willed-away little creature, without
her enamel, waving farewell to the stages departing for the
ferry ; and to hear the disappearing ones calling out to her :
" By-by, Flora, dear ; Eddy ought to see you now with your
natural complexion." "*Au revoir*, Pet.   You'd better
hurry in now ; here comes a man ! "   " Don't stay out in
the sun for us, Darling, or the belladonna may lose its
effect."

Oh, rosebud-garden of girls !   Oh, fresh young blossoms,
to which we of the male and cabbage growth are as cheap
vegetables !• Cling together while ye may in the fair bou-
quet of sweet school friendship, of musical parlor-sisterhood.
So shall your thorns be known only to each other in such
fragrant clustering, and never known at all to Men unless
they insensately persist in giving you their hands.

While the Flowerpot was thus receiving fond good-byes, Edwin Drood, on his way to see her, suffered an indecision of purpose which might have bred disquiet in a more gigantic mind than his. With the package containing the memorial stay-lace in one pocket, and his hands in two others, he strode up the Bumsteadville turnpike in a light overcoat and a brown study. But for good Mr. Dibble's undeniably truthful picture of a modern lover's actual situation, he might have allowed matters to go as they would, and sunk into an early marriage without one prayer to Heaven for mercy. Now, however, that picture troubled him even more than the bump which he had got upon his head from the tilting table in the lawyer's office, and he was disposed to send the stay-lace back to the candid old man. "Flora and I have about equal intellects," reasoned he to himself. "Shall I leave the whole question to her, or my own decision! One would be about as profound in wisdom as the other. Which? I guess I'll toss-up for it."

He stepped aside from the road, under a leafless tree, and drew from a pocket a badly speckled nickel coin. "Heads for her, tails for me," he said, with some awe in his tone. The tasteful coin was tossed, and "Heads" stared up at him from the frozen ground. "It's her inning," he muttered, and, repocketing the money and his hands, went on whistling. Thus the great crises of our laborious human lives are settled by the idle inspiration of a moment, and fate, for good, or evil, comes as it is cent.

The Flowerpot, expecting him, was ready in her walking dress, and, by tacit permission of Miss Carowthers, the two started upon a promenade for the nearest confidential cross-road, each eating half of an apple which Mr. Drood had brought to disguise his feelings.

"My dear, absurd Eddy," said Flora, when they had arrived in a secluded lane not far from St. Cow's Church, "I want to give you something very serious, and oh! I'm so ridiculously nervous about doing so, — especially after your giving me this apple."

"Never mind the apple, Flora. It was the fruit of our First Parents, and has constituted the most available pie of the poor ever since. Don't allow it to fetter your freedom of speech, and please try to eat it without such a gashing noise."

"Thank you, Eddy. You have always been liberal with me. And now are you sure you won't be angry with me if I give you something?"

He fell away from her a moment, as half anticipating a kiss, but promised that he would restrain his temper.

"Then here you are, Eddy;" and she drew from a pocket in her dress and held out to him a small worsted mitten.

"You give this to me?" he said, accepting it, and tossing it from one hand to the other, as though it were something hot.

"Yes, dear, ridiculous friend; and from this day forth let

us give up the cold indifference of people engaged to each other, and be as truly affectionate as brother and sister."

" Never get married ? "

" Not to each other." ·

Under the ecstatic influence of the moment, the emancipated young bondman began dancing and turning somersaults like one possessed; but, quickly remembering himself, hastened to regain a perpendicular position at her side, and coughed energetically, as though the recent gymnastics had been prescribed for his cold.

"My own sister ! " he exclaimed, "a weight is now lifted from both of our minds, and both of us should be the better for the lifting-cure.   It is noble in you to let me off so."

" And it's perfectly splendid in you, Eddy, to make no horrid fuss about it."

The beautiful contest of generosities between these two young souls made each as tender toward the other as though the parents of both had been alive and frantically opposed to their mutual attachment.

" We are both sorry that we have ever had any absurd engagement between us," said Flora, with a manner of exquisite softness, "and, now, that we are like brother and sister, we need not be all the time playing the Pretty with each other and needn't be putting on our best things every time we have to meet.   You think that my hair always curls in this way, don't you, Eddy ? "

" Why, you don't mean to say, Flora, that it's *all* — "

" — False ? No, you absurd thing ! But curling irons, and oil, and crimping pins have to be used hours and hours."

" Ha ! ha !" laughed Edwin Drood, " I see the point : you've had to make-up for me. Now I dare say that you have thought my boots, which I have worn in your company, were the right size for me ? They're really one and a half sizes too small, and almost kill me. As for gloves, I never wear any except when I come to see you."

" And my complexion, dear brother ? "

" Oh, I know all about that, darling sister. I couldn't find any fault with *that*, so long as my own seal-ring which you thought so rich-looking, was only plated."

The little creature burst into a laugh of delight, and pressed his arm with sisterly enthusiasm. " And we can be perfectly honest with each other ; can't we, Eddy ? As a partnership for life until death should us part is no longer our object, we have no need to utterly deceive each other in everything."

" No," answered the equally happy young man ; " as we're not trying to marry now, we may as well drop the swindle."

"And just suppose we'd gone on and got married," cried the Flowerpot, with dancing eyes. " When it was too late, you'd have found out what I really was — "

" And you'd have found *me* out," interrupted Edwin, vivaciously.

" I should have wanted more expenditure upon myself, for giving me my proper place in society, than you, with your limited means, could have possibly afforded — "

"And I should have told you it would ruin me — "

"And that would have made me more disappointed in you than ever, and provoked me to call you a pauper-monster — "

" And then I would have twitted you about being anything but an heiress yourself when I married you — "

"— Which would have thrown me into hysterics — "

"— Which would have made *me* lock you up in your room, and leave the house — "

" — For which *I* would have sued you for an Indiana divorce — "

"Thus driving *me* to commit suicide — "

" — And bringing myself under a cruel public prejudice seriously detrimental to my future prospects."

Gloriously excited and made nearly breathless by their friendly rivalry in thus specifying what must have been the successive results of their union without plenty of money, the animated pair panted at each other in a kind of imaginative intoxication, and then shook hands almost deliriously.

In a moment after, however, Mr. Drood thrust his hands into his pockets and presented an aspect of sudden discomfiture.

"I forgot about my uncle, Jack Bumstead," he said, uneasily. "It will be a dreadful blow for Jack; he's counted

so much upon my having a wife for him to flirt with. —
There he is, now ? "

" *Where ?* "

"Amongst those trees down there — Look ! "

In a small grove, skirting the road some distance behind
them, Mr. Bumstead could indeed be seen, dodging wildly
from one tree to another in an extraordinary manner, and
occasionally leaping high in the air and slashing excitedly
around him with his alpaca umbrella. A hoop from a bar-
rel, possibly cast out upon the road by somebody, had, apparently, become entangled around the legs and in the
coat-tails of the Ritualistic organist ; and, he, in his extreme
nervous sensibility, precipitately mistaking it for one of his
old enemies, the snakes, had evidently fled headlong with it
as far as the grove, and was there engaging it in frantic
single-combat.

"Oh, take me home, at once, please ! " begged Flora,
alarmed at the remarkable sight.

" Poor dear old fellow ! " exclaimed her companion, obe-
diently hurrying onward with her, " I shall never have the
heart to tell him of our separation, and must leave it to
your guardian. He'll think he's been the cause of it, by
stealing your heart from me.— Here he comes ! "

They had barely time to conceal themselves in the Macassar porch, when, with umbrella in full play, and the barrel-
hoop half-way up to his waist, Mr. Bumstead came bound-
ing along the turnpike with frenzied agility. " Shoo ! 'S'cat,

you viper! Get out!" cried he; and stopped, with an unearthly culminating scream of terror, immediately in front of the Alms-House, where the hoop suddenly fell at his feet. A moment he beat his fallen enemy with the umbrella, as though madly striving to actually hammer it into the earth; then, as suddenly, suspended his attack, stooped low to eye his victim more closely, and, with a fierce pounce, had it in his grasp. "Was it only thisss?" he hissed, holding it at arm's length: "Sold again: signed, J. Bumstead." And, hanging it over his umbrella, he stalked moodily onward.

"What a struggle his whole lonely life is!" said Edwin Drood, coming out from the porch.

Flora's parting look, as she entered the door, was as though she had said, "Oh! don't you understand?" But the young man went away unconscious of its meaning.

CHAPTER XIV.

CLOVES FOR THREE.

CHRISTMAS EVE in Bumsteadville. Christmas Eve all over the world, but especially where the English language is spoken. No sooner does the first facetious star wink upon this Eve, than all the English-speaking millions of this Boston-crowned earth begin casting off their hatreds, meannesses, uncharities, and Carlyleisms, as a garment, and, in a beautiful spirit of no objections to anybody, proceed to think what can be done for the poor in the way of sincerely wishing them well. The princely merchant, in his counting-room, involuntarily experiences the softening, humanizing influence of the hour, and, in tones tremulous with unwonted emotion, privately directs his Chief-Clerk to tell all the other clerks, that, on this night of all the round year, they may, before leaving the store at 10 o'clock, take almost any article from that slightly damaged auction-stock down in the front cellar, at actual cost-price. This, they are to understand, implies their Employer's hearty wish of a Merry Christmas to them ; and is a sign that, in the grand spirit of the festal season, he can even forget and forgive those unnatural leaner entry-clerks who are always whining for more than their allotted \$7 a week. The President of the great railroad corporation, in the very middle of a growling fit over the extra cost involved in purchasing his last Legislature, (owing to the fact that some of its Members had been elected upon a fusion of Radical-Reform and Honest-Workingman's Tickets,) is suddenly and mysteriously impressed with the recollection that this is Christmas Eve. " Why, bless my soul, so it is ! " he cries, springing up from his littered rosewood desk like a boy. " Here, you General Superintendent out there in the office ! " sings he, cheerily, " send some one down to Washington Market this instant, to find out whether or not any of those luscious anatomical western turkies that I saw in the barrels this morning are left yet. If the commercial hotels down-town haven't taken them all, buy every remaining barrel at once ! Not a man nor boy in this Company's service shall go home to-night without his Christmas dinner in his hand ! Lively, now, Mr. Jones ! and just oblige me by picking out one of the birds for yourself, if you can find one at all less blue than the rest. It's Christmas Eve, sir ; and upon my word I'm really sorry our boys have to work to-morrow as usual. Ah ! it's hard to be poor, Jones ! A merry Christmas to us all. Here's my carriage come for me." And even in returning to their homes from their daily avocations, on Christmas Eve, how the most grasping, penurious souls of men will soften to the world's unfortunate ! Who is this poor old lady, looking as though she might be some-

7

body's grandmother, sitting here by the wayside, shivering, on such an Eve as this? No home to go to? — Relations all dead? — Eaten nothing in two days? — Walked all the way from the Woman's Rights Bureau in Boston? — Dear me? *can* there be so much suffering on Christmas Eve? I must do something for her, or my own good dinner to-morrow will be a reproach to me. "Here! Policeman! just take this poor old lady to the Station-House, and give her a good warm home there until morning. There! cheer-up, Aunty; you're all right *now*. This gentleman in the uniform has promised to take care of you. Merry Christmas!" — Or, when at home, and that extremely bony lad, in the thin summer coat, chatters to you, from the snow on the front-stoop, about the courage he has taken from Christmas Eve to ask you for enough to get a meal and a night's-lodging — how differently from your ordinary style does a something soft in your breast impel you to treat him. "No work to be obtained?" you say, in a light tone, to cheer him up. "Of course there's none *here*, my young friend. All the work here at the East is for foreigners, in order that they may be used at election-time. As for you, an American boy, why don't you go to h—— I mean to the West. *Go West*, young man! Buy a good, stout farming outfit, two or three serviceable horses, or mules, a portable house made in sections, a few cattle, a case of fever medicine — and then go out to the far West upon Government-land. You'd better go to one of the hotels for to-night, and then purchase Mr. Greeley's 'What I Know About Farming', and start as soon as the snow permits in the morning. Here are ten cents for you. Merry Christmas!" — Thus to honor the natal Festival of Him — the Unselfish incarnate, the Divinely insighted — Who said unto the lip-server : Sell all that thou hast, and give it to the Poor, and follow Me; and from Whom the lip-server, having great possessions, went away exceeding sorrowful !

Three men are to meet at dinner in the Bumsteadian apartments on this Christmas Eve. How has each one passed the day?

Montgomery Pendragon, in his room in Gospeller's Gulch, reads Southern tragedies in an old copy of the *New Orleans Picayune*, until two o'clock, when he hastily tears up all his soiled paper collars, packs a few things into a travelling satchel, and, with the latter slung over his shoulder, and a Kehoe's Indian club* in his right hand, is met in the hall by his tutor, the Gospeller.

"What are you doing with that club, Mr. Montgomery?" asks the Reverend Octavius, hastily stepping back into a corner.

"I've bought it to exercise with in the open air," answers the young Southerner, playfully denting the wall just over his tutor's head with it.

"After this dinner with Mr. Drood, at Bumstead's, I reckon I shall start on a walking match, and I've procured

*.In the original, a very heavy, iron-shod walking-stick.

the club for exercise as I go. Thus : " He twirls it high
in the air, grazes Mr. Simpson's nearer ear, hits his own
head accidentally, and breaks the glass in the hat-stand.

"I see ! I see !" says the Gospeller, rather hurriedly.
"Perhaps you *had* better be entirely alone, and in the open
country, when you take that exercise."

Rubbing his skull quite dismally, the prospective pedestrian goes straightway to the porch of the Alms-House, and
there waits until his sister comes down in her bonnet and
joins him.

"Magnolia," he remarks, hastening to be the first to
speak, in order to have any conversational chance at all
with her, "it is not the least mysterious part of this Mystery
of ours, that keeps us all out of doors so much in the un-
seasonable winter month of December,* and now I am peculiarly a meteorological martyr in feeling obliged to go
walking for two whole freezing weeks, or until the Holidays
and this — this marriage-business, are over. I didn't tell
Mr. Simpson, but my real purpose, I reckon, in having this
club, is to save myself, by violent exercise with it, from per-
ishing of cold."

"Must you do this, Montgomery?" asks his colloquial

---

* In the original English story there is, considering the bitter time of year given, a
truly extraordinary amount of solitary sauntering, social strolling, confidential confab-
ulating, evening-rambling, and general lingering, in the open air. To "adapt" this
novel peculiarity to American practice, without some little violation of probability, is
what the present conscientious Adapter finds almost the hardest artistic requirement
of his task.

sister, thoughtfully. "Perhaps if I were to talk long enough with you —"

"— You'd literally exhaust me into not going? Certainly you would," he returns, confidently. "First, my head would ache from the constant noise; then it would spin; then I should grow faint and hear you less distinctly; then your voice, although you were talking-on the same as ever, would sound like a mere steady hum to me; then I should become unconscious, and be carried home, with you still whispering in my ear. But do *not* talk, Magnolia; for I must do the walking-match. The prejudice here against my Southern birth makes me a damper upon the festivities of others at this general season of forgiveness to all mankind, and I can't stand the sight of that Drood and Miss Potts together. I'd better stay away until they have gone."

He pauses a moment, and adds, "I wish I were not going to this dinner, or that I were not carrying this club there."

He shakes her hand and his own head, glances up at the storm-clouds now gathering in the sky, goes onward to Mr. Bumstead's boarding-house, halts at the door a moment to moisten his right hand and balance the Indian club in it, and then enters.

Edwin Drood's day before merry Christmas is equally hilarious. Now that the Flowerpot is no longer on his mind, the proneness of the masculine nature to court misfortune causes him to think seriously of Miss Pendragon, and wonder whether *she* would make a wife to ruin a man? It will be rather awkard, he thinks, to be in Bumsteadville for a week or two after the Macassar young ladies shall have heard of his matrimonial disengagement, as they will all be sure to sit symmetrically at every front window in the Alms-House whenever he tries to go by; and he resolves to escape the danger by starting for Egypt, Illinois, immediately after he has seen Mr. Dibble and explained the situation to him. Finding that his watch has run down, he steps into a jeweller's to have it wound, and is at once subjected to insinuating overtures by the man of gems. What does he think of this ring, which is exactly the thing for some particular Occasions in Life? It is made of the metal for which nearly all young couples marry now-a-days, is as endless as their disagreements, and, by the new process, can be stretched to fit the Second wife's hand also. Or look at this pearl set. Very chaste, really soothing; intended as a present from a Husband after First Quarrel. These cameo earrings were never known to fail. Judiciously presented, in a velvet case, they may be depended upon to at once divert a young Wife from Returning to her Mother, as she has threatened. Ah! Mr. Drood cares for no more jewellery than his watch, chain, and seal-ring? To be sure! when Mr. Bumstead was in yesterday for the regular daily new crystal in his own watch — how *does* he break so many! — *he* said that his beloved nephews wore only watches and rings, or he would buy paste breastpins for them. Your oroide is now wound up, Mr. Drood, and set at twenty minutes past Two.

" Dear old Jack ! " thinks Edwin to himself, pocketing his watch as he walks away; "he thinks just twice as much of me as any one else in the world, and I should feel doubly grateful."

As dusk draws on, the young fellow, returning from a long walk, espies an aged Irish lady leaning against a tree on the edge of the turnpike, with a pipe upside-down in her mouth, and her bonnet on wrong-side afore.

" Are you sick ? " he asks kindly.

" Divil a sick, gintlemen," is the answer, with a slight catch of the voice, — " bless the two of yez ! "

Edwin Drood can scarcely avoid a start, as he thinks to himself, "Good Heaven ! how much like Jack ! "

" Do you eat cloves, madame ? " he asks, respectfully.

" Cloves is it, honey? ah, thin, I do that, whin I'm expectin' company. Odether-nodether, but I've come here the day from New York for nothing. Sure phat's the names of you two darlints ? "

" Edwin," he answers, in some wonder, as he hands her a currency stamp, which, on account of the large hole worn in it, he has been repeatedly unable to pass himself.

" Eddy is it ? Och hone, och hone, machree ! " exclaims the venerable woman, hanging desolately around the tree by her arms while her bonnet falls over her left ear : "I've heard that name threatened. Och, acushla wirasthu ! "

Believing that the matron will be less agitated if left
alone, and, probably, able to get a little roadside sleep, Edwin Drood passes onward in deep thought.   The boarding-
house is reached, and *he* enters.

J. Bumstead's day of the dinner is also marked by exhilarating experiences.   With one coat-tail unwittingly tucked
far up his back, so that it seems to be amputated, and his
alpaca umbrella under his arm, he enters a grocery-store of
the village, and abstractedly asks how strawberries are selling to-day?   Upon being reminded that fresh fruit is very
scarce in late December, he changes his purpose, and orders
two bottles of Bourbon flavoring-extract sent to his address.
And now he wishes to know what they are charging for
sponges?   They tell him that he must seek those articles at
the druggist's, and he compromises by requesting that four
lemons be forwarded to his residence.   Have they any good
Canton-flannel, suitable for a person of medium complexion? — No? — Very well, then : send half a pound of cloves
to his house before night.

There are Ritualistic services at Saint Cow's, and he
renders the organ-accompaniments with such unusual freedom from reminiscences of the bacchanalian repertory, that
the Gospeller is impelled to compliment him as they leave
the cathedral.

"You're in fine tone to-day, Bumstead.   Not quite so
much volume to your playing as sometimes, but still the
tune could be recognized."

"That, sir," answers the organist, explainingly, "was because I held my right wrist firmly with my left hand, and played mostly with only one finger. The method, I find, secures steadiness of touch and precision in hitting the right key."

"I should think it would, Mr. Bumstead. You seem to be more free than ordinarily from your occasional indisposition."

"I am less nervous, Mr. Simpson," is the reply. "I've made up my mind to swear off, sir. — I'll tell you what I'll do, Simpson," continues the Ritualistic organist, with sudden confidential affability. "I'll make an agreement with you, that whichever of us catches the other slipping-up first in the New Year, shall be entitled to call for whatever he wants."

"Bless me! I don't understand," ejaculates the Gospeller.

"No matter, sir. No matter!" retorts the mystic of the organ-loft, abruptly returning to his original gloom. "My company awaits me, and I must go."

"Excuse me," cries the Gospeller, turning back a moment; "but what's the matter with your coat?"

The other discovers the condition of his tucked-up coat-tail with some fierceness of aspect, but immediately explains that it must have been caused by his sitting upon a folding-chair just before leaving home.

So, humming a savage tune in make-believe of no em-

7*

barrassment at all in regard to his recently disordered garment, Mr. Bumstead reaches his boarding-house. At the
door he waits long enough to examine his umbrella, with
scowling scrutiny, in every rib ; and then *he* enters.

Behind the red window-curtain of the room of the dinner-
party shines the light all night, while before it a wailing December gale rises higher and higher.   Through leafless
branches, under eaves and against chimneys, the savage
wings of the storm are beaten, its long fingers caught, and
its giant shoulder heaved.   Still, while nothing else seems
steady, that light behind the red curtain burns unextin-
guished ; the reason being that the window is closed and the
wind cannot get at it.

At morning comes a hush on nature ; the sun arises with
that innocent expression of countenance which causes some
persons to fancy that it resembles Mr. Greeley after shav-
ing ; and there is an evident desire on the part of the wind
to pretend that it has not been up all night.   Fallen chimneys, however, expose the airy fraud, and the clock blown
completely out of Saint Cow's steeple reveals what a high
time there has been.

Christmas morning though it is, Mr. McLaughlin is summoned from his family-circle of pigs, to mount the Ritualistic church and see what can be done ; and while a small
throng of early idlers a restaring up at him from Gospeller's
Gulch, Mr. Bumstead, with his coat on in the wrong way,

and a wet towel on his head, comes tearing in amongst them like a congreve rocket.

"Where's them nephews? — where's Montgomeries? — where's that umbrella?" howls Mr. Bumstead, catching the first man he sees by the throat, and driving his hat over his eyes.

"What's the matter, for goodness sake?" calls the Gospeller from the window of his house. "Mr. Pendragon has gone away on a walking match. Is not Mr. Drood at home with you?"

"Norrabit' v it," pants the organist, releasing his man's throat, but still leaning with heavy affection upon him: "m'nephews wen' out with'm — f'r li'lle walk — er mir'night; an' 've norseen'm — since."

There is no more looking up at Saint Cow's steeple with a McLaughlin on it now. All eyes fix upon the agitated Mr. Bumstead, as he wildly attempts to step over the tall paling of the Gospeller's fence at a stride, and goes crashing headlong through it instead.

CHAPTER XV.

" SPOTTED. "

WHEN the bell of St. Cow's began ringing for Ritualistic morning service, with a sound as of some incontinently rambling daughter of the lacteal herd — now near at hand in cracked dissonance, as the wind blows hither ; now afar, in tinkling distance, as the wind blows hence — Montgomery Pendragon was several miles away from Bumsteadville upon his walking-match, with head already bumped like a pine-apple, and face curiously swelled, from amateur practice with the Indian Club. Being by that time cold enough for break-fast, and willing to try the virtues of some soothing applica-tion to his right eye, which, from a bruise just below it, was nearly closed, the badly bandaged young man suspended his murderous calisthenics at the door of a rustic hotel, and there entered to secure a wayside meal.

The American country "hotel," or half-way house, is, per-haps, one of the most depressing fictions ever encountered by stage-passenger, or pedestrian afield : and depends so exclusively upon the imagination for any earthly distinction from the retired and neglected private hiding-place of some decayed and morbid agricultural family, that only the conven-

tional swinging sign-board before the door saves the cogni-
zant mind from a painfully dense confusion.   Smelling about
equally of eternal wash-day, casual cow-shed, and passing
feather-bed, it sustains a lank, middle-aged, gristly man to
come out at the same hour every day and grunt unintelligibly
at the stage-driver, an expressionless boy in a. bandless
straw hat and no shoes, to stare blankly from the doorway at
the same old pole-horse he has mechanically thus inspected
from infancy, and one speckled hen of mature years to poise
observingly on single leg at the head of the shapeless black
dog asleep at the sunny end of the low wooden stoop.   It
is the one rural spot on earth where a call for fresh eggs
evokes remonstrative and chronic denial; where chickens
for dinner are sternly discredited as mere freaks of legendary
romance, and an order for a glass of new milk is incredulously answered by a tumblerful of water which tastes of
whitewash-brush.   Whosoever sleeps there of a night shall
be crowded by walls which rub off, into a faint feather-bed of
the flavor and consistency of geese used whole, and have
for his feverish breakfast in the morning a version of broiled
ham as racy of attic-salt as the rasher of Bacon's essays.
And to him who pays his bill there, ere he straggles weakly
forth to repair his shattered health by frenzied flight, shall be
given in change such hoary ten-cent shreds of former postal
currency as he has not hitherto deemed credible, sticking
together in inextricable conglomeration by such fragments
of fish-scales as he never before believed could be gathered

by handled small-money from palms not sufficiently washed
after piscatorial diversion.

It was in at a country hotel, then, that the young Southern
pedestrian turned for temporary rest and a meal, and pitiless
was the cross-examination instituted by the inevitable lank,
middle-aged, gristly man, before he could reconcile it with
his duty as a cautious public character to reveal the treasures
of the larder.   Those bumps on the head, that swollen eye,
and nose, came — did they ? — from swinging this here club
for exercise.   Well, he wanted to know, now !   People generally used two of the clubs at once — did they ? — but one
was enough for a beginner.   Well, he *wanted* to know, now !
Could he supply a couple of poached eggs and a cup of milk ?
No, young man ; but a slice of corned pork and a bowl of
tea were within the resources of the establishment.

When at length upon the road again, the bruised youth resolved to follow a cattle-track " across lots," for the greater
space in which to exercise with his Indian Club as he walked.
Like any other novice in the practice, he could not divest
his mind of the impression, that the frightful thumps he continually received, in twirling the merciless thing around and
behind his devoted head, were due to some kind of crowd-
ing influence from the boundaries on either side the way, and
it was to gain relief from such damaging contractions of area
that he left the highway for the wider wintry fields.   Going
onward in these latter at an irregular pace ; sometimes momentarily stunned into a rangy stagger by a sounding blow

on the cerebrum or the cerebellum; and again, irritated almost to a run by contusion of shoulder-blade or funny-bone ; he finally became aware that two men were following him through the lots, and that with a closeness of attention indicating more than common interest. To the perception of his keenly sensitive Southern nature they at once became ribald Yankee vandals, hoping for unseemly amusement from the detection of some awkwardness in the Indian club-play of a defeated but not conquered Southern Gentleman ; and, in the haughty sectional pride of his contemptuous soul, he indignantly determined to show not the least conscious-ness of their disrespectful observation. Twirling the club around and around his battered head with increasing velocity, he smiled scornfully to himself, nor deigned a single back-ward glance at the one of his two followers who approached more rapidly than the other. He heard the hindermost say to the foremost, "Leave him alone, I tell you, and he'll knock himself down in a minute," and, in a passionately reckless effort of sheer bravado to catch the club from one hand with the other while it yet circled swiftly over his skull, he accidentally brought the ungovernable weapon into tre-mendous contact with the top of his head, and dashed him-self violently to the earth.

"Didn't I tell you he'd do it?" cried the hindermost of the two strangers, coming up ; while the other coolly seated himself upon the prostrated victim. "These here Indian clubs always throw a man if he ain't got muscle in his arms ;

and this here little Chivalry has got arms like a couple of canes."

"Arise from me instantly, fellow! You're sitting upon my breast-pin," exclaimed Montgomery to the person sitting upon him.

They suffered him to regain his feet, which he did with extreme hauteur, and surveyed his bumped head and swollen countenance with undisguised wonder.

"How dare you treat a Southerner in this way?" continued the young man, his head aching inexpressibly. "I thought the war was over long ago. If money is your object, seek out a citizen of some other section than mine; for the South is out of funds just now, owing to the military. outrages of Northern scorpions."

"We're constables, Mr. Pendragon," was the reply, "and it is our duty to take you back to the main road, where a couple of your friends are waiting for you."

Staring from one to the other in speechless wonder at what this fresh outrage upon the down-trodden South could mean, Montgomery allowed them to replace his Indian club in his hand, and conduct him back to the public road ; where, to his increased bewilderment, he found Gospeller Simpson and the Ritualistic organist.

"What is the matter, gentlemen?" he asked, in great agitation : "must I take the oath of Loyalty ; or am I required by Yankee philanthropy to marry a negress?"

At the sound of his voice, Mr. Bumstead left the shoulder

of Mr. Simpson, upon which he had been leaning with great weight, and, coming forward in three long skips, deliberately wound his right hand in the speaker's neck-tie.

"Where are those nephews — where's that umbrella?" demanded the organist, with considerable ferocity.

"Nephews ! — umbrella !" gasped the other.

"The Edwins — bone handle," explained Mr. Bumstead, lurching toward his captive.

"Mr. Montgomery," interposed the Gospeller, sadly, "Mr. Drood went out with you last night, late, from his estimable uncle's lodgings, and has not been seen since. Where is he ?"

"He went back into the house again, sir, after I had walked him up and down the road a few times."

"Well, then, where's that umbrella ?" roared the organist, who seemed quite beside himself with grief and excitement.

"Mr. Bumstead, pray be more calm," implored the Reverend Octavius.

"Mr. Montgomery, this agitated gentleman's nephew has been mysteriously missing ever since he went out with you at midnight : also an alpaca umbrella."

"Upon my honor, I know nothing of either," ejaculated the unhappy Southerner.

Mr. Bumstead, still holding him by the neck-tie, cast a fiery and unsettled glance around at nothing in particular ; then ground his teeth audibly, and scowled.

"My boy's missing!" he said, hissingly. — "Y'understand? — he's missing.   I must insist upon searching the prisoner."

In the presence of Gospeller and constables, and loftily regardless alike of their startled wonder and the young man's protests, the maddened uncle of the lost Drood deliberately examined all the captive's pockets in succession.   In one of them was a penknife, which, after thoughtfully trying it upon his pink nails, he abstractedly placed in his own pocket. Searching next the overwhelmed Southerner's travelling-satchel, he found in it an apple, which he first eyed with marked suspicion, and then bit largely into, as though half expecting to find in it some traces of his nephew.

"I'll keep this suspicious fruit," he remarked, with a hollow laugh; and, bearing unreservedly upon the nearer arm of the hapless Montgomery, and eating audibly as he surged onward, he started on the return march for Bumsteadville.

Not a word more was spoken until, after a cool Christmas stroll of about eight and a quarter miles, the whole party stood before Judge Sweeney, in the house of the latter.   There, when the story had been sorrowfully repeated by the Gospeller, Mr. Bumstead exhibited the core of the apple, and tickled the magistrate almost into hysterics by whispering very closely in his ear, that it was a core curiously similar to that of the last apple eaten by his nephew; and, having been found in an apple from the prisoner's satchel, might be useful in evidence.   Judge Sweeney wished to know if Mr. Pendragon had any political relations, or could influence any votes;

and, upon being answered in the negative, eyed the young man sternly, and said that appearances were decidedly against him. He could not exactly commit him to jail without accusation, although the apple-core and his political unimportance subjected him to grave suspicion; but he should hold the Gospeller responsible for the youth's appearance at any time when his presence should be required. Mr. Bumstead, whose eyes were becoming very glassy, then suggested that a handbill should be at once printed and circulated, to the effect that there had been Lost, or Stolen, two Black Alpaca Nephews, about five feet eight inches high, with a bone handle, light eyes and hair, and whalebone ribs, and that if the said Edwin would return, with a brass ferule slightly worn, the finder should receive earnest thanks, and be seen safely to his home by J. Bumstead. Mr. Gospeller Simpson and Judge Sweeney agreed that a handbill should be issued: but thought it might confuse the public mind if the missing nephew and the lost umbrella were not kept separate.

"Has either 'f yougen'l'men ever been 'n Uncle?" asked the Ritualistic organist, with dark intensity.

They shook their heads.

"*Then,*" said Mr. Bumstead, with great force, "THEN, gen'l'men, you-knownor-wahritis-to-lose-'n-umbrella!"

Before they could decide in their weaker minds what the immediate connection was, he had left them, at a sharp slant, in great intellectual disturbance, and was passing out through the entry-way with both his hands against the wall.

Early next morning, while young Mr. Pendragon was locked in his room, startled and wretched, the inconsolable uncle of Edwin Drood was energetically ransacking every part of Bumsteadville for the missing man. House after house he visited, like some unholy inspector : peering up chimneys, prodding under carpets, and staying a long time in cellars where there was cider. Not a bit of paper or cloth blew along the turnpike but he eagerly picked it up, searched in it with the most anxious care, and finally placed it in his hat. Going to the pond, with a borrowed hatchet, he cut a hole in the thick ice, lost the hatchet, and, after bathing his head in the water, declared that his alpaca nephew was not there. Finding an antique flask in one of his pockets, he gradually removed all the liquid contents therefrom with a tubular straw, but still could discern no traces of Edwin Drood. All the live-long day he prosecuted his researches, to the great discomposure of the populace ; and, with whitewash all over the back of his coat, and very dingy hands, had just seated himself at his own fireside in the evening, when Mr. Dibble came in.

" This is a strange disappearance," said Mr. Dibble.

" And it was good as new," groaned the organist, with but one eye open.

" Almost new ! — *what* was ? "

" Th'umbrella."

"Mr. Bumstead," returned the old man, coldly, "I am not talking of an umbrella, but of Mr. Edwin."

"Yesh, I know," said the uncle. "Awright. I'm li'lle sleepy ; tha'sall."

"I've just seen my ward, Mr. Bumstead."

"She puerwell, shir ? "

"She is *not* pretty well. Nor is Miss Pendragon."

"I'm vahr' sorry," said Mr. Bumstead, just audibly.

"Miss Pendragon scorns the thought of any blame for her brother," continued Mr. Dibble, eyeing the fire.

"It had a bun — bone handle," muttered the other, dreamily. Then, with a momentary brightening, "'Scuse me, shir : whah'll y' take ? "

"Nothing, sir !" was the sharp response. "I'm not at all thirsty. But there is something more to tell you. At the last meeting of my ward and your nephew, — just before your dinner here, — they concluded to break their engagment of marriage, for certain good reasons, and thenceforth be only brother and sister to each other."

Starting forward in his chair, with partially opened eyes, the white-washed and dingy Mr. Bumstead managed to get off his hat, covering himself with a bandanna handkerchief and innumerable old pieces of paper and cloth, as he did so, from head to foot ; made a feeble effort to throw it at the aged lawyer ; and, then, chair and all, tumbled forward with a crash to the rug, where he lay in a refreshing sleep.

CHAPTER XVI.

AVUNCULAR DEVOTION.

HAVING literally *fallen* asleep from his chair to the rug, J. Bumstead, Esquire, was found to have reached such an extraordinary depth in slumber, that Mr. and Mrs. Smythe, his landlord and landlady, who were promptly called in by Mr. Dibble, had at first some fear that they should never be able to drag him out again. In pursuance, however, of a mode of treatment commended to their judgment by frequent previous practice with the same patient, the good couple poured a pitcher of water over his fallen head ; hauled him smartly up and down the room, first by a hand and then by a foot ; singed his whiskers with a hot poker, held him head-downward for a time, and tried various other approved allopathic remedies. Seeing that he still slept profoundly, though appearing, by occasional movements of his arms, to entertain certain passing dreams of single combats, the quick womanly wit of Mrs. Smythe finally hit upon the homœopathic expedient of softly shaking his familiar antique flask at his right ear. Scarcely had the soft, liquid sound therefrom resulting been addressed for a minute to the auricular orifice, when a singularly pleasing smile wreathed the countenance of the Ritualistic organist, his eyelids flew up like the spring-covers of two valuable hunting-case watches, and he suddenly arose to a sitting position upon the rug, and began feeling around for the bed-clothes.

"There!" cried Mrs. Smythe, greatly affected by his pathetic expression of countenance, "you're all right now, sir. How worn-out you must have been, to sleep so!"

"Do you always go to sleep with such alarming suddenness?" asked Mr. Dibble.

"When I have to go anywhere, I make it a rule to go at once : — similarly, when going to sleep," was the answer. "Excuse me, however, for keeping you waiting, Mr. Dibble. We've had quite a rain, sir."

His hair, collar, and shoulders being very wet from the water which had been poured upon him during his slumber, Mr. Bumstead, in his present newly-awake frame of mind, believed that a hard shower had taken place, and thereupon turned moody.

"We've had quite a rain, sir, since I saw you last," he repeated, gloomily, "and I am freshly reminded of my irreparable loss."

"Such an open, spring-like character!" apostrophized the lawyer, staring reflectively into the grate.

"Always open when it rained, and closing with a spring," said Mr. Bumstead, in soft abstraction lost.

"*Who* closed with a spring?" queried the elder man, irascibly.

" The umbrella," sobbed John Bumstead.

" I was speaking of your nephew, sir ! " was Mr. Dibble's impatient explanation.

Mr. Bumstead stared at him sorrowfully for a moment, and then requested Mrs. Smythe to step to a cupboard in the next room and immediately pour him out a bottle of soda-water which she should find there.

" Won't you try some ? " he asked the lawyer, rising limply to his feet when the beverage was brought, and drinking it with considerable noise.

" No, thank you," returned Mr. Dibble.

" As you please, then," said the organist, resignedly. " Only, if you have a headache, don't blame me. (Mr. and Mrs. Smythe, you may place a few cloves where I can get them, and retire.) What you have told me, Mr. Dibble, concerning the breaking of the engagement between your ward and my nephew, relieves my mind of a load. As a right-thinking man, I can no longer suspect you of having killed Edwin Drood."

" Suspect ME ? " screamed the aged lawyer, almost leaping into the air.

"Calm yourself," observed Mr. Bumstead, quietly, the while he ate a sedative clove. " I say that I can *not* longer suspect you. I can not think that a person of your age would wantonly destroy a human life merely to obtain an umbrella."

Absolutely purple in the face, Mr. Dibble snatched his hat

from a chair just as the Ritualistic organist was about to sit upon it, and was on the point of hurrying wrathfully from the room, when the entrance of Gospeller Simpson arrested him.

Noting his agitation, Mr. Bumstead instantly resolved to clear him from suspicion in the new-comer's mind also.

"Reverend Sir," he said to the Gospeller, quickly, "in this sad affair we must be just, as well as vigilant. . I believe Mr. Dibble to be as innocent as ourselves. Whatever may be his failings so far as liquor is concerned, I wholly acquit him of all guilty knowledge of my nephew and umbrella."

Too apoplectic with suffocating emotions to speak, Mr. Dibble foamed slightly at the mouth and tore out a lock or two of his hair.

"And I believe that my unhappy pupil, Mr. Pendragon, is as guiltless," responded the puzzled Gospeller. "I do not deny that he had a quarrel with Mr. Drood, in the earlier part of their acquaintance ; but, as you, Mr. Bumstead, yourself, admit, their meeting at the Christmas-eve . dinner was amicable ; as I firmly believe their last mysterious parting to have been."

The organist raised his fine head from the shadow of his right hand, in which it had rested for a moment, and said, gravely : "I cannot deny, gentlemen, that I have had my terrible distrusts of you all. Even now, while, in my deepest heart, I release Mr. Dibble and Mr. Pendragon from all suspicion, I cannot entirely rid my mind of the impression that you, Mr. Simpson, in an hour when, from undue indul-

8

gence in stimulants, you were not wholly yourself, may have been tempted, by the superior fineness of the alpaca, to slay a young man inexpressibly dear to us all."

"Great heavens, Mr. Bumstead!" panted the Gospeller, livid with horror, "I never —"

—"Not a word, sir!" interrupted the Ritualistic organist, —"not a word, Reverend sir, or it may be used against you at your trial."

Pausing not to see whether the equally overwhelmed old lawyer followed him, the horribly astounded Gospeller burst precipitately from the house in wild dismay, and was presently hurrying past the pauper burial-ground. Whether he had been drawn to that place by some one of the many mystic influences moulding the fates of men, or because it happened to be on his usual way home, let students of psychology and topography decide. Thereby he was hurrying, at any rate, when a shining object lying upon the ground beside the broken fence, caused him to stop suddenly and pick up the glittering thing. It was an oroide watch, marked E. D.; and, a few steps further on, a coppery-looking seal-ring also attracted the finder's grasp. With these baubles in his hand the genial clergyman was walking more slowly onward, when it abruptly occurred to him, that his possession of such property might possibly subject him to awkward consequences if he did not immediately have somebody arrested in advance. Perspiring freely at the thought, he hurried to his house, and, there securing the company of Montgomery

Pendragon, conveyed his beloved pupil at once before Judge Sweeney, and made affidavit of finding the jewelry. Tha jeweller, who had wound Edwin Drood's watch for him oi the day of the dinner, promptly identified the timepiece bj the innumerable scratches around the keyhole; Mr. Bumstead, though at first ecstatic with the idea that the seal-ring was a ferule from an umbrella, at length allowed himself to be persuaded into a gloomy recognition of it as a part of his nephew, and Montgomery was detained in custody for further revelations.

News of the event circulating, the public mind of Bumsteadville lost no time in deploring the incorrigible depravity of Southern character, and recollecting several horrors of human Slavery. It was now clearly remembered that there had once been rumors of terrible cruelties by a Pendragon family to an aged colored man of great piety; who, because he incessantly sang hymns in the cotton-field, was sent to a field farther from the Pendragon mansion, and ultimately died. Citizens reminded each other, that when, during the rebellion, a certain Pendragon of the celebrated Southern Confederacy met a former religious chattel of his confronting him with a bayonet in the loyal ranks, and immediately afterwards felt a cold, tickling sensation under one of his ribs, he drew a pistol upon the member of the injured race, who subsequently died in Ohio of fever and ague. What wonder was it, then, that this young Pendragon with an Indian club and a swelled head should secretly slaughter the

nephew and appropriate the umbrella of one of the most
loyal and devoted Ritualists' that ever sent a substitute to
battle? In the mighty metropolis, too, the Great Dailies —
those ponderous engines of varied and inaccurate intelligence — published detailed and mistaken reports of the
whole affair, and had subtle editorial theories as to the
nature of the crime. The *Sun*, after giving a cut of an old-
fashioned parlor-grate as a diagram of Mr. Bumstead's house,
said : " The retention of Mr. Fish as Secretary of State
" by the present venal Administration, and the official coun-
" tenance otherwise corruptly given to friends of Spanish
" tyranny who do not take the *Sun*, are plainly among the
" current encouragements to such crime as that in the full re-
" porting of which to-day the *Sun's* advertisements are
" crowded down to a single page, as usual. Judge Connolly,
" after walking all the way from Yorkville, agrees with the
" *Sun* in believing, that something more than an umbrella
" tempted this young Montmorency Padregon to waylay
" Edwin Wood. To-morrow we shall give the public still
" further exclusive revelations, such as the immense circula-
" tion of the New York *Sun* enables us especially to obtain.
" On this, as upon every occasion of the publication of the
" *Sun*, we shall leave out columns upon columns of profit-
" able advertising, in order that no reader of the *Sun* shall
" be stinted in his criminal news. The *Sun* (price two cents)
" has never yet been bought by advertisers, and never will
" be." The *Tribune* said : " What time the reader can spare

"from perusing our special dispatches concerning the pro-
"gress of Smalleyism*͏ in Europe, shall, undoubtedly, be
"given to our female reporter's account of the alleged·
"tragedy at Bumperville. There are reasons of manifest
"propriety to restrain us, as superior journalists, from the
"sensational theorizing indulged by editors choosing to ex-
"pend more care and money upon local news than upon
"European rumors; but we may not injudiciously hazard
"the assumption, that, were the police under any other than
"Democratic domination, such a murder as that alleged to
"have been committed by Manton Penjohnson on Baldwin
"Good had not been possible. Penjohnson, it shall be
"noticed, is a Southerner, while young Good was strongly
"Northern in sentiment; and it requires no straining of a
"point to trace in these known facts a sectional antagonism
"to which even a long war has not yielded full sanguinary
"satiation." The *World* said: "*Acerrima proximorum*
"*odia;* and, under the present infamous Radical abuse of
"empire, the hatred between brothers, first fostered by the
"eleutheromaniacs of Abolitionism, is bearing its bitter fruit
"of private assassination at last. Somewhere amongst our
"*loci communes* of to-day may be found a report of the sup-
"posed death, at Hampsteadville (*not* Bumperville, as a
"radical contemporary has it), of a young Northerner named
"Goodwin Blood, at the hands of a Southern gentleman be-

* "Mr. Smalley" was the amusing name of a London reporter to this entertaining journal, which, it is believed, had hopes, at one time, of his selection for the vacant throne of Spain.

"longing to the stately old Southern family of Pentorrens.
"The Pentorrens are related, by old cavalier stock, to the
"Dukes of Mandeville, whose present ducal descendant
"combines the elegance of an Esterhazy with the intellect
"of an Argyle.   That a scion of such blood as this has re-
"duced a fellow-being to a condition of inanimate proto-
"plasm, is to be regretted for his sake ; but more for that of
"a country in which the philosophy of Comte finds in a cor-
"rupt radical pantarchy all-sufficient first-cause of whatso-
"ever is rotten in the State of Denmark."   The *Times* said :
"We give no details of the Burnstableville tragedy to-day,
"not being willing to pander to a vitiated public taste ; but
"shall do so to-morrow."

After reading these articles in the Great Dailies with considerable distraction, and inferring therefrom, that at least
three different young Southerners had killed three different
young Northerners in three different places on Christmas-
Eve, Judge Sweeney had a rush of blood to the brain, and
discharged Montgomery Pendragon as a person of undistinguishable identity.   But, when set at large, the helpless
youth could not turn a corner without meeting some bald-
headed reporter who raised the cry of " Stop thief ! " if he
sought to fly, and, if he paused, interviewed him in a magis-
terial manner, and almost tearfully implored him to Confess
his crime in time for the Next Edition.

Father Dean, Ritual Rector of St. Cow's, meeting Gospeller Simpson upon one of their daily strolls through the snow, said to him : —

"This young man, your pupil, has sinned, it appears; and a Ritualistic church, Mr. Gospeller, is no sanctuary for sin- ners."

"I cannot believe that the sin is his, Holy Father," answered the Reverend Octavius, respectfully : "but, even if it is, and he is remorseful for it, should not our Church cover him with her wings?"

"There are no wings to St. Cow's yet," returned the Father, coldly, — "only the main building; and that is too small to harbor any sinner who has not sufficient means to build a wing or two for himself."

"Then," said the Gospeller, bowing his head and speaking slowly, "I suppose he must go to the Other Church."

"What Other Church."

The Gospeller raised his hat and spoke reverently : —

"That which is all of God's world outside this little church of ours. That in which the Altar is any humble spot pressed by the knees of the Unfortunate. That in which the priest is whoso doeth a good, unselfish deed, even if in the shadow of the scaffold. That in which the anthem of visible charity for an erring brother sinks into the listening soul an echo of an unseen Father's pity and forgiveness, and the choral service is the music of kind words to all who ever found but unkind words before."

"You must mean the Church of the Pooritans," said the Ritual Rector.

So, Montgomery Pendragon went forth from Gospeller's Gulch to seek harbor where he might; and, a day or two afterwards, Mr. Bumstead exhibited to Mr. Simpson the following entry in his famous Diary : —

"No signs of that umbrella yet. Since the discovery of the watch and seal-ring, I am satisfied that my umbrella, only, was the temptation of the murderer. I now swear that I will no more discuss either my nephew or my umbrella with any living soul, until I have found once more the familiar boyish form and alpaca canopy, or brought vengeance upon him through whom I am nephewless and without protection in the rain."

CHAPTER XVII.

INSURANCE AND ASSURANCE.

Six months had come and gone and done it; the weather was as inordinately hot as it had before been intolerably cold; and the Reverend Octavius Simpson stood waiting, in the gorgeous office of the Boreal Life Insurance Company,* New York, for the appearance of Mr. Melancthon Schenck.

Having been directed by a superb young clerk, who parted his hair in the middle, to "just stand out of the passage-way and amuse yourself with one of our Schedules for awhile," until the great life-Agent should come in, the Gospeller read a few schedulistic pages, proving, that if a person had his life Insured at the age of Thirty, and paid his premiums regularly until he was Eighty-five, the cost to him and profit to the Company would, probably, be much more than the amount he had insured for. It must, then, be evident to him, that, upon his death, at Ninety, the Company would have received, in all, sufficient funds from him to pay the full amount of his Policy to the lady whom he had always introduced as his wife, and still retain enough to

* In the original, the "chief offices of the Haven of Philanthropy."

8*

declare a handsome Dividend for itself. Such was the sound business-principle upon which the Boreal was conducted; and the merest child must perceive, that only the extremely unlikely coincidence of at least four insurers all dying before Eighty-five could endanger the solvency of the beneficent institution.— Having mastered this convincing argument, and become greatly confused by its plausibility, Mr. Simpson next gave some attention to what was going on around him in the Office, and allowed his overwrought mind to relax cheerfully in contemplation thereof. One of human nature's peculiarities was quite amusingly exemplified in the different treatment accorded to callers who were "safe risks," and to those who where not. Thus the whisper of "Here comes old Tubercles, again !" was prevalent amongst the clerks upon the entrance of a very thin, narrow-chested old gentleman, whom they informed, with considerable humor, that he was only wasting hours which should be spent with a spiritual adviser, in his useless attempts to take out a Policy in *that* office. The Boreal couldn't insure men who ought to be upon their dying beds instead of coughing around Insurance offices. Ha, ha, ha! Another gentleman, florid of countenance, and absolutely without neck, was quickly checked in the act of giving his name at one of the desks; one clerk desiring another clerk to look, under the head of "A," in his book, for "*Apoplexy*," and let this man see that we can't take such a risk as he is on any terms. A third caller, who really looked quite healthy except around the eyes, was also assured that he need not call again — "Because, you see," explained the clerkly wag, "it's no go for you to try to play your Bright's Disease on *us !*" When, however, the applicant was a robustious, long-necked, fresh individual, he was almost lifted from his feet in the rush of obliging young Boreals to show him into the room of the Medical Examiner; and when, now and then, an agent, or an insurance-broker, came dragging in, by the collar, some Safe Risk, just captured, there was an actual contest to see who should be most polite to the panting but healthy stranger, and obtain his private biography for the consideration of the Company.

The Reverend Octavius studied these sprightly little scenes with unspeakable interest until the arrival of Mr. Schenck, and then followed that popular benefactor into his private office with the air of a man who had gained a heightened admiration for his species.

"So you have come to your senses at last !" said Mr. Schenck, hastily drawing his visitor toward a window in the side-room to which they had retired. "Let me look at your tongue, sir."

"What do you mean ?" asked the Gospeller, endeavoring to draw back.

"I mean what I say. Let — me— see —your — tongue. Or, stop !" said Mr. Schenck, seized with a new thought, "I may as well examine your general organization first." And, flying at the astounded Ritualistic clergyman, he had

sounded his lungs, caused a sharp pain in his liver, and felt
his pulse, before the latter could phrase an intelligent protest.

"You may die at any moment, and probably will," concluded Mr. Schenck, thoughtfully; "but still, on the score
of friendship, we'll give you a Policy for a reasonable
amount, and take the chance of being able to compromise
with your mother on a certain per centage after the funeral."

"I don't want any of your plagued policies!" exclaimed
the irritated Gospeller, pushing away the hand striving to
feel his pulse again.

"As you have expressed a desire to resign the guardianship of your wards, Mr. and Miss Pendragon, and I have
agreed to accept it, my purpose in calling here is to obtain
such statement of your account with those young people as
you may be disposed to render."

"Ah!" returned the other, in sullen disappointment.
"That is all, eh? Allow me to inform you, then, that I
have cancelled the Boreal policies which have been granted
to the Murderer and his sister; and allow me also to remark, that a dying clergyman like yourself might employ his
last moments better than encouraging a Southern destroyer
of human life."

"I do not, cannot believe that Montgomery Pendragon is
guilty," said Mr. Simpson, firmly. "Having his full confidence, and thoroughly knowing his nature, I am sure of his
innocence, let appearances be what they may. Consequently, it is my determination to befriend him."

" And you will not have your life insured ? "

" I will not, sir. Please stop bothering me."

" And you call yourself a clergyman ! " cried Mr. Schenck, with intense scorn. "You pretend to be a Ritualistic spiritual guide ; you champion people who slay the innocent and steal devout men's umbrellas ; and yet you do not scruple to leave your own high-church Mother entirely without provision at your death. — In such a case," continued the speaker, rising, while his manner grew ferocious with determination — "in such a case, all other arguments having failed, my duty is plain. You shall not leave this room, ` sir, until you have promised to take out a Boreal Policy."

He started, as he spoke, for the door of the private office, intending to lock it and remove the key ; but the unhappy Ritualist, fathoming his design, was there before him, and tore open the door for his own speedy egress.

" Mr. Schenck," observed the Gospeller, turning and pausing in the doorway, " you allow your business energy to violate all the most delicate amenities of private life, and will yet drive some maddened mortal to such resentful use of pistol, knife, or poker, as your mourning family shall sincerely deplore. The articles on Free Trade and Protection in the daily papers have hitherto been regarded as the climax of all that utterly wearies the long-suffering human soul ; but I tell you, as a candid friend, that they are but little more depressing and jading to the vital powers ·than your unceasing mention of life-insurance."

"These are strong words, sir," answered Mr. Schenck, incredulously. "The editorial articles to which you refer are considered the very drought of journalism; those by Mr. Greeley, especially, being so dry that they are positively dangerous reading without a tumbler of water."

"You brought the comparison upon yourself, Mr. Schenck. Good-day."

Thus speaking, the Reverend Octavius Simpson hurried nervously from the Boreal temple; not fairly satisfied that he had escaped a Policy until he found himself safely emerged on Broadway and turning a corner toward Nassau Street. Reaching the latter by-way, after a brief interval of sharp walking, he entered a building nearly opposite that in which was the office of Mr. Dibble; and, having ascended numerous flights of twilight stairs to the lofty floor immediately over the saddened rooms occupied by a great American Comic Paper, came into a spidery garret where lurked Montgomery Pendragon.

"Hard at it?" he asked, approaching a rickety table at which sat the persecuted Southerner, reading a volume of Hoyle's Games.

"My only friend!" ejaculated the lonely reader, hurriedly covering the book with an arm. "I am, as you see, studying law here, all alone with these silent friends."

He waved his thin hand toward a rude shelf on which were several well-worn City Directories of remote dates, volumes of Patent Office Reports for the years '57 and '59, a copy of Mr. Greeley's Essays on Political Economy, an edition of the Corporation Manual, the Coast Survey for 1850, and other inflaming statistical works, which had been sent to him in his exile by thoughtful friends who had no place to keep them.

" Cheer up, brother ! " exhorted the good Gospeller, " I'll send you some nice theological volumes to add to your library, which will then be complete. Be not despondent. All will come right yet."

" I reckon it will, in time," returned the youth, moodily. " I suppose you know that my sister is determined to come here and stay with me ? "

" Yes, Montgomery, I have heard of her noble resolution. May her conversation prove sustaining to you."

" There will be enough of it, I reckon, to sustain half a dozen people," was the despondent answer. " This is a gloomy place for her, Mr. Simpson, situated, as it is, immediately over the offices of a Comic Paper."

" And do you think she would care for cheerful accessories while you are in sorrow? " asked the Gospeller, reproachfully.

" But it is *so* mournful — that floor below," persisted the brother, doubtfully. " If there were only something the least bit more lively down there — say an Undertaker's."

" A Sister's Love can lessen the most crushing gloom, Montgomery."

A silent pressure of the hand rewarded this encouraging

reminder of sanguine friendship; and, after the depressed law-student had promised the Reverend Octavius to walk with him as far as the ferry in a few moments, the said Reverend departed for a hasty call upon the old lawyer across the street.

Benignant Mr. Dibble sat near a front window of his office, and received the visitor with legal serenity.

"And how does our young friend enjoy himself, Mr. Simpson, in the retreat which I had the honor of commending to you for him?"

The visitor replied, that his young friend's retreat, by its very loftiness, was calculated to inspire any occupant with a room-attic affection.

"And how, and when, and where did you leave Mr. Bumstead?" inquired Mr. Dibble.

"As well as could be expected; this morning, at Bumsteadville," said the Gospeller, with answer as terse and comprehensive as the question.

— "Because," added the lawyer, quickly, "there he is, now, coming out of a refreshment saloon immediately under the building in which our young friend takes refuge."

"So he is!" exclaimed the surprised Mr. Simpson, staring through the window.

There, indeed, as indicated, was the Ritualistic organist; apparently eating cloves from the palm of his right hand as he emerged from the place of refreshment, and wearing a linen coat so long and a straw hat of such vast brim, that his

sex was not obvious at first glance. While the two behold-
ers gazed, in unspeakable fascination, Mr. Bumstead suddenly made a wild dart at a passing elderly man with a dark
sun-umbrella, ecstatically tore the latter from his grasp, and
passionately tapped him on the head with it. Then, before
the astounded elderly man could recover from his amazement, or regain the gold spectacles which had been knocked
from his nose, the umbrella, after an instant of keen exam-
ination, was restored to him with a humble, almost abjectly
apologetic air, and Mr. Bumstead hurried back, evidently
crushed, into the refreshment saloon.

"His brain must be turned by the loss of his relative,"
murmured the Gospeller, pitifully.

"His umbrellative, you mean," said Mr. Dibble.

When these two gentlemen had parted, and the Reverend
Octavius Simpson had been escorted to the ferry, as promised, by Montgomery Pendragon, the latter, after a long,
insane walk about the city, with the thermometer at 98 degrees, returned to his attic in time to surprise a stranger
climbing in through one of the back windows.

"Who are you?" exclaimed the Southern youth, much
struck by the funereal aspect, sexton-like dress, and inordinately long countenance of the pallid, light-haired intruder.

"Pardon! pardon!" answered he at the window, with
much solemnity. "I am a proprietor of the Comic Paper
down below, and am eluding the man who comes every day
to tell me how such a paper *should* be conducted. He is

now talking to the young man writing the mail-wrappers, who, being of iron constitution and unmarried, can bear more than I. There was just time for me to glide out of the window at sound of that fearful voice, and I climbed the iron shutter and found myself at your casement. — Hark ! Do you hear the buzz down there ? He's now telling the young man writing the mail-wrappers what kind of Cartoons should be got-up for *this* country. — Hark, again ! He and the young man writing the mail-wrappers have clinched and are rolling about the floor.— Hark, once more ! The young man writing the mail-wrappers has put him out."

"Won't you come in ? " asked Montgomery, sincerely sorry for the agitated being.

"Alas, no ! " responded the fugitive, in the tone of a cathedral bell. "I must go back to my lower deep once more. My name is Jeremy Bentham ; * I am very unhappy in my mind ; and, with your permission, will often escape this way from him who is the bane of my existence."

Being assured of welcome on all occasions, he of the long countenance went clanging down the iron shutter again ; and the lonely law-student, burying his face in his hands, prayed Providence to forgive him for having esteemed his own lot so hopelessly gloomy, when there were Comic Paper men on the very next floor.

That night, before going home to Gowanus, the old law-

---

* In the original, *Mr. Tartar*, a retired naval officer.

yer across the way glanced up toward Montgomery's retreat, and shook his head as though he couldn't make something out. Whether he had a difficult idea in his brain, or only a fly on his nose, was for the observer to discover for himself.

CHAPTER XVIII.

A SUBTLE STRANGER.

THE latest transient guest at the Roach House — a hotel
kept on the entomological plan in Bumsteadville — was a
gentleman of such lurid aspect as made every beholder burn
to know whom he could possibly be. His enormous head
of curled red hair not only presented a central parting on
top and a very much one-sided parting and puffing-out
behind, but actually covered both his ears; while his ruddy
semi-circle of beard curled inward, instead of out, and
greatly surprised, if it did not positivly alarm, the looker-on,
by appearing to remain perfectly motionless, no matter how
actively the stranger moved his jaws. This ball of improb-
able inflammatory hair and totally independent face, rested
in a basin of shirt collar; which, in its turn, was supported
by a rusty black neck-tie and a very loose suit of gritty
alpaca; so that, taking the gentleman for all in all, such an
incredible human being had rarely been seen outside of literary circles.

"Landlord," said the stranger, to the brown linen host of
the Roach House, who was intently gazing at him with the
appreciative expression of one who beholds a comic ghost,

— "landlord, after you have finished looking at my head and involuntarily opening your mouth at some occasional peculiarity of my whiskers, I should like to have something to eat. As you tell me that woodcock is not fit to eat this year, and that broiled chicken is positively prohibited by the Board of Health in consequence of the sickly season, you *may* bring me some pork and beans, and some crackers. Bring plenty of crackers, landlord, for I'm uncommon fond of crackers. By absorbing the superfluous moisture in the head, they clear the brain and make it more subtle."

Having been served with the wholesome country fare he had ordered, together with a glass of the heady native wine called applejack, the gentleman had but just moved a slice of pork from its bed in the beans, when, with much interest, he closely inspected the spot of vegetables he had uncovered, and expressed the belief that there was something alive in it.

"Landlord," said he, musingly, "there is something amongst these beans that I should take for a raisin, if it did not move."

Placing upon his nose a pair of vast silver spectacles, which gave him an aspect of having two attic windows in his countenance, the landlord bowed his head over the plate until his nose touched the beans, and thoughtfully scrutinized the living raisin.

"As I thought, sir, it is only a water-bug," he observed,

rescuing the insect upon his thumb-nail. "You need not have been frightened, however, for they never bite."

Somewhat reassured, the stranger went on eating until his knife encountered resistance in the secondary layer of beans; when he once more inspected the dish, with marked agitation.

"Can this be a skewer, down here?" inquired he, prodding out some hard, springy object with his fork.

The host of the Roach House bore both fork and object to a window, where the light was less deceptive, and was presently able to announce confidently that the object was only a hair-pin. Then, observing that his guest looked curiously at a cracker, which, from the gravelly marks on one side, seemed to have been dug out of the earth, like a potato, he hastened to obviate all complaint in that line by carefully wiping every individual cracker with his pocket handkerchief.

"And now, landlord," said the stranger, at last, pulling a couple of long, unidentified hairs from his mouth as he hurriedly retired from the meal, "I suppose you are wondering who I am?"

"Well, sir," was the frank answer, "I can't deny that there are points about you to make a plain man like myself thoughtful. There's that about your hair, sir, with the middle-parting on top and the side-parting behind, to give a plain person the impression that your brain must be slightly turned, and that, by rights, your face ought to be where your

neck is. Neither can I deny, sir, that the curling of your
whiskers the wrong way, and their peculiarity in remaining
entirely still while your mouth is going, are circumstances
calculated to excite the liveliest apprehensions of those who
wish you well."

"The peculiarities you notice," returned the gentleman,
"may either exist solely in your own imagination, or they
may be the result of my own ill-health. My name is Tracey
Clews,* and I desire to spend a few weeks in the country
for physical recuperation. Have you any idea where a dead
beat,† like myself, could find inexpensive lodgings in Bumsteadville?"

The host hastily remarked, that his own bill for those
pork and beans was fifty cents; and upon being paid,
coldly added, that a Mrs. Smythe, wife of the sexton of
Saint Cow's Ritualistic Church, took hash-eaters for the
summer. As the gentleman preferred a high-church private
boarding-house to an unsectarian first-class hotel, all he had
to do was to go out on the road again, and keep inquiring
until he found the place.

Donning his Panama hat, and carrying a stout cane, Mr.
Clews was quickly upon the turnpike; and, his course taking

---

* In the original, Dick Datchery.

† "Buffer" is the term used in the English story. Its nearest native equivalent
is, probably, our "Dead Beat;" meaning, variously, according to circumstances, a
successful American politician ; a wife's male relative ; a watering-place correspondent
of a newspaper ; a New York detective policeman ; any person who is uncommonly
pleasant with people, while never asking them to take anything with him; a pious
boarder; a French revolutionist.

him near the pauper burial-ground, he presently perceived an extremely disagreeable child throwing stones at pigeons in a field, and generally hitting the beholder.

"You young Alderman! what do you mean?" he exclaimed, with marked feeling, rubbing the place on his knee which had just been struck.

"Then just give me a five-cent stamp to aim at yer, and yer won't ketch it onc't," replied the boyish trifler. "I couldn't hit what I was to fire at if it was my own daddy."

"Here are ten cents, then," said the gentleman, wildly dodging the last shot at a distant pigeon, "and now show me where Mrs. Smythe lives."

"All right, old brick-top," assented the merry sprite, with a vivacious dash of personality. "D'yer see that house as yer skoot past the Church and round the corner?"

"Yes."

"Well, that's Smythe's, and Bumstead lives there too — him as is always tryin' to put a head on me. I'll play my points on him yet, though. *I'll* play my points!" And the rather vulgar young chronic absentee from Sunday-school retired to a proper distance, and from thence began stoning his benefactor, to the latter's perfect safety.

Reaching the boarding-house of Mrs. Smythe, as directed, Mr. Tracey Clews soon learned from the lady that he could have a room next to the apartment of Mr. Bumstead, to whom he was referred for further recommendation of the establishment. Though that broken-hearted gentleman was

mourning the loss of a beloved umbrella, accompanied by a
nephew, and having a bone handle, Mrs. Smythe was sure
he would speak a good word for her house. Perhaps Mr.
Clews had heard of his loss?

Mr. Clews could not exactly recall that particular case;
but had a confused recollection of having lost several umbrellas himself, at various times, and had no doubt that the
addition of a nephew must make such a loss still heavier.

Mr. Bumstead being in his room when the introduction
took place, and having Judge Sweeney for company over a
bowl of lemon tea, the new boarder lifted his hat politely to
both dignitaries, and involuntarily smacked his lips at the
mixture they were taking for their coughs.

"Excuse me, gentlemen," said Mr. Tracey Clews, in a
manner almost stealthy; "but, as I am about to take summer board with the lady of this house, I beg leave to inquire
if she and the man she married are strictly moral except in
having cold dinner on Sunday?"

Mr. Bumstead, who sat very limply in his chair, said that
she was a very good woman, a very good woman, and would
spare no pains to secure the comfort of such a head of hair
as he then saw before him.

"This is my dear friend, Judge Sweeney," continued the
Ritualistic organist, languidly waving a spoon toward that
gentleman, "who has a very good wife in the grave, and
knows much more about women and gravy than I. As for
me," exclaimed Mr. Bumstead, suddenly climbing upon the

9

arm of his chair and staring at Mr. Clews' head rather wildly,
" my only bride was of black alpaca, with a brass ferule,
and I can never care for the sex again." Here Mr. Bumstead, whose eyes had been rolling in an extraordinary manner, tumbled into his chair again, and then, frowning intensely,
helped himself to lemon tea.

"I am referred to your Honor for further particulars,"
observed Mr. Tracey Clews, bowing again to Judge Sweeney.
" Not to wound our friend further by discussion of the fair
sex, may I ask if Bumsteadville contains many objects of interest for a stranger, like myself ? "

"One, at least, sir," answered the Judge. "I think I
could show you a tombstone which you would find very good
reading. An epitaph upon my late better-half. If you are
a married man you can not help enjoying it."

Mr. Clews regretted to inform his Honor, that he had
never been a married man, and, therefore, could not presume to fancy what the literary enjoyment of a widower
must be at such a treat.

"A journalist, I presume ? " insinuated Judge Sweeney,
more and more struck by the other's perfect pageant of in-
comprehensible hair and beard.

" His Honor flatters me too much."

" Something in the lunatic line, then, perhaps ? "

"I have told your Honor that I never was married."

Since last speaking, Mr. Bumstead had been staring at the
new boarder's head and face, with a countenance expressive

of mingled consternation and wrath. and now made a start-ling rush at him, from his chair, and fairly forced half a glass of lemon tea down his throat.

"There, sir!" said the mourning organist, panting with suppressed excitement. "That will keep you from taking cold until you can be walked up and down in the open air long enough to get your hair and beard sober. They have been indulging, sir, until the top of your head has fallen over backwards, and your whiskers act as though they belonged to somebody else. The sight confuses me, sir, and in my present state of mind I can't bear it."

Coughing from the lemon tea, and greatly amazed by his hasty dismissal, Mr. Clews followed Judge Sweeney from the room and house in precipitate haste, and, when they were fairly out of doors, remarked, that the gentlemen they had just left had surprised him unprecedentedly, and that he was very much put out by it.

"Mr. John Bumstead, sir," explained the Judge, "is al-most beside himself at the double loss he has sustained, and I think that the sight of your cane, there, maddened him with the memory it revived."

"Why," exclaimed the gentleman of the hair, staring in wonder, "you don't mean to tell me that my cane looks at all like his nephew?"

"It looks a little like the stick of his umbrella, which he lost at the same time," was the grave answer.

After walking on in thoughtful silence for a while, as

though deeply pondering the striking character of a man
whose great nature could thus at once unite the bereaved
uncle with the sincere mourner for the dumb friend of his '
rainier days, Mr. Tracey Clews asked whether suspicion yet
pointed to any one ?

Yes, he was told, suspicion did point very decidedly at a
certain person ; but, as no specific reward had yet been offered in sufficient amount to justify the exertions of police
officials having families to support ; and as no lifeless body
had yet been found ; and as it was not exactly certain
that the abstraction of an umbrella by unknown parties
would justify the criminal prosecution of a person for having
in his possession an Indian Club : — in view of all these
complicated circumstances, the law did not feel itself author-
ized to execute any assassin at present.

"And here we are, sir, at last, near our Ritualistic
Church," continued Judge Sweeney, "where we stand up for
the Rite so much that strangers sometimes complain of it as
fatiguing.   Upon that monument yonder, in the graveyard,
you may find the epitaph I have mentioned.   What is more,
here comes a rather interesting local character of ours, who
cut the inscription and put up the monument."

Mr. McLaughlin came shuffling up the road as he spoke,
followed in the distance by the inevitable Smalley and a
shower of promiscuous stones.

"Here, you boy !" roared Judge Sweeney, beckoning the
amiable child to him with a bit of small money, "aim at *all*

of us — do you hear? — and see that you don't hit any windows. And now, McLaughlin, how do you do? Here is a
gentleman spending the summer with us, who would like to
know you."

Old 'Mortarity stared at the hair and beard thus introduced to him, with undisguised amazement, and grimly remarked, that if the gentleman would come to see him any
evening, and bring a social bottle with him, he would not
allow the gentleman's head to stand in the way of a further
acquaintance.

" I shall certainly call upon you," assented Mr. Clews,
" if our young friend, the stone-thrower, will accept a trifle
to show me the way."

Before retiring to his bed that night, the same Mr. Tracey
Clews took off his hair and beard, examined them closely,
and then broke into a strange smile. " No wonder they all
looked at me so !" he soliloquized, "for I did have my locks
on the topside backmost, and my whiskers turned the wrong
way. However, for a dead beat, with all his imperfections
on his head, I've formed a pretty large acquaintance for
one day." *

* In both conception and execution, the original of the above Chapter, in Mr.
Dickens's work, is, perhaps, the least felicitous page of fiction ever penned by the
great novelist ; and, as this Adaptation is in no wise intended as a burlesque, or carica-
ture, of the *style* of the original (but rather as a conscientious imitation of it, so far as
practicable), the Adapter has not allowed himself that license of humor which, in the
most comically effective treatment of said Chapter, might bear the appearance of such
an intention.

CHAPTER XIX.

THE H. AND H. OF J. BUMSTEAD.

THE exquisitely sweet month of the perfectly delicious summer-vacation having come, Miss Carowthers' Young Ladies have returned again, for a time, to their respective homes, Magnolia Pendragon has gone to the city and her brother, and Flora Potts is ridiculously and absurdly alone.

Under the ardent sun of August, Bumsteadville slowly bakes, like an ogre's family-dish of stuffed cottages and greens, with here and there some slowly moving object, like a loose vegetable on a sluggish current of tidal gravy, and the spire of the Ritualistic church shooting up at one end like an incorrigibly perpendicular leg of magnified mutton.

Hotter and hotter comes the fiery breath of nature's cookery, until some of the stuffing boils out of one cottage, in the shape of the Oldest Inhabitant, who makes his usual annual remark, that this is the Warmest Day in ninety-eight years, and then simmers away to some cooler nook amongst the greens. More and more intolerably quivers the atmosphere of the sylvan oven with stifling fervency, until there oozes from beneath the shingled crust of a vegetarian country-boarding-house a parboiled guest from the City, who, believing himself almost ready to turn, drifts feebly to where the roads fork and there is a shade more dun ; while, to the speculative mind, each glowing field of corn, or buckwheat, is an incipient Meal, and each chimney, or barn, a mere temptation to guess how many Swallows there may be in it.

Upon the afternoon of such a day as this, Miss Potts is informed, by a servant, that Mr. Bumstead has arrived, and, sending her his love, would be pleased to have her come down stairs to him and bring a fan.

"Why didn't you tell him I wasn't at home, you absurd thing?" cries the young girl, hurriedly practising a series of agitated looks and pensive smiles before her mirror.

"So I did, Miss," answers the attached menial, "but he'd seen you looking at him with an opera-glass as he came up the path, and said that he could hear you taking a clean handkerchief out of the drawer, on purpose to receive him with, before he'd got to the door."

"Oh, what shall I do? My hands are *so* red to-day!" sighs Flora, holding her arms above her head, that the blood may retire from the too pinkish members.

After a pause, and an adjustment of a curl over her right eye and the scarf at her waist, to make them look innocent, she yields to the meteorological mania so strikingly prevalent amongst all the other characters of this narrative, and says that she will receive the visitor in the yard, near the pump. Then, casting carelessly over her shoulder that web-like shawl without which no woman nor spider is complete, she arranges her lips in the glass for the last time, and, with a garden-hat hanging from the elbow latest singed, goes down, humming unsuspiciously, into the open-air, with the guileless bearing of one wholly unprepared for company.

Resting an elbow upon a low iron patent-pump, near a rustic seat, the Ritualistic organist, in his vast linen coat and imposing straw hat, looks not unlike an eccentric garden statue, upon which some prudish slave of modern conventionalities has placed the summer attire of a western editor. The great heat of the sun upon his back makes him irritable, and when Miss Potts sharply smites with her fan the knuckles of the hand which he has affably extended to take her by the chin, more than the usual symptoms of acute inflammation appear at the end of his nose, and he blows hurriedly upon his wounded digits.

"That hurt like the mischief!" he remarks in some anger. "I don't know when I've felt anything smart so."

"Then don't be so horrid," returns the pensive girl, taking a seat before him upon the rustic settee, and abstractedly arranging her dress so that only two-thirds of a gaiter-boot can be seen.

Munching cloves, the aroma of which ladens the air all around him, Mr. Bumstead contemplates her with a calmness which would be enthralling, but for the nervous twisting of his features under the torments of a singularly adhesive fly.

"I have come, dear," he observes, slowly, "to know how

soon you will be ready for me to give you your next music-lesson?"

" I prefer that you would not call me your ' dear,' " is the chilling answer.

The organist thinks for a moment, and then nods his head intelligently. " You are right," he says gravely, " — there *might* be somebody listening who could not enter into our real feelings. And now, how about those music-lessons ?"

"I don't want any more, thank you," says Flora, coldly. "While we are all in mourning for our poor, dear, absurd Eddy, it seems like a perfectly ridiculous mockery to be practising the scales."

Fanning himself with his straw hat, Mr. Bumstead shakes his bushy head several times. " You do not discriminate sufficiently," he replies. " There are kinds of music which, when performed rapidly upon the violin, fife, or kettle-drum, certainly fill the mind with sentiments unfavorable to the deeper anguish of human sorrow. Of such, how-ever, is not the kind made by young girls, which is at all times a help to the intensity of judicious grief. Let me assure you, with the candor of an idolized friend, that some of the saddest hours of my life have been spent in teaching you to try to sing a humorous aria from Donizetti ; and the moments in which I have most sincerely regretted ever hav-ing been born were those in which you have played, in my hearing, the Drinking-song from *La Traviata.* Believe me, then, my devoted pupil, there can be nothing at all incon-

9*

sistent with a prevalence of profound melancholy in your continued piano-playing; whereas, on the contrary, your sudden and permanent cessation might at least surprise your friends and the neighborhood into a light-heartedness temporarily oblivious of the memory of that dear missing boy, to whom you could not, I hear, give the love already bestowed upon me."

" I loved him ridiculously, absurdly, with my whole heart," cries Flora, not altogether liking what she has heard. - " I'm real sorry, too, that they think somebody has killed him."

Mr. Bumstead folds his brown linen arms as he towers before her, and the dark circles around his eyes appear to shrink with the intensity of his gaze.

" There are occasions in life," he remarks, "when to acknowledge that our last meeting with a friend who has since mysteriously disappeared, was to reject him and imply a preference for his uncle, may be calculated to associate us unpleasantly with that disappearance, in the minds of the censorious, and invite suspicions tending to our early cross-examination by our Irish local magistrate. I do not say, of course, that you actually destroyed my nephew for fear he should try to prejudice me against you; but I cannot withhold my earnest approval of your judicious pretence of a sentiment palpably incompatible with the shedding of the blood of its departed object. If you will move your dress a little, so that I can sit beside you and allow your head to rest upon my shoulder, that fan will do for both of us, and we may converse in whispers."

"My head upon *your* shoulder!" exclaims Miss Potts, staring swiftly about to see if anybody is looking. "I prefer to keep my head upon my own shoulders, sir."

"Two heads are better than one," the Ritualistic organist reminds her. "If a little hair-oil and powder *does* come off upon my coat, the latter will wash, I suppose. Come, dearest, if it is our fate to never get through this hot day alive, let us be sunstruck together."

She shrinks timidly from the brown linen arm which he begins insinuating along the back of the rustic settee, and tells him that she couldn't have believed that he could be so absurd. He draws back his arm, and seems hurt.

"Flora," he says, tenderly, "how beautiful you are, especially when fixed up. The more I see of you, the less sorry I am that I have concluded to be yours. All the time that my dear boy was trying to induce you to release him from his engagement, I was thinking how much better you might do; yet, beyond an occasional encouraging wink, I never gave the least sign of reciprocating your attachment. I did not think it would be right."

The assertion, though superficially true, is so imperfect in its delineation of habitual conduct liable to another construction, that the agitated Flowerpot returns, with quick indignation: "Your arm was always reaching out whenever you sat in a chair anywhere near me, and whenever I sang

you always kept looking straight into my mouth until it
tickled me. You know you did, you hateful thing! Besides, it wasn't you that I preferred at all; it was — oh, it's
too ridiculous to tell!"

In her bashful confusion she is about to arise and trip
shyly away from him into the house, when he speaks again.

"Miss Potts, is your friendship for Miss Pendragon and
her brother such, that their execution upon some Friday of
next month would be a spectacle to which you could give
no pleased attention?"

"What do you mean, you absurd creature?"

"I mean," continues Mr. Bumstead, "simply this : you
know my double loss. You know that, upon the person of
the male Pendragon was found an apple looking and tast-
ing like one which my nephew once had. You know, that
when Miss Pendragon went from here she wore an alpaca
waist which looked as though it had been exposed more than
once to the rain.— See the point?"

Flora gives a startled look, and says, "I don't see it."

"Suppose," he goes on — "suppose that I go to a magistrate, and say : 'Judge, I voted for you, and can influence a
large foreign vote for you again. I have lost a nephew who
was very fond of apples, and a black alpaca umbrella of
great value. A young Southerner, who has not lived in this
State long enough to vote, has been found in possession
of an apple singularly like the kind generally eaten by my

missing relative, and his sister has come out in a waist made of second-hand alpaca?'— See the point now?"

"Mr. Bumstead," exclaims Flora, affrighted by the terrible menace of his manner, "I don't any more believe that Mr. Pendragon is guilty than that I, myself, am; and as for your old umbrella —"

"Stop, woman!" interrupts the bereaved organist, imperiously. "Not even your lips shall speak disrespectfully of my lost bone-handled friend. By a chain of unanswerable argument, I have shown you that I hold the fate of your Southern acquaintances in my hands, and shall be particularly sorry if you force me to hang Mr. Pendragon as a rival."

Flora puts her hands to her temples, to soothe her throbbing head and display a bracelet.

"Oh, what shall I do! I don't want anybody to be hung! It must be so perfectly awful!"

Her touching display of generous feeling does not soften him. On the contrary, he stands more erect, and smiles rather triumphantly under his straw hat.

"Beloved one," he murmurs, in a rich voice, "I find that I cannot induce you to make the first advance towards the mutual avowal we are both longing for, and must therefore precipitate our happiness myself. My poor boy would not have given you perfect satisfaction, and your momentary liking for the male Pendragon was but the effect of a temporary despair undoubtedly produced by my seeming coldness.

That coldness had nothing to do with my heart, but resulted partially from my habit of wearing a wet towel on my head. I now propose to you —"

"Propose to me?" ejaculates Miss Potts, with heightened color.

—"That you pick out a worthy man belonging to your own section of the Union," he continues hastily. — "Here's my Heart," he adds, going through the motions of taking something from a pocket and placing it in his outstretched palm, "and here's my Hand,"— placing therein an equally imaginary object from another pocket. — "Try the H. and H. of J. Bumstead."

His manner is as though he were commending some patent article of unquestionable utility.

"But I can't bear the sight of you!" she cries, pushing away the brown linen arm coming after her again.

Taking away her fan, he pats her on the head with it, and seems momentarily surprised at the hollow sound.

"Future Mrs. Bumstead," he cheerfully replies, at last, "my observation and knowledge of the women of America teach me that there never was a wife going to Indiana for a divorce, who had not at first sworn to love, as well as honor and obey, her husband. Such is woman, that if she had felt and said at the altar that she couldn't bear the sight of him, it wouldn't have been in the power of masculine brutality and dissipated habits to drive her from his side through all their lives. There can be no better sign of our future happiness, than for you to say, beforehand, that you utterly detest the man of your choice."

There is something terrible to the young girl in the original turn of thought of this fascinating man. Say what she may, he at once turns it into virtual devotion to himself. He appears to have a perfectly dreadful power to hang everybody; he considers her strongest avowal of present personal dislike the most promising indication she can give of eternal future infatuation with him, and his powerful mode of reasoning is more profound and confusing than an article in a New York newspaper on a War in Europe. Rendered dizzy by his metaphysical conversation, she arises from the rustic seat, and is flying giddily into the house, when he leaps athletically after her, and catches her in the doorway.

" I merely wish to request," he says, quietly, "that you place sufficient restraint upon your naturally happy feelings to keep our engagement a secret from the public at present, as I can't bear to have the boys calling out after me, 'There's the feller that's goin' to get married ! There's the feller that's goin' to get married !' When a man is about to make a fool of himself, it is not for children to remind him of it."

The door being opened before she can answer, Flora receives a parting bow of Grandisonian elegance from Mr. Bumstead, and hastens upstairs to her room in a destraction of mind not uncommon to those having conversational relations with the Ritualistic organist.

CHAPTER XX.

AN ESCAPE.

THE bewildered Flowerpot had no sooner gained her own room, enjoyed her agitated expression of face in the mirror, and tried four differently colored ribbon-bows upon her collar in succession, than the thought of becoming Mr. Bumstead's bride lost the charm of its first wild novelty, and became utterly ridiculous.   He was a man of commanding stature, which his linen "duster" made appear still more long ; the dark circles around his eyes would disappear in time, and he had an abusive way of referring to women which made him inexpressibly grand to women as a true poet-soul; but would it be safe, would it be religiously right, for a young girl, not yet conscious of her own full power of annual monetary expenditure, to blindly risk her necessary expenses for life upon one whom the cost of a single imported bonnet, in the contingency of a General European War, might plunge into inextricable pecuniary embarrassment?   Possibly, the General European War might not occur in an ordinary married-lifetime, as France was no longer in a condition to menace England, Russia would be wary about provoking the new Prussian giant, and Austria and Italy were not likely soon to forget their last military misadventures : yet, while all the great American journals had, for the last twenty years, published daily editorials, by young writers from the country, to show that such a War could not possibly be averted longer than about the day after to-morrow, would it be judicious for a young girl to marry as though that War were absolutely impossible? No! Her woman's heart sternly reiterated the pitiless negative ; and, as the Ritualistic organist had plainly evinced an earnest intention to let no foreign military complications prevent her marriage with him, she felt that her only safety from his matrimonial violence must be sought in flight.

With whom, though, could she take refuge? If she went to Magnolia Pendragon, all her dearest schoolmates would say, that they had always loved her, despite her great faults, yet could not disguise from themselves that she seemed at last to be fairly running after Miss Pendragon's brother. Besides, Mr. Bumstead, offended by the seeming want of confidence in him evinced by her flight, would, probably, take measures publicly to identify Magnolia's alpaca garment with the covering of his lost umbrella, and thus direct new suspicion against a sister and brother already bothered almost into hysterics.

During the last few weeks, an attack of dyspepsia had laid the foundation of a mind in the Flowerpot, as it generally does in other young female American boarding-school thinkers, and she was now capable of that subtle line of rea-

soning which is the great commendation of her sex to a
recognized perfect intellectual equality with man. Once decided, by her apprehension of a General European War,
against marriage with J. Bumstead, she took a rather irritable view of that too attractive devotional musician, and
inferred, from his not being wealthy enough to stand the test
of possible transatlantic hostilities, that he must, himself,
have killed Edwin Drood. His umbrella, it was well known,
had been present at that fatal Christmas dinner; and a
thoughtless insult offered to it, even by his nephew, might
have made a demon of him. Suppose that Edwin, upon returning to the dining-room that night, after his temporary
exercise in the open air with Montgomery Pendragon, had
found his uncle, flushed with cloves, endeavoring to force a
social glass of lemon tea upon the umbrella, under the impression that it was a person, and had unthinkingly accused
him thereat of being momentarily unsettled in his faculties?
Probably, then, hot words would have passed between them;
each telling the other that he would have a nice headache in
the morning and find it impossible not to look very sleepy
even if he fixed his hair ever so elaborately. Blows might
have followed : the uncle, in his anger, hewing the nephew
limb from limb with the carving knife from the table, and
subsequently carrying away the remains to the Pond and
there casting them in. Suppose, in his natural excitement,
the uncle had hurriedly used the umbrella, opened and held
downward, to carry the remains in ; and, after coming home

again, and snatching a nap under the table, had forgotten all about it, and thus been ever since inconsolable for his alpaca loss? As the young orphan argued thus exhaustively to herself, the extreme probability of her suppositions made her more and more frenzied to fly instantly beyond the reach of one who, in the event of a General European War, would not be a husband whom her head could approve.

After penning a hasty farewell note to Miss Carowthers, to the effect that urgent military reasons obliged her to see her guardian at once, Flora lost no time in packing a small leather satchel for travel. Two bottles of hair-oil, a jar of glycerine, one of cold cream, two boxes of powder, a package of extra back-hair, a phial of belladonna, a camel's-hair brush for the eyebrows, a rouge-saucer for pinking the nails, four flasks of perfumery, a depilatory in a small flagon, and some tooth-paste, were the only articles she could pause to collect for her precipitate escape: and, with them in the satchel on her arm, and a bonnet and shawl hurriedly thrown on, she stole away down-stairs, and thus from the house.

Hastening to the Roach House, from whence started an omnibus for the ferry, she was quickly rattling out of Bum-steadville in a vehicle remarkable for the great number and variety of noises it could make when maddened into motion by a span of equine rivals in an immemorial walking-match.

"Now, Bonner," she said to the driver, taking leave of him at the ferry-boat, "be sure and let Miss Carowthers

know that you saw me safely off, and that I was not a bit
more tired than if I had walked all the way."

Blushing with pleasure at the implied compliment to his
equipage from such lips, the skilful horseman had not the .
heart to object to the wildly mutilated fragment of currency
with which his fare had been paid, and went back to where
his steeds were taking turns in holding each other up, as
happy a man as ever lost money by the change in woman.

Reaching the city, Miss Potts was promptly worshipped by
a hackman of marked conversational powers, who, whip in
hand, assured her that his carriage was widely celebrated
under the titles of the "Rocking Chair," the "Old Shoe,"
and the "Glider," on account of its incredible ease ot motion ; and that, owing to its exquisite abbreviation of travel
to the emotions, those who rode in it had actually been
known to dispute that they had ridden even half the distance
for which they were charged.   Did he know where Mr. Dibble, the lawyer, lived, in Nassau Street, near Fulton?*   If
.she meant lawyer Dibble, near Fulton Street, in Nassau,
next door but one to the second house below, and directly
opposite the building across the way, there was just one
span of buckskin horses in the city that could take a carriage built expressly for ladies to that place, as naturally as
though it were a stable.   It was a place that he — the hackman — always associated with his own mother, because he

---

* In the original, *Staple Inn*, London, is the lawyer's address.

was so familiar with it in childhood, and had often thought of driving to it blindfolded for a wager.

Proud to learn that her guardian was so well known in the great city, and delighted that she had met a charioteer so minutely familiar with his house of business, Flora stepped readily into the providential hack, which thereupon instantly began Rocking-Chair-ing, Old-Shoe-ing, and Gliding. Any one of these celebrated processes, by itself, might have been desirable ; but their indiscriminate and impetuous combination in the present case gave the Flowerpot a confused impression that her whole ride was a startling series of incessant sharp turns around obdurate street corners, and kept her plunging about like an early young Protestant tossed in a Romish blanket. Instinctively holding her satchel aloft, to save its fragile contents from fracture, she rocked, shoed, and glided all over the interior of the vehicle, without hope of gaining breath enough for even one scream, until, nearly unconscious, and, with her bonnet driven half-way into her chignon, she was helped out by the hackman at her guard- ian's door.

" I am dying ! " she groaned.

" Then please remember me in your will, to the extent of two dollars," returned the hackman with much humor. " You're only a little sea-sick, miss ; as often happens to people in humble circumstances when they ride in a ker-ridge for the first time."

Still panting, Miss Potts paid and discharged this friendly

man, and, weariedly entering the building, followed the signs upstairs to her guardian's office.

After knocking several times at the right door, without reply, she turned the knob, and entered so softly that the venerable lawyer was not aroused from the slumber into which he had fallen in his chair by the window. With a copy of *Old and New* still grasped in his honest right hand, good Mr. Dibble slept like a drugged person ; nor could the young girl awaken him until, by a happy inspiration, she had snatched away the monthly and cast it through the casement.

"Am I dreaming ?" exclaimed the aged man, when thus suddenly rescued from his deadly lethargy at last. "Is that you, my dear; or are you your late mother ? "

"I am your ridiculously unhappy ward," answered the Flowerpot, tremulously. "Oh, poor, dear, absurd Eddy ! "

"And you have come here all alone ? "

"Yes ; and to escape being married to Eddy's perfectly hateful uncle, who has the same as ordered me to become his utterly disgusted bride. Oh, why is it, why is it, that I must be thus persecuted by young men without property ! Why is it that perfectly horrid madmen on salaries are allowed to claim me as their own ! "

"My dear," cried the old lawyer, leading her to a chair, and striving to speak soothingly, "if Mr. Bumstead desires to marry you he must indeed be insane. Such a man ought really to be confined," he continued, pacing thoughtfully up and down the room. "This must have been the idea that was already turning his brain when — bless my soul ! — he actually intimated, first, that I, and then, that Mr. Simpson, had killed his nephew !"

"He thinks, now, that I, or Magnolia Pendragon, may have done it, — the hateful creature !" said Flora, passionately.

"I see, I see," assented Mr. Dibble, nodding. "When he has you in his head, my dear, he himself must clearly be out of it. You shall stay here and take tea with me, and then I will take you to French's Hotel for your accommodation during the night."

It was a sight to see him tenderly help her off with her bonnet ; and suggestive to hear him say, that if a man could only take off his brains as easily as a woman hers, what a relief it would be to him occasionally. It was curious to see him peep into her bottle-filled satchel, with an old man's freedom ; and to hear him audibly wonder thereat, whether after all, men were any more addicted than women to the social glass when they wanted to put a better face on affairs. And, after the waiter, bringing him toast and tea from a neighboring restaurant, had brought an additional slice and cup for the guest, it was pleasant to behold him smiling across the office-table at that guest, and encouraging her to eat as much as she would if a member of his sex were not looking.

"It must be absurdly ridiculous to stay here all alone, as you do, sir," observed Flora.

"But I am not always alone," answered Mr. Dibble. "My clerk, Mr. Bladams, now taking a vacation in the country, is generally here; though, to be sure, I may lose 'him before long. He's turned literary."

"How perfectly frightful!" said Miss Potts.

"He has set up for a genius, my child, and is now engaged upon a great American novel. Discontented with the law, he is giving great attention to this; but Free Trade will not, I am afraid, allow any American publisher to bring it out."

"Free Trade?" repeated Flora.

"Yes, my dear, Free Trade; that is, while American publishers can steal foreign novels for nothing, they are not going to pay anything for native fiction."

Yawning behind her hand, the Flowerpot murmured something about Free Trade being positively absurd, and her guardian went on : —

"Nevertheless, Mr. Bladams is going on with his work, which he calls 'The Amateur Detective;' and if it ever does come out you shall have a copy. — But, by the by," added the lawyer, suddenly, "you have not yet fully described to me the interview in which poor Mr. Edwin's uncle offered to become your husband."

She gave him a full history of the Ritualistic organist's handsome offer to her of his H. and H. ; adding her own final decision in the matter as precipitated by the possibility of a General European War; and Mr. Dibble heard the whole with an air of studious attention.

"Although I have certainly no particular reason for be-friending Mr. Bumstead," said he, reflectively, "I shall take measures to keep him from you. Now come with me to French's Hotel.* To-morrow I will call there for you, you know, and then, perhaps, you may be taken to see your friend, Miss Pendragon."

Having obtained for his ward a room in the hotel named, and seen her safely to its shelter, the good old lawyer visited the bar-room of the establishment, for the purpose of ascer-taining whether any evil-disposed person could get in through that way for the disturbance of his fair charge. After which he departed for his home in Gowanus.

* In the original, *Furnival's Inn.*

19

CHAPTER XXI.

BENTHAM TO THE RESCUE.

EUROPEAN travellers in this country — especially if one
economical condition of their coming hither has not been
the composition of works of imagination on America, sufficiently contemptuous to pay all the expenses of the trip —
have, occasionally — and particularly if they have been in-
vited to write for New York magazines, take professorships
in native colleges, or lecture on the encouraging Conti-
nental progress of scientific atheism before Boston audi-
ences; — such travellers, we say, convinced that they shall
lose no money by it, but, on the contrary, rather sanguine
of making a little thereby in the long run, have occasionally
remarked, that, in the United States, women journeying
alone are treated with a chivalric courtesy and deference
not so habitually practised in any other second-class new
nation on the face of the earth.*

What, oh, what can be more true than this? A lady well-
stricken in years, and of adequate protraction of nose and
rectilinear undeviation of figure, can travel alone from Maine
to Florida with as perfect immunity from offensive mascu-

---

* Shades of Quintilian and Dr. Johnson, what a sentence!

line intrusion as though she were guarded by a regiment; while a somewhat younger girl, with curls and an innocent look, can not appear unaccompanied by an escort in an American omnibus, car, ferry-boat, or hotel, without appealing at once to the finest fatherly feelings of every manly middle-aged observer whose wife is not watching him, and exciting as general a desire to make her trip socially delightful as though each gentlemanly eye seeking hers were indeed · that of a tender sire.

Thus, although Miss Potts's lonely stay in her hotel had been so brief, the mysterious American instinct of chivalry had discovered it very early on the first morning after her arrival, and she arose from her delicious sleep to find at least half a dozen written offers of hospitality from generous strangers, sticking under her door. Understanding that she was sojourning without natural protectors in a strange city, the thoughtful writers, who appeared to be chiefly Western men of implied immense fortunes, begged her (by the delicate name of "Fair Unknown") to take comfort in the thought that they were stopping at the same hotel, and would protect her from all harm with their lives. In proof of this unselfish disposition on their parts, several of them were respectively ready to take her to a circus-matinée, or to drive in Central Park, on that very day: and her prompt acceptance of these signal evidences of a disinterested friendship for womanhood without a natural protector could not be more simply indicated to those who now freely offered such friendship, than by her dropping her fork *twice* at the public breakfast table, or sending the waiter back *three* times with the boiled eggs to have them cooked rightly.

Flora had completed her chemical toilet, put all the bottles, jars, and small round boxes back into her satchel again, and sat down to a second reading of these gratifying intimations that a prepossessing female orphan is not necessarily without assiduous paternal guardianship at her command wherever there are Western fathers, when Mr. Dibble appeared, as he had promised, accompanied by Gospeller Simpson.

"Miss Carowthers was so excited by your sudden flight, Miss Potts," said the latter, "that she came at once to me and Oldy with your farewell note, and would not stop saying 'Did you ever!' until, to restrain my aggravated mother from fits, I promised to follow you to your guardian's and ascertain what your good-by note would have meant, if it had actually been punctuated."

"Our reverend friend reached me about an hour ago," added Mr. Dibble, "saying, that a farewell note without a comma, colon, semicolon, or period in it, and with every other word beginning with a capital, and underscored, was calculated to drive friends to distraction. I took the liberty of reminding him, my dear, that young girls from boarding-school should hardly be expected to have advanced as far as English composition in their French and musical studies; and I also related to him what you had told me of Mr. Bumstead."

"And I don't know that, under the circumstances, you could do a better thing than you have done," continued the Gospeller. "Mr. Bumstead, himself, explains your flight upon the supposition that you were possibly engaged with myself, my mother, Mr. Dibble, and the Pendragons, in killing poor Mr. Drood."

"Oh, oughtn't he to be ashamed of himself, when he knows that I never did kill any absurd creature," cried the Flowerpot, in earnest deprecation. "And just to think of darling Magnolia, too, with her poor, ridiculous brother! You're a lawyer, Mr. Dibble, and I should think you could get them a *habeas corpus*, or a divorce, or some other perfectly absurd thing about courts, that would make the judges tell the juries to bring them in Not Guilty."

Fixing upon the lovely young reasoner a look expressive of his affectionate wonder at her inspired perception of legal possibilities, the old lawyer said, that the first thing in order was a meeting between herself and Miss Pendragon; which, as it could scarcely take place (all things considered) with propriety in the private room of that lady's brother, nor without publicity in his own office, or in a hotel, he hardly knew how to bring about.

And here we have an example of that difference between novels and real life which has been illustrated more than once before in this conscientious American Adaptation of what all our profoundly critical native journals pronounce the "most elaborately artistic work" of the grandest of English novelists. In an equivalent situation of real life, Mr. Dibble's quandary would not have been easily relieved; but, by the magic of artistic fiction, the particular kind of extemporized character absolutely necessary to help him and the novel continuously along was at that moment coming up the stairs of the hotel.*

At that critical instant, a servant knocked, to say, that there was a gentleman below, "with a face as long as me arrum, sir, who axed me was there a man here av the name av Simpson, miss?"

"It is John — it is Mr. Bumstead!" shrieked Flora, hastening involuntarily toward a mirror, — "and just see how my dress is wrinkled!"

"My name is Bentham — Jeremy Bentham," said a deep voice in the doorway; and there entered a gloomy figure, with smoky, light hair, a curiously long countenance, and black worsted gloves. "Simpson! — Old Octavius! — did you never, never see me before?"

"If I am not greatly mistaken," returned the Gospeller, sternly, "I saw you standing in the bar-room of the hotel, just now, as we came up."

"Yes," sighed the stranger, "I was there — waiting for a

---

* Quite independently of any specific design to that end by the Adapter, this Adaptation, carefully following the original narrative, as it does, can not avoid acting as a kind of practical — and, of course, somewhat exaggerative — commentary upon what is strained, forced, or out of the line of average probabilities, in the work Adapted.

Western friend — when you passed in. And has sorrow, then, so changed me, that you do not know me? Alas! Alack! Woe's me!"

"Bentham, you say?" cried the Ritualistic clergyman, with a start, and sudden change of countenance. "Surely you're not the rollicking fellow-student who saved my life at Yale."

"I am! I am!" sobbed the other, smiting his bosom. "While studying theology, you'd gone to sleep in bed reading the Decameron. I, in the next room, suddenly smelt a smell of wood burning. Breaking into your apartment, I saw your candle fallen upon your pillow and your head on fire. Believing that, if neglected, the flames would spread to some vital part, I seized the water-pitcher and dashed the contents upon you. Up you instantly sprang, with a theological expression upon your lips, and engaged me in violent single combat. "Madman!" roared I, "is it thus you treat one who has saved your life?" Falling upon the floor, with a black eye, you at once consented to be reconciled; and from that hour forth, we were both members of the same secret society."

Leaping forward, the Reverend Octavius wrung both the black worsted gloves of Mr. Bentham, and introduced the latter to the old lawyer and his ward.

"He did indeed save all but my head from the conflagration, and extinguished that, even, before it was much

charred," cried the grateful Ritualist, with marked emotion.
— "But, Jeremy, why this aspect of depression ?"

"Octavius, old friend," said Bentham, his hollow voice
quivering, "let no man boast himself upon the gayety of his
youth, and fondly dream — poor self-deceiver ! — that his
maturity may be one of revelry. You know what I once
was. Now I am conducting a first-class American Comic
Paper.

Commiseration, earnest and unaffected, appeared upon
every countenance, and Mr. Dibble was the first to break
the ensuing deep silence.

"If I am not mistaken, then," observed the good lawyer,
quietly, "the scene of your daily loss of spirits is in the
same building with our young friend, Mr. Pendragon, whom
you may know."

"I do know him, sir ; and that his sister has lately come
unto him. His room, by means of outside shutters, was
once a refuge to me from the Man " — here Mr. Bentham's
face flamed with inconceivable hatred — "who came to tell
me just how an American first-class Comic Paper *should* be
conducted."

"At what time does your rush of subscribers cease ? "

"As soon as I begin to charge anything for my paper."

"And the newsmen, who take it by the week, — what is
their usual time for swarming in your office ?"

"On the day appointed for the return of unsold copies."

"Then I *have* an idea," said Mr. Dibble. "It appears

to me, Mr. Bentham, that your office, besides being so near Mr. Pendragon's quarters, furnishes all the conditions for a perfectly private confidential interview between this young lady here, and her friend, Miss Pendragon. Mr. Simpson, if you approve, be kind enough to acquaint Mr. Bentham with Miss Potts's history, without mentioning names; and explain to him, also, why the ladies' interview should take place in a spot whither that singular young man, Mr. Bumstead, would not be likely to prowl, if in town, in his inspection of umbrellas."

The Gospeller hurriedly related the material points of Flora's history to his recovered friend, who moaned with all the more cheerful parts, and seemed to think that the serious ones might be worked-up in comic miss-spelling for his paper. — "For there is nothing more humorous in human life," said he, gloomily, "than the defective orthography of a fashionable young girl's education for the solemnity of matrimony."

Finally, they all set off for the appointed place of retirement, upon nearing which Mr. Dibble volunteered to remain outside as a guard against any possible interruption. The Gospeller led the way up the dark stairs of the building, when they had gained it; and the Flowerpot following, on Jeremy Bentham's arm, could not help glancing shyly up into the melancholy face of her escort, occasionally. "Do you *never* smile?" she could not help asking.

8*

"Yes," he said, mournfully, "sometimes : when I clean my teeth."

No more was said; for they were entering the room of which the tone and atmosphere were those of a receiving-vault.

CHAPTER XXII.

A CONFUSED STATE OF THINGS.

THE principal office of the Comic Paper was one of those amazingly unsympathetic rooms in which the walls, windows, and doors all have a stiff, unsalient aspect of the most hard-finished indifference to every emotion of humanity, and a perfectly rigid insensibility to the pleasures or pains of the tenants within their impassive shelter. In the whole configuration of the heartless, uncharacterized place, there was not one gracious inequality to lean against; not a ledge to rest elbow upon ; not a panel, not even a stove-pipe hole, to become dearly familiar to the wistful eye ; not so much as a genial crack in the plastering, or a companion-able rattle in casement, or a little human obstinacy in a door to base some kind of an acquaintance upon and make one feel less lonely. Through the grim, untwinkling windows, gaping sullenly the wrong way with iron shutters, came a discouraged light, strained through the narrow intervals of the dusty roofs above, to discover a large coffin-colored desk surmounted by ghastly busts of Hervey, Keble, and Blair ; * a smaller desk, over which hung a picture of

* Author of "The Grave."

the Tomb of Washington, and at which sat a pallid assistant-
editor in deep mourning, opening the comic contributions
received by last mail; a still smaller desk, for the nominal
writer of subscription-wrappers; files of the *Evangelist*,
Observer, and *Christian Union* hanging along the wall; a
dead carpet of churchyard-green on the floor; and a print
of Mr. Parke Godwin just above the mantel of monumental
marble.

Upon finding themselves in this temple of Momus, and
observing that its peculiar arrangement of sunshine made
their complexions look as though they had been dead a few
days, Gospeller Simpson and the Flowerpot involuntarily
spoke in whispers behind their hands.

"Does that room belong to your establishment, also,
Bentham?" whispered the Gospeller, pointing rather fear-
fully, as he spoke, towards a side-door leading apparently
into an adjoining apartment.

"Yes," was the low response.

"Is there — is there anybody dead in there?" whispered
Mr. Simpson, tremulously.

"No. — Not yet."

"Then," whispered the Ritualistic clergyman, "you
might step in there, Miss Potts, and have your interview
with Miss Pendragon, whom Mr. Bentham will, I am sure,
cause to be summoned from upstairs."

The assistant-editor of the Comic Paper stealing softly
from the office to call the other young lady down, Mr. Jer-

emy Bentham made a sign that Flora should follow him to the supplementary room indicated; his low-spirited manner being as though he had said: " If you wish to look at the body, miss, I will now show you the way."

Leaving the Gospeller lost in dark abstraction near the black mantel, the Flowerpot allowed the sexton of the establishment to conduct her funereally into the place assigned for her interview, and stopped aghast before a huge black object standing therein.

"What's this?" she gasped, almost hysterically.

"Only a safe," said Mr. Bentham, with inexplicable bitterness of tone. "Merely our fire-and-burglar-proof receptacle for the money constantly pouring in from first-class American Comic Journalism." — Here Mr. Bentham slapped his forehead passionately, checked something like a sob in his throat, and abruptly returned to the main office.

Scarcely, however, had he closed the door of communication behind him, when another door, opening from the hall, was noiselessly unlatched, and Magnolia Pendragon glided into the arms of her friend.

" Flora!" murmured the Southern girl, "I can scarcely credit my eyes! It seems so long since we last met! You've been getting a new bonnet, I see."

"It's like an absurd dream!" responded the Flowerpot, wonderingly caressing her. " I've thought of you and your poor, ridiculous brother twenty times a day. How much you must have gone through here !   Are they wearing skirts full, or scant, this season ? "

"About medium, dear.   But how do you happen to be here, in Mr. Bentham's office ? "

In answer to this question, Flora related all that had happened at Bumsteadville and since her flight from thence ; concluding by warning Magnolia, that her possession of a black alpaca waist, slightly worn, had subjected her to the ominous suspicion of the Ritualistic organist.

"I scorn and defy the suspicions of that enemy of the persecuted South, and high-handed wooer of exclusively Northern women !" exclaimed Miss Pendragon, vehemently. "Is this Mr. Bentham married?" '

"I suppose not."

"Is he visiting any one ? "

"I shouldn't think so, dear."

"Then," added Magnolia, thoughtfully, "if dear Mr. Dibble approves, he might be a friend to Montgomery and myself; and, by being so near us, protect us both from Mr. Bumstead.   Just think, dear Flora, what heaps of sorrow I should endure, if that base man's suspicions about my alpaca waist should be only a pretence, to frighten me into ultimately receiving his addresses."

"I don't think there's any danger, love," said Miss Potts, rather sharply.

"Why, Flora, precious ?"

"Oh, because he's so absurdly fastidious, you know, about regularity of features in women."

"More than he is about brains, I should think, dear, from what you tell me of his making love to you."

Here both young ladies trembled very much, and said they never, never would have believed it of each other; and were only reconciled when Flora sobbed that she was a poor unmarried orphan, and Miss Pendragon moaned piteously that an unwedded Southern girl without money had better go away somewhere in the desert, with her crushed brother, and die at once for their down-trodden section. Then, indeed they embraced tearfully; and, in proof of the perfect restoration of their devoted friendship, agreed never to marry if they could avoid it, and told each other the prices of all their best clothes.

"You *won't* tell your brother that I've been here?" said the Flowerpot. "I'm so absurdly afraid that he can't help blaming me for causing some of his trouble."

"Can't I tell him, even if it would serve to amuse him in his desolation?" asked the sister, persuasively. "I want to see him smile again, just as he does some days when a hand-organ-man's monkey climbs up to our windows from the street."

"Well, you *may* tell him, then, you absurd thing!" returned Flora, blushing; and, with another embrace, they parted, and the deeply momentous interview was over.

When Miss Potts and Mr. Simpson rejoined Mr. Dibble,

in the office of the latter, across the street, it was decided
that the flighty young girl should be made less expensive to
her friends by temporary accommodation in an economical
boarding-house, and that the Gospeller, returning to Bumsteadville, should persuade Miss Carowthers to come and
stay with her until the time for the reopening of the Macassar Female College.

Subsequently, with his homeless ward upon his arm, the
benignant old lawyer underwent a series of scathing rebuffs
from the various high-strung descendants of better days at
whose once luxurious but now darkened homes he applied
for the desired board. Time after time was he reminded,
by unspeakably majestic middle-aged ladies with bass voices,
that when a fine old family loses its former wealth by those
vicissitudes of fortune which bring out the noblest traits of
character and compel the letting-out of a few damp rooms,
it is significant of a weak understanding, or a depraved dis-
respect of the dignity of adversity, to expect that such families shall lose money and lower their hereditary high tone by
waiting upon a parcel of young girls. A few single Gentlemen desiring all the comforts of a home would not be considered insulting unless they objected to the butter, and a
couple of married Childless Gentlemen with their wives
might be pardoned for respectfully applying; but the idea of
a parcel of young girls! Wherever he went, the reproach
of not being a few Single Gentlemen, or a couple of married
Childless Gentlemen with their wives, abashed Mr. Dibble

into helpless retreat; while Flora's increasing guilty consciousness of the implacable sentiment against her as a parcel of young girls, culminated at last in tears. Finally, when the miserable lawyer was beginning to think strongly of the House of the Good Shepherd, or the Orphan Asylum, as a last resort, it suddenly occurred to him that Mrs. Skammerhorn,* a distant widowed aunt of his clerk, Mr. Bladams, had been known to live upon boarders in Bleecker Street; and thither he dragged hastily the despised object on his arm.

Being a widow without children, and relieved of nearly all the weaknesses of her sex by the systematic refusal of the opposite sex to give her any encouragement in them, Mrs. Skammerhorn was a relentless advocate of Woman's Inalienable Rights, and only wished that Man could just see himself in that contemptible light in which he was distinctly visible to One, who sooner than be his Legal Slave, would never again accompany him to the Altar.

"I tell you candidly, Dibble," said she, in answer to his application, "that if you had applied to be taken yourself, I should have said 'Never!' and at once called in the police. Since Skammerhorn died delirious, I have always refused to have his sex in the house, and I tell you, frankly, that I consider it hardly human. If this girl of yours, however, and the elderly female whom, you say, she expects to join her in a few days, will make themselves generally useful about the

---

* In the original, *Mrs. Billickin,* "of Southampton Street, Bloomsbury Square."

house, and try to be companions to me, I can give them the very room where Skammerhorn died."

Perceiving that Flora turned pale, her guardian whispered to her that she would not be alone in the room, at any rate; and then respectfully asked whether the late Mr. Skammerhorn had ever been seen around the house since his death?

"To be frank with you," answered the widow, "I did think that I came upon him once in the closet, with his back to me, as often I'd seen the weak creature in life going after a bottle on the top shelf. But it was only his coat hanging there, with his boots standing below and my muff hanging over to look like his head."

"You think, then," said Mr. Dibble, inquiringly, "that it is such a room as two ladies could occupy, without awaking at midnight with a strange sensation and thinking they felt a supernatural presence?"

"Not if the bed was rightly searched beforehand, and all the joints well peppered with magnetic powder," was the assuring answer.

"Could we see the room, madam?"

"If the shutters were open you could; as they're not," returned the widow, not offering to stir; "but ever since Skammerhorn, starting up with a howl, said, 'Here he comes again, red-hot!' and tried to jump out of the window, I've never opened them for any single man, and never shall. I couldn't bear it, Dibble, to see one of your sex in that room again, and hope you will not insist."

Broken in spirit as he was by preceding humiliations, the old lawyer had not the heart to contest the point, and it was agreed, that, upon the arrival of Miss Carowthers from Bumsteadville, she and Flora should accept the memorable room in question.

Upon their way back to the hotel, guardian and ward met Mr. Bentham, who, from the moment of becoming a character in their Story, had been possessed with that mysterious madness for open-air exercise which afflicted every acquaintance of the late Edwin Drood, and now saluted them in the broiling street and solemnly besought their company for a long walk. "It has occurred to me," said the Comic Paper man, who had resumed his black worsted gloves, "that Mr. Dibble and Miss Potts may be willing to aid me in walking-off some of the darker suicidal inclinations incident to first-class Humorous Journalism in America. Reading the 'proof' of an instalment of a comic serial now publishing in my paper, I contracted such gloom, that a frantic rush into the fresh air was my only hope of an escape from self-destruction. Let us walk, if you please."

Led on, in the profoundest melancholy, by this chastened character, Mr. Dibble and the Flowerpot were presently toiling hotly through a succession of grievous side-streets, and forlorn short-cuts to dismal ferries; the state of their conductor's spirits inclining him to find a certain refreshingly solemn joy in the horrors of pedestrianism imposed by obstructions of merchandise on sidewalks, and repeated climb-

ings over skids extending from store doors to drays. Inspired to an extraordinary flow of malignant animal spirits
by the complexities of travel incident to the odorous mazes
of some hundred odd kegs of salt mackerel and boxes of
brown soap impressively stacked before one very enterprising
Commission house, Mr. Bentham lightened the journey with
anecdotes of self-made Commission men who had risen in
life by breaking human legs and city ordinances ; and dwelt
emotionally upon the scenes in the city hospitals when
ladies and gentlemen were brought in, with nails from the
hoops of sugar-hogsheads sticking into their feet, or limbs
dislocated from too-loftily piled firkins of butter falling upon
them.   Through incredible hardships, and amongst astound-
ing complications of horse-cars, target companies, and bar-
rels of everything, Mr. Bentham also amused his friends with
circuits of several of the fine public markets of New York ;
explaining to them the relations of the various miasmatic
smells of those quaint edifices with the various devastat-
ing diseases of the day, and expatiating quite eloquently
upon the political corruption involved in the renting of the
stalls, and the fine openings there were for Cholera and
Yellow Fever in the Fish and Vegetable departments.
Then, as a last treat, he led his panting companions through
several lively up-hill blocks of drug-mills and tobacco firms,
to where they had a distant view of a tenement house next
door to a kerosene factory, where, as he vivaciously told
them, in the event of a fire, at least one hundred human

beings would be slowly done to a turn. After which all three returned from their walk, firmly convinced that an unctuous vein of humor had been conscientiously worked, and abstractedly wishing themselves dead.*

The exhilarating effect of the genial Comic Paper man upon Flora did not, indeed, pass away, until she and Miss Carowthers were in their appointed quarters under the roof of Mrs. Skammerhorn, whither they went immediately upon the arrival of the elder spinster from Bumsteadville.

"It could have been wished, my good woman," said Miss Carowthers, casting a rather disparaging look around the death-chamber of the late Mr. Skammerhorn, "that you had assigned to educated single young ladies, like ourselves, an apartment less suggestive of Man in his wedded aspects. The spectacle of a pair of pegged boots sticking out from under a bed, and a razor and a hone grouped on the mantel-shelf, is not such as I should desire to encourage in the dormitory of a pupil under my tuition."

"That's much to be deplored, I'm sure, Carowthers," returned Mrs. Skammerhorn, severely, "and sorry am I that I ever married, on that particular account. I'd not have done it, if you'd only told me. But, seeing that I married

---

* Ordinary readers, while admiring the heavy humor of this unexpected open-air episode, may wonder what on earth it has to do with the Story; but the cultivated few, understanding the ingenious mechanics of novel-writing, will appreciate it as a most skilful and happy device to cover the interval between the hiring of Mrs. Skammerhorn's room, and the occupation thereof by Flora and her late teacher — another instance of what our profoundly critical American journals call " artistic elaboration." (See corresponding Chapter of the original English Story.)

Skammerhorn, and then he died delirious, his boots and razor must remain, just as he often wished to throw the former at me in his ravings. Once married is enough, say I ; and those who never were, through having no proposals, must bear with those who have, and take things as they come."

"There are those, I'd have you know, Mrs. Skammerhorn, to whom proposals have been no inducement," said Miss Carowthers, sharply ; " or, if being made, and then withdrawn, have given our sex opportunities to prove, in courts of law, that damages can still be got. I'm afraid of no Man, my good woman, as a person named Blodgett once learned from a jury; but boots and razors are not what I would have familiar to the mind of one who never had a husband to die in raging torments, nor yet has sued for breach."

"Miss Potts is but a chicken, I'll admit," retorted Mrs. Skammerhorn ; "but you're not such, Carowthers, by many a good year. On the contrary, quite a hen. Then, you being with her, if the boots and razor make her think she sees that poor, weak Skammerhorn a-ranging round the room, when in his grave it is his place to be, you've only got to say, ' A fool you are, and always were,' — as often I, myself, called at him in his lifetime, — and off he'll go into his tomb again for fear of broomsticks."

" Flora, my dear," said Miss Carowthers, turning with dignity to her pupil, " if I know anything of human nature, the man who has once got away from here, will stay away.

Only single ghosts have attachments for the houses in which they once lived. So, never mind the boots and razor, darling; which, after all, if seen by peddlers, or men who come to fix the gas, might keep us safe from robbers."

"As safe as any man himself, young woman, with pistols under his head that he would never dare to fire if robbers were no more than cats rampaging," added Mrs. Skammerhorn, enthusiastically. "With nothing but an old black hat of Skammerhorn's, and walking-cane, kept hanging in the hall, I haven't lost a spoon by tramps or census-takers for six mortal years. So make yourselves at home, I beg you both, while I go down and cook the liver for our dinner. You'll find it tender as a chicken, after what you've broke your teeth upon in boarding-schools; though Skammerhorn declared it made him bilious in the second year, forgetting what he'd drank with sugar to his taste, beforehand."

Thus was sweet Flora Potts introduced to her new home; where, but for looking down from her windows at the fashions, making-up hundreds of bows of ribbons for her neck, and making-over all her dresses, her woman's mind must have been a blank. What time Miss Carowthers told her all day how she looked in this or that style of wearing her hair, and read her to sleep each night with extracts from the pages of cheery Hannah More. As for the object nearest her young heart, to say that she was wholly unruffled by it would be inaccurate; but by address she kept it hidden from all eyes save her own.

CHAPTER XXIII.

GOING HOME IN THE MORNING.

AFTER having thrown all his Ritualistic friends at home into a most unholy and exasperated condition of mind, by a steady series of vague remarks as to the extreme likelihood of their united implication in the possible deed of darkness by which he has lost a broadcloth nephew and an alpaca umbrella, the mournful Mr. Bumstead is once more awaiting the dawn in that popular retreat in Mulberry Street where he first contracted his taste for cloves. The Assistant-Assessor and the Alderman of the Ward are again there, tilted back against the wall in their chairs ; their shares in the Congressional Nominating Convention held in that room earlier in the night having left them too weary for further locomotion. The decanters and tumblers hurled by the Nominating Convention over the question of which Irishman could drink the most to be nominated, are still scattered about the floor ; here and there a forgotten slung-shot marks the places where rival delegations have confidently presented their claims for recognition ; and a few bullet-holes in the wall above the bar enumerate the various pauses in the great debate upon the perils of the public peace from Negro Suffrage.

Reclining with great ease of attitude upon an uncushioned settee, the Ritualistic organist is aroused from dreamy slumber by the turning-over of the pipe in his mouth, and majestically motions for the venerable woman of the house to come and brush the ashes from his clothes.

"Wud yez have it filled again, honey?" asks the woman. "Sure, wan pipe more would do ye no harrum."

"I'mtooshleepy," he says, dropping the pipe.

"An' are yez too shlapey, asthore, to talk a little bissiness wid an ould woman?" she asks, insinuatingly. "Couldn't yez be afther payin' me the bit av a schore I've got agin ye?"

Mr. Bumstead opens his eyes reproachfully, and wishes to know how she can dare talk about money matters to an organist who, at almost any moment, may be obliged to see a Chinaman hired in his place on account of cheapness?

"Could the haythen crayture play, thin?" she asks, wonderingly.

"Thairvairimitative," he tells her; — "Cookwashiron' n' eatbirdsnests."

"An' vote would they, honey?"

"Yesh —'f course — thairvairimitative, I tell y'," snarls he: "do't-cheapzdirt."

"Is it vote chaper they would, the haythen naygurs, than daycint, hardworkin' white min?" she asks, excitedly

"Yesh. Chinesecheaplabor," he says, bitterly.

11

"Och, hone !" cries the woman, in anguish ; "and f'hat's the poor to do then, honey ? "

"Gowest; go'nfarm !" sobs Mr. Bumstead, shedding tears. "I'd go m'self if a-hadn't lost dear-re-er relative. — Nephew'n' umbrella."

"Saint Payther ! an' f'hat's that ?"

"Edwins !" cries the unhappy organist, starting to his feet with a wild reel. "Th' pride of'sunckle'sheart ! I see 'm now, in'sh'fectionatemanhood, with whalebone ribs, made 'f alpaca, andyetsoyoung. 'Help me !' hiccries ; 'Pendragon'sash'nate'n me !' hiccries — and I go !"

While uttering this extraordinary burst of feeling, he has advanced toward the door in a kind of demoniac can-can, and, at its close, abruptly darts into the street and frantically makes off.

"The cross of the holy fathers !" ejaculates the woman, momentarily bewildered by this sudden termination of the scene. Then a new expression comes swiftly over her face, and she adds, in a different tone, "Odether-nodether, but it's coonin' as a fox he is, and it's off he's gone again widout payin' me the schore ! Sure, but I'll follow him, if it's to the wurruld's ind, and see f'hat he is and where he is."

Thus it happens that she reaches Bumsteadville almost as soon as the Ritualistic organist, and, following him to his boarding-house, encounters Mr. Tracey Clews upon the steps.

" Well now ! " calls that gentleman, as she looks inquiringly at him ; "who do you want ? "

"Him as just passed in, your Honor."

" Mr. Bumstead ? "

"Ah.   Where does he play the organ ? "

" In St. Cow's Church, down yonder.   Mass at seven o'clock, and he'll be there in half an hour."

" It's there, I'll be, thin," mumbles the woman ; "and bad luck to it that I didn't know before ; whin I came to ax him for me schore, and might have gone home widout a cint but for a good lad named Eddy, who gave me a sthamp. — The same Fddy, I'm thinkin', that I've heard him mutter about in his shlape at my shebang in town, when he came there on political business."

After a start and a pause, Mr. Clews repeats his information concerning the Ritualistic church, and then cautiously follows the woman as she goes thither.

Unconscious of the remarkable female figure intently watching him from under a corner of the gallery, and occasionally shaking a fist at him, Mr. Bumstead attends to the musical part of the service with as much artistic accuracy as a hasty head-bath and a glass of soda-water are capable of securing.   The worshippers are too busy with risings, kneelings, bowings, and miscellaneous devout gymnastics, to heed his casual imperfections, and his headache makes him fiercely indifferent to what any one else may think.   .

Coming out of the athletic edifice, Mr. Clews comes upon the woman again, who seems excited.

"Well?" he says.

"Sure he saw me in time to shlip out of a back dure," she returns savagely; "but it's shtrait to his boording-house I'm going afther him, the spalpeen."

Again Mr. Tracey Clews follows her; but this time he allows her to go up to Mr. Bumstead's room, while he turns into his own apartment where his breakfast awaits him. " I can make a chalk mark for the trail I've struck to-day," he says; and then thoughtfully attacks the meal upon the table.*

* At this point, the English original — the "*Mystery of Edwin Drood*" — breaks off forever.

CHAPTER XXIV.

MR. CLEWS AT HIS NOVEL.*

THROWN into Rembrandtish relief by the light of a garish kerosene lamp upon the table : with one discouraged lock of hair hanging over his nose, and straw hat pushed so far back from his phrenological brow that its vast rim had the fine artistic effect of a huge saintly nimbus : Mr. Bumstead sat gymnastically crosswise in an easy-chair, over an arm of which his slender lower limbs limply dangled, and elaborately performed one of the grander works of Bach upon an irritable accordion. Now, winking with intense rapidity, and going through the muscular motions of an excitable person resolutely pulling out an obstinate and inexplicable drawer from somewhere about his knees, he produced sustained and mournful notes, as of canine distress in the backyard; anon, with eyes nearly closed and the straw nimbus sliding still further back, his manipulation was that of an excessively

---

* The few remaining chapters, which conclude this Adaptation of " *The Mystery of Edwin Drood*," should not be construed as involving any presumptuous attempt to divine that full solution of the latter which the pen of its lamented author was not permitted to reach. No further correspondence with the tenor of the unfinished English story is intended than the Adapter will endeavor to justify to his own conscience, and that of his reader, by at least one unmistakable foreshadowing circumstance of the original publication.

weary gentleman slowly compressing a large sponge, thereby squeezing out certain choking, snorting, guttural sounds,
as of a class softly studying the German language in another
room ; and, finally, with an impatient start from the unexpected slumber into which the last shaky *pianissimo* had momentarily betrayed him, he caught the untamed instrument
in mid-air, just as it was treacherously getting away from him,
frantically balanced it there for an instant on all his clutching
finger-tips, and had it prisoner again for a renewal of the
weird symphony.

Seriously offended at the discovery that he could not drop
asleep in his own room, for a minute, without the music
stopping and the accordion trying to slip off, the Ritualistic
organist was not at all softened in temper by almost simultaneously realizing that the further skirt of his long linen
coat was standing out nearly straight from ·his person, and,
apparently, fluttering in a heavy draught.

"Who's-been-ope'nin'-th'-window ? " he sternly asked.
" What's-meaning-'f-such-a-gale-at thistime-'f-year ? "

"Do I intrude ?" inquired a voice close at hand.

Looking very carefully along the still extended skirt of his
coat toward exactly the point of the compass from which
the voice seemed to come, Mr. Bumstead at last awoke to
the conviction that the tension of his garment and its breezy
agitation were caused by the tugging of a human figure.

"Do I intrude ?" repeated Mr. Tracey Clews, dropping

the skirt as he spoke. "Have I presumed too greatly in coming to request the favor of a short private interview?"

Slipping quickly into a more genteel but rather rigid position on his chair, the Ritualistic organist made an airy pass at him with the accordion.

"Any doors where youwasborn, sir?"

"There were, Mr. Bumstead."

"People ever knock when th' wanted t'-come-in, sir?"

"Why, I did knock at *your* door," answered Mr. Clews, conciliatingly. "I knocked and knocked, but you kept on playing; and after I finally took the liberty to come in and pull you by the coat, it was ten minutes before you found it out."

In an attempt to look into the speaker's inmost soul, Mr. Bumstead fell into a doze, from which the crash of his accordion to the floor aroused him in time to behold a very curious proceeding on the part of Mr. Clews. That gentleman successively peered up the chimney, through the windows, and under the furniture of the room, and then stealthily took a seat near his rather languid observer.

"Mr. Bumstead, you know me as a temporary boarder under the same roof with you. Other people know me merely as a dead-beat. May I trust you with a secret?"

A pair of blurred and glassy eyes looked into his from under a huge straw hat, and a husky question followed his:—

" Did y' ever read Wordsworth's poem-'f-th' Excursion, sir ? "

" Not that I remember."

" Then, sir," exclaimed the organist, with spasmodic animation — " then's not in your hicsperience to know hows-sleepy-I am-jus'-now."

" You had a nephew," said his subtle companion, raising his voice, and not appearing to heed the last remark.

" An' 'numbrella," added Mr. Bumstead, feebly.

" I say you had a nephew," reiterated the other, " and that nephew disappeared in a very mysterious manner. Now I'm a literary man — "

" C'd tell that by y'r-headerhair," murmured the Ritualistic organist. " Left y'r wife yet, sir ? "

" I say I'm a literary man," persisted Tracey Clews, sharply. " I'm going to write a great American Novel, called 'The Amateur Detective,' founded upon the story of this very Edwin Drood, and have come to Bumsteadville to get all the particulars. I've picked up considerable from Gospeller Simpson, John McLaughlin, and even the woman from the Mulberry Street place who came after you the other morning. But now I want to know something from you. — What has become of your nephew ? "

He put the question suddenly, and with a kind of suppressed leap at him whom he addressed. Immeasurable was his surprise at the perfectly calm answer, —

" I can't r'member hicsactly, sir."

" Can't remember !— Can't remember what ? "

" Where-I-put't."

" *It ?*"

" Yes.   Th' umbrella."

"What on earth are you talking about ? " exclaimed Mr. Clews, in a rage.   " — Come ! Wake up ! — What have umbrellas to do with this ? "

Rousing himself to something like temporary consciousness, Mr. Bumstead slowly climbed to his feet, and, with a wild kind of swoop, came heavily down with both hands upon the shoulders of his questioner.

"What now ? " asked that startled personage.

" You want t' know 'bout th' umbrella ? " said Bumstead with straw hat amazingly awry, and linen coat a perfect map of creases.

" Yes ! — You're crushing me ! " panted Mr. Clews.

" Th' umbrella ! " cried Mr. Bumstead, suddenly withdrawing his hands and swaying before his visitor like a linen person on springs, — " This 's what there's 'bout 't :   *Where th' umbrella is, there is Edwins also !*"

Astounded by this bewildering confession, and fearful that the uncle of Mr. Drood would be back in his chair and asleep again if he gave him a chance, the excited inquisitor sprang from *his* chair, and slowly and carefully backed the wildly glaring object of his solicitation until his shoulders and elbows were safely braced against the mantel-piece.   Then, like one inspired, he grasped a bottle of soda water from the table, and forced the reviving liquid down his staring patient's throat; as quickly tore off his straw hat, newly moistened the damp sponge in it at an eighboring wash-stand, and replaced both on the aching head; and, finally, placed in one of his tremulous hands a few cloves from a saucer on the mantel-shelf.

"You are better now? You can tell me more?" he said, resting a moment from his violent exertions.

With the unsettled air of one coming out of a complicated dream, Mr. Bumstead chewed the cloves musingly; then, after nodding excessively, with a hideous smile upon his countenance, suddenly threw an arm about the neck of his restorer and wept loudly upon his bosom.

"My fr'en'," he wailed, in a damp voice, "lemme confess to you. I'm a mis'able man, my fr'en'; perfectly mis'able. These cloves — these insidious tropical spices — have been thebaneofmyexistence. On Chrishm's night — *that* Chrishm's night — I toogtoomany. Wha'scons'q'nce? I put m' nephew an' m' umbrella away somewhere, an 've neverb'n able terremembersince!"

Still sustaining his weight, the author of "The Amateur Detective" at first seemed nonplussed; but quickly changed his expression to one of abrupt intelligence.

"I see, now; I begin to see," he answered, slowly, and almost in a whisper. "On the night of that Christmas dinner here, you were in a clove-trance, and made some secret disposition (which you have not since been able to remem-

ber), of your umbrella — and nephew. Until very lately —
until now, when you are nearly, but *not quite*, as much under
the influence of cloves again — you have had a vague general idea that somebody else must have killed Mr. Drood
and stolen your umbrella. But now, that you are partially
in the same condition, physiologically and psychologically, as
on the night of the disappearance, you have once more a
partial perception of what were the facts of the case. Am
I right ?"

"Tha's it, sir. You're a ph'los'pher," murmured Mr.
Bumstead, trying to brush from above his nose the pendent
lock of hair, which he took for a fly.

"Very well, then," continued Tracey Clews, his extraordinary head of hair fairly bristling with electrical animation:
"You've only to get yourself into *exactly the same* clove-y
condition as on the night of the double disappearance, when
you put your umbrella and nephew away somewhere, and
you'll remember all about it again. You have two distinct
states of existence, you see : a cloven one, and an uncloven
one : and what you have done in one you are totally oblivious of in the other."

Something like an occult wink trembled for a moment in
the right eye of Mr. Bumstead.

"Tha's ver' true," said he, thoughtfully. "I've been 'bliv-
ious m'self, frequently. Never c'd r'member whar I-owed."

"The idea I've suggested to you for the solution of this
mystery," went on Mr. Clews, "is expressed by one of the

greatest of English writers : who, in his very last work, says :
'— *in some cases of drunkenness, and in others of animal
magnetism, there are two states of consciousness which never
clash, but each of which pursues its separate course as though
it were continuous instead of broken. Thus, if I hide my
watch when I am drunk, I must be drunk again before I can
remember where.*' " *

"I'm norradrink'n'man, sir," returned Mr. Bumstead,
drawing coldly back from him, and escaping a fall into the
fireplace by a dexterous surge into the nearest chair. " Th'
lemon tea which I take for my cold, or to pr'vent the cloves
from disagreeing with me, is norrintoxicating."

" Of course not," assented his subtle counsellor : " but in
this country, at least, chronic inebriation, clove-eating, and
even opium-taking, are strikingly alike in their aspects, and ·
the same rules may be safely applied to all. My advice to
you is what I have given. Cause a table to be spread in
this room, exactly as it was for that memorable Christmas-
dinner ; sit down to it exactly as then, and at the same hour ;
go through all the same processes as nearly as you can remember ; and, by the mere force of association, you will
enact all the final performances with your umbrella and
your nephew."

Mr. Bumstead's arms were folded tightly across his manly
breast, and the fine head with the straw hat upon it tilted
heavily toward his bosom.

* See Chapter III., *The Mystery of Edwin Drood.*

" I see't now," said he softly ; " bone han'le 'n ferule. I r'member threshing 'm with it. I can r'memb'r carry'ng — "
Here Mr. Bumstead burst into tears, and made a frenzied dash at the lock of hair which he again mistook for a fly.

" To sum up all," concluded Mr. Tracey Clews, shaking him violently by the shoulder, that he might remain awake long enough to hear it, — " to sum up all, I am satisfied, from the familiar knowledge of this mystery I have already gained, that the end will have something to do with exercise in the Open Air ! You'll have to go outdoors for something important. And now good-night."

" Goornight, sir."

Retiring softly to his own room, under the same roof, the author of "The Amateur Detective" smiled at himself before the mirror with marked complacency. " You're a long-headed one, my dead-beat friend," he said archly, " and your great American Novel is likely to be a respectable success."

There sounded a crash upon a floor, somewhere in the house, and he held his breath to listen. It was the Ritualistic organist going to bed.

.

CHAPTER XXV.

THE SKELETON IN MCLAUGHLIN'S CLOSET.

NIGHT, spotted with stars, like a black leopard, crouched once more upon Bumsteadville, and her one eye to be seen in profile, the moon, glared upon the helpless place with something of a cat's nocturnal stare of glassy vision for a stupefied mouse. Midnight had come with its twelve tinkling drops more of opiate, to deepen the stupor of all things almost unto death, and still the light shone luridly through the window-curtains of Mr. Bumstead's room, and still the lonely musician sat stiffly at a dinner-table spread for three, whereof only a goblet, a curious antique black bottle, a bowl of sugar, a saucer of lemon-slices, a decanter of water,

and a saucer of cloves appeared to have been used by the
solitary diner.

Unconscious that, through the door ajar at his back, a
pair of vigilant human orbs were upon him, the Ritualistic
organist, who was in very low spirits, drew an emaciated
and rather unsteady hand repeatedly across his perspiring
brow, and talked in deep bass to himself.

" He came in, af'r' bein' brisgly walked up'n-down the
turnpike by Pendragon, and slammed himself down-'n-that-
chair," ran the soliloquy, with a ghostly nod towards an
opposite chair, drawn back from the table. "'Inebrious
boy !' says I, sternly, 'how-are-y'-now?' He said 'Poora-
well ; ' 'n' wen' down on-er-floor fas'hleep ! I w's scan'l'ized.
— Whowoonbe ? — I took m' umbrella 'n' thrashed ' m with
it, remarking 'F'shame ! waygup ! mis'able boy ! 's poory-
sight-f'r-'nuncle-t'   see-'s-nephew-'n-this-p'litical-c'ndit'n.' —
H'slep on ; 'n' 't last I picked up him, 'n' umbrella, 'n' took
'm out t' some cool place t'shleep 't off. *Where'd'* I take
him ? Thashwazmarrer — *Where'd'* I leave 'm ?' "

Repeating this question to himself, with an almost frenzied
intensity, the gloomy victim of a treacherous memory threw
an unearthly stare of bloodshot questioning all over the
room, and, after a swaying motion or two of the upper half
of his body, pitched forward, with his forehead crashing upon
the table. Instantly recovering himself, and starting to rub
his head, he as suddenly checked that palliative process by a
wild run to his feet and a hideous bellow.

"*I r'memb'r, now!*" he ejaculated, walking excitedly at a series of obtuse angles all over the apartment. "Got-'t-knockedinto-m'-head-'t-last. Pauper bur'l ground — J. M'-CLAUGHLIN. Down'n cellar — cool placefa' man's tight — lef' m' umbrella there by m'stake — go'n' get't thishmin't —."

Managing, after several inaccurate aims at the doorway, to plunge into the adjacent bedroom, he presently reappeared from thence, veering hard-aport, with a lighted lantern in his right hand. Then, circuitously approaching the neglected dining-table, he grasped with his disengaged digits at the antique black bottle, missed it, went all the way around the board before he could stop himself, clutched and missed again, went clear around once more, and finally effected the capture. "Th 'peared t' be, two," he muttered, placing the prize in one of his pockets ; and, with a triumphant stride, made for the half-open hall-door through which the eyes had been watching him.

The owner of those eyes, and of a surprising head of florid hair, had barely time to draw back into the shadow of the corridor and notice an approaching face like that of one walking in his sleep, when the clove-eater swung disjointedly by him, with jingling lantern, and went fiercely bumping down the stairway. Closely, without sound, followed the watcher, and the two, like man and shadow, went out from the house into the quarry of the moon-eyed black leopard.

Fully bound now in the sinister spell of the spice of the

Molucca islands, Mr. Bumstead had regained that condition of his duplex existence to which belonged the disposition he had made of his lethargic nephew and alpaca umbrella on that confused Christmas night ; and with such realization of a distinct duality came back to him at least a partial recollection of where he had put the cherished two. Finding Mr. E. Drood rather overcome by the more festive features of the meal, — notwithstanding his walk at midnight with Mr. Pendragon, — he had allowed his avuncular displeasure thereat to betray itself in a threshing administered with the umbrella. Observing that the young man still slept beside the chair from which he fell, he had ultimately, and with the umbrella still under his arm, raised the dishevelled nephew head-downward in his arms, and impatiently conveyed him from the heated room and house to the coolest retreat he could think of. There depositing him, and, in his hurry, the umbrella also, to sleep off, under reviving atmospheric influences, the unseemly effect of the evening's banquet, he had gone back on both sides of the road to his boarding-house, and, with his boots upon the pillow, sunk into an instantaneous sleep of unfathomable depth. Dreaming, towards morning, that he was engaging a large boa-constrictor in single combat, and struggling energetically to restrain the ferocious reptile from getting into his boots, he had suddenly awakened, with a crash, upon the floor — to miss his umbrella and nephew, to forget where he had put them, and to fly to Gospeller's Gulch with incoherent charges of larceny and manslaughter. All this he could now vaguely recall, his present pyschological condition, or trance-state, being the same as then; and was going entrancedly back to the hiding-place where, with the best of motives, he had forgetfully left the two objects dearest to him in life.

On, then, proceeded the Ritualistic organist, in the tawny light of the black leopard's eye : his stealthy follower trailing closely after in the shade of the roadside trees where the star-spotted leopard's black paws were plunged deepest. On he went, in zig-zag profusion of steps and occasional high skips over incidental shadows of branches which he took for snakes, until the Pauper Burial Ground was reached, and McLaughlin's hidden subterranean retreat therein attained. It was the same weird spot to which he had been brought by Old Mortarity on the wintry night of their unholy exploring party ; and, without appearing to be surprised that the entrance to the excavation was open, he eagerly descended by the rickety step-ladder, and held himself steady by the latter while throwing the light of his lantern around the mouldy walls.

His immediate hiccup, provoked by the dampness of the situation, was answered by a groan, which, instead of being solid, was very hollow ; and, as he peered vivaciously forward behind his extended lantern, there advanced from a far corner — O, woeful man ! O, thrice unhappy uncle ! — the spectral figure of the missing Edwin Drood !

After a moment's inspection of the apparition, which

paused terribly before him with hand hidden in breast, Mr. Bumstead placed his lantern upon a step of the ladder, drew and profoundly labiated his antique black bottle, thoughtfully crunched a couple of cloves from another pocket — staring stonily all the while — and then addressed the youthful shade : —

"Where's th' umbrella?"

"Monster of forgetfulness! murderer of memory!" spoke the spirit, sternly. " In this, the last rough resting place of the impecunious dead, do you dare to discuss commonplace topics with one of the departed? Look at me, O uncle, clove-befogged, and shrink appalled from the dread sight, and pray for mercy."

"Ishthis `prop'r language t' address-t'-y'r-relative?" inquired Mr. Bumstead, in a severely reproachful manner.

"Relative!" repeated the apparition, sepulchrally. — "What sort of relative is he, who, when his sister's orphaned son is sleeping at his feet, conveys the unconscious orphan, head downward, through a midnight tempest, to a place like this, and leaves him here, and then forgets where he has put him?"

"I give 't up," said the organist, after a moment's consideration.

"The answer is: he's a dead-beat," continued the young ghost, losing his temper. "And what, John Bumstead, did you do with my oroide watch and other jewels?"

"Musht've spilt'm on the road here," returned the musing

uncle, faintly remembering that they had been found upon
the turnpike, shortly after Christmas, by Gospeller Simpson.

" Are you dead, Edwin ? "

" Did you not bury me here alive, and close the opening
to my tomb, and go away and charge everybody with my
murder ? " asked the spectre, bitterly.   " O, uncle, hard of
head and paralyzed in recollection ! is it any good excuse for
sacrificing my poor life, that, in your cloven state, you put
me down a cellar, like a pan of milk, and then could not remember where you'd put me ?   And was it noble, then, to
go to her whom you supposed had been my chosen bride,
and offer wedlock to her on your own account ? "

" I was acting as y'r-executor, Edwin," explained the uncle.   " I did ev'thing forth' besht."

" And does the sight of me fill you with no terror, no re-
morse, unfeeling man ? " groaned the ghost.

" Yeshir," answered Mr. Bumstead, with sudden energy.
" Yeshir.   I'm r'morseful on 'count of th' umbrella. Who-d'-
y'-lend-'t-to ? "

It is an intellectual characteristic of the more advanced
degrees of the clove-trance, that, while the tranced individual can perceive objects, even to occasional duplexity, and
hear remarks more or less distinctly, neither objects nor remarks are positively associated by him with any perspicuous
idea.   Thus, while the Ritualistic organist had a blurred perception of his nephew's conversational remains, and was
dimly conscious that the tone of the supernatural remarks

addressed to himself was not wholly congratulatory, he still presented a physical and moral aspect of dense insensibility.

Momentarily nonplussed by such unheard-of calmness under a ghostly visitation, the apparition, without changing position, allowed itself to roll one inquiring eye toward the opening above the step-ladder, where the moonlight revealed an attentive head of red hair. Catching the glance, the head allowed a hand belonging to it to appear at the opening and motion downward.

"Look there, then," said the intelligent ghost to its uncle, pointing to the ground near its feet.

Mr. Bumstead, rousing from a brief doze, glanced indifferently toward the spot indicated; but in another instant, was on his knees beside the undefined object he there beheld. A keen, breathless scrutiny, a frenzied clutch with both hands, and then he was upon his feet again, holding close to the lantern the thing he had found.

The barred light shone on a musty skeleton, to which still clung a few mouldy shreds left by the rats ; and only the celebrated bone handle identified it as what had once been the maddened finder's idolized Alpaca Umbrella.

"Aha!" twitted the apparition; "then you have some heart left, John Bumstead?"

"Heart!" moaned the distracted organist, fairly kissing the dear remains, and restored to perfect speech and comprehension by the awful shock. "I had one, but it is broken now! — Allie, my long-lost Allie!" he continued, tenderly apostrophizing the skeleton, "do we meet thus at last again? —

'What thought is folded in thy leaves!
What tender thought, what speechless pain!
I hold thy faded lips to mine,
Thou darling of the April rain!'

Where is thine old familiar alpaca dress, my Allie? Where is the canopy that has so often sheltered thy poor master's head from the storm? Gone! gone! and through my own forgetfulness!"

"And have you no thought for your nephew?" asked the persevering apparition, hoarsely.

"Not under the present circumstances," retorted the mourner; he and the ghost both coughing with the colds which they had taken from standing still so long in such a damp place — "not under the present circumstances," he repeated, wildly, making a fierce pass at the spectre with the skeleton, and then dropping the latter to the ground in nerveless despair. "To a single man, his umbrella is wife, mother, sister, venerable maiden aunt from the country — all in one. In losing mine, I've lost my whole family, and want to hear no more about relatives. Good-night, sir."

"Here! hold on! Can't you leave the lantern for a moment?" cried the ghost. But the heart-stricken Ritualist had swarmed up the ladder and was gone.

Then, going up too, the spectre appeared also unto two

other men, who crawled from behind pauper headstones at his summons; the face of the one being that of J. McLaughlin, that of the other Mr. Tracey Clews'. And the spectre walked between these two, carrying Mr. Bumstead's skeleton in his hand.*

---

* The *cut* accompanying the above chapter is from the illustrated title-page of the English monthly numbers of *The Mystery of Edwin Drood ;* — in which it is the last of a series of border-vignettes ; — and plainly shows that it was the author's intention to bring back his hero a living man before the conclusion of the story.

4

CHAPTER XXVI.

FOR BETTER, FOR WORSE.

MISS CAROWTHERS having gone out with Mrs. Skammer-horn to skirmish with the world of dry-goods clerks for one of those alarming sacrifices in feminine apparel which wo-man onselfishly, yet never needlelessly, is always making, Flora sat alone in her new home, working the latest beaded pin-cushion of her useful life. Frequently experiencing the truth of the adage, that as you sew so shall you rip, the fair young thing was passing half her valuable time in ripping out the mistaken stitches she had made in the other half; and the severe moral discipline thus endured made her mad, as equivalent vexation would have made a man the reverse of that word. Flippant social satirists cannot dwell with sufficient sarcasm upon the difference between the invincible amiability affected by artless girls in society and their occa-sional bitterness of aspect in the privacy of home ; never stopping to reflect that there are sore private trials for these industrious young crochet creatures in which the thread of the most equable female existence is necessarily worsted. Miss Potts, then, although looking up from her trying worsted oc-cupation at the servant who entered with a rather snappish

expression of countenance, was guilty of no particularly hypo-
critical assumption in at once suffering her features to relax
into a sweetly pensive smile upon learning that there was a
gentleman to see her in the parlor.

"'Montgomery Pendragon,'" she softly read from the
card presented. "Is he alone, Bridget, dear?"

"Sorra any wan with him but his cane, Miss; and that he
axed me wud I sthand it behind the dure for him."

There was a look of desperate purpose about this. When
a sentimental young man seeks a private interview with a
marriageable young woman, and recklessly refuses at the
outset to retain at least his cane for the solution of the intri-
cate conversational problem of what to do with his hands, it
is an infallible sign that some madly rash intention has temporarily overpowered his usual sheepish imbecility, and that
he may be expected to speak and act with almost human intelligence.

With hand instinctively pressed upon her heart, to mod-
erate its too sanguine pulsations and show the delicate lace
around her cuffs, Flora shyly entered the parlor, and surprised Mr. Pendragon striding up and down the apartment
like one of the more comic of the tragic actors of the day.

"Miss Potts!" ejaculated the wild young Southern pedestrian, pausing suddenly at her approach, with considerable
excitement of manner, "scorn me, spurn me, if you will;
but do not let sectional embitterment blind you to the fact
that I am here by the request of Mr. Dibble."

" I wasn't scorning and spurning anybody," explained the startled orphan, coyly accepting the chair he pushed forward. " I'm sure I don't feel any sectional hatred, nor any other ridiculous thing."

" Forgive me ! " pleaded Montgomery. " I reckon I'm a heap too sensitive about my Southern birth ; but only think, Miss. Potts, what I've had to go through since I've been amongst you Yankees ! Fancy what it is to be suspected of a murder, and have no political influence."

" It must be *so* absurd ! " murmured Flora.

" I've felt wretched enough about it to become a contributor to the first-class American comic paper on the next floor below me," he continued, gloomily. "And here, to-day, without any explanation, your guardian desires me to come here and wait for him."

" I'm sorry that's such a trial for you, Mr. Pendragon," simpered the Flowerpot. " Perhaps you'd prefer to wait on the front stoop, and appear as though you'd just come, you know ? ".

" And can you think," cried the young man with increased agitation, " that it would be any trial for me to be in your society, if—— ? But tell me, Miss Potts, has your guardian the right to dispose of your hand in marriage ? "

" I suppose so," answered Flora, with innocent surprise and a pretty blush ; " he has charge of *all* my money matters, you know."

" Then it is as I feared," groaned her questioner, smiting

his forehead. " He is coming here to-day to tell you what man of opulence he wants you to have, and I am to be witness to my own hopelessness ! "

" What makes you think anything so ridiculous, you absurd thing ? " asked the orphan, not unkindly.

" He as good as said so," sighed the unhappy Southerner. " He told me, with his own mouth, that he wanted to get you off his hands as soon as possible, and thought he saw his way clear to do it."

The girl knew what bitter, intolerable emotions were tearing the heart of the ill-fated secessionist before her, and, in her own gentle heart, pitied him.

" He needn't be so sure about it," she said, with indignant spirit. " I'll never marry *any* stranger, unless he's awful rich — oh, as rich as anything ! "

" Oh, Miss Potts ! " roared Montgomery, suddenly, folding down upon one knee before her, and scratching his nose with a ring upon the hand he sought to kiss, " why will you not bestow upon me the heart so generously disdainful of everything except the most extreme wealth ? Why waste your best years in waiting for proposals from a class of Northern men who occasionally expect that their brides, also, shall have property, when here I offer you the name and hand of a loving Southern gentleman, who only needs the paying off of a few mortgages on his estate in the South to be beyond all immediate danger of starvation ? "

Turning her pretty head aside, but unconsciously allowing

him to retain her hand, she faintly asked how they were to live?

"Live!" repeated the impetuous lover. "On love, hash, mutual trust, bread pudding : anything that's cheap. I'll do the washing and ironing myself."

"How perfectly ridiculous!" said the orphan, bashfully turning her head still further aside, and bringing one ear-ring to bear strongly upon him. "You'd never be able to do fluting and pinking in the world."

"I could do anything, with you by my side!" he retorted, eagerly. "Oh, Miss Potts!— Flora!— think how lonely I am. My sister, as you may have heard, has accepted Gos-peller Simpson's proposal, by mail, for her hand, and is already so busy quarrelling with his mother, that she is no longer any company for me. My fate is in your hands; it is in woman's power to either make or marry the man who loves her —— "

"Provided, always, that her legal guardian consents," in-terrupted the benignant voice of Mr. Dibble, who, unper-ceived by them, had entered the room in time to finish the sentence.

Springing alertly to an upright position, and coughing ex-cessively, Mr. Pendragon was a shamefaced reproach to his whole sex, while the young lady used the edge of her right foot against a seam of the carpet with that extreme solicitude as to the result which, in woman, is always so entirely deceiving to those who have hoped to see her show signs of painful embarrassment.

After surveying them in thoughtful silence for a moment, the old lawyer bent over his ward, and hugged and kissed her with an unctuousness justified by his great age and extreme goodness. It was his fine old way of bestowing an inestimable blessing upon all the plump younger women of his acquaintance, and the benediction was conferred on the slightest pretexts, and impartially, up to a certain age.

"Am I to construe what I have seen and heard, my dear as equivalent to the conclusion of my guardianship?" he asked, smilingly.

"Oh, please don't be so ridiculous — oh, I never was so exquisitely nervous," pleaded the helpless, fluttered young creature.

"I reckon I've betrayed your confidence, sir," said Montgomery, desperately; "but you must have known, from hearsay at least, how I have felt toward this young lady ever since our first meeting, and should not have exposed me to a temptation stronger than I could bear. I have, indeed, done myself the honor to offer her the hand and heart of one who, although but a poor gentleman, will be richer than kings if she deigns to make him so."

"Why, how absurd!" ejaculated the orphan, quickly. "It's perfectly ridiculous to call me well off; and how *could* I make you richer than kings and things, you know!"

The old and the young man exchanged looks of unspeakable admiration at such touching artlessness.

"Sweet innocence !" exclaimed her guardian, playfully pinching her cheek and privately surprised at its floury feeling. "What would you say if I told you that, since our shrewd Eddy retired from the contest, I have been wishing to see you and our Southern friend here brought to just such terms as you appear to have reached ? What would you say if I added that, such consummation seeming to be the best you or your friends could do for yourself, I have determined to deal with you as a daughter, in the matter of seeing to it that you begin your married life with a daughter's portion from my own estate ? "

Both the young people had his hands in theirs, on either side of him, in an instant.

"There ! there !" continued the excellent old gentleman, "don't try to express yourselves. Flota, place one of your hands in the breast of my coat, and draw out the parcel you find there. . . . That's it. The article it contains once belonged to your mother, my dear, and has been returned to me by the hands to which I once committed it in the hope that *they* would present it to you. I loved your mother well, my child, but had not enough property at the time to contend with your father. Open the parcel in private, and be warned by its moral : Better is wilful waist than woful want of it."

It was the stay-lace by which Mrs. Potts, from too great

persistence in drawing herself up proudly, had perished in her prime.

" Now come into the open air with me, and let us walk to Central Park," continued Mr. Dibble, shaking off his momentary fit of gloom. "I have strange things to tell you both. I have to teach you, in justice to a much-injured man, that we have, in our hearts, cruelly wronged that excellent and devout Mr. Bumstead, by suspecting him of a crime whereof he is now proved innocent — at least *I* suspected him. To-morrow night we must all be in Bumsteadville. I will tell you why as we walk."

CHAPTER XXVII.

SOLUTION.

IN the darkness of a night made opaque by approaching showers, a man stands under the low-drooping branches of the edge of a wood skirting the cross-road leading down to Gospeller's Gulch.

"Not enough saved from the wreck even to buy the merciful rope that should end all my humor and impecuniosity!" he mutters, over his folded arms and heaving chest. "I have come to this out-of-the-way suburb to end my miserable days, and not so much as one clothes-line have I seen yet. There is the pond, however; I can jump into that, I suppose: but how much more decent were it to make one's quietus under the merry greenwood tree with a cord—"

He stops suddenly, holding his breath; and, almost simultaneously with a sharp, rushing noise in the leaves overhead, something drops upon his shoulder. He grasps it, cautiously feels of it, and, to his unspeakable amazement, discovers that it is a rope apparently fastened to the branches above!

"Wonderful!" he ejaculates, in an awe-stricken whisper. "Providence helps a wretch to die, if not to live. At any other time I should think this very strange, but just now I've got but one thing to do. Here's my rope, here's my neck, and here goes!"

Heedless of everything but his dread intention, he rapidly ties the rope about his throat, and is in the act of throwing forward his whole weight upon it, when there is a sharp jerk of the rope, he is drawn up about three feet in the air, and, before he can collect his thoughts, is as abruptly let down upon his feet again. Simultaneously, a sound almost like suppressed swearing comes very clearly to his ear, and he is conscious of something dimly white in the profound darkness, not far away.

"Sold again : signed, J. Bumstead," exclaims a deep voice "I thought the rope was caught in a crotch ; but 'twasn't. Try't once more."

The astounded hearer feels the rope tugging at his own neck again, and, with a half comprehension of the situation, calls "Stop!" in a suffocating voice.

"Who's there ?" comes from the darkness.

"Jeremy Bentham, late proprietor of first-class American Comic Paper. — Died of Comic Serial. — Want to hang myself," is the jerky reply from the other side.

"Got your own rope, sir?"

"No. One fell down on my shoulders just as I was wishing for it ; but it seems to be too elastic."

"That's the other end 'f *my* rope, sir," rejoins the second voice, as in wrath. "I threw't over the branches and thought it had caught, and instead of that it let me down, sir."

"And drew me up," says Mr. Bentham.

Before another word can be spoken by either, the light of a dark-lantern is flashed upon them. There is Mr. Bumstead, not three yards from Mr. Bentham; each with an end of the same rope about his neck, and the head of the former turbaned with a damp towel.

"Are ye men?" exclaims the deep voice of Mr. Melancthon Schenck from behind the lantern, "and would ye madly incur death before having taken out life-policies in the Boreal?"

"And would my uncle celebrate my return in this style?" cries still another voice from the darkness.

"Who's that spoke just then?" cries the Ritualistic organist.

The answer comes like the note of a trumpet : —

"Edwin Drood!"

At the same instant a great glare of light breaks upon the scene from a bonfire of tar-barrels, ignited at the higher end of the cross-road by young Smalley; and, to the mingled bewilderment and exasperation of Mr. Bumstead, the radiance reveals, as in noonday, Mr. Schenck and his long-lost nephew standing before him; and, coming toward the min festive procession from Gospeller's Gulch, Montgomery Pendragon with Flora on his arm, the Reverend Octavius Simpson escorting Magnolia, Mr. Dibble guarding Mrs. Simpson,

Mr. Clews arm in arm with John McLaughlin, Father Dean and Judge Sweeney, Miss Carowthers, and the Smythes.

"Trying to hang yourselves!" exclaims Mr. Dibble, as the throng gathers curiously around the two gentlemen of the rope.

"And my old friend Bentham, too!" cries the Gospeller.

"How perfectly ridiculous!" warbles Flora.

Staring majestically from one face to the other, and from thence toward the illuminating bonfire, Mr. Bumstead, quite unconscious of the picturesque effect of the towel on his head, deliberately draws an antique black bottle from his pocket, moistens his lips therewith, passes it to the Comic Paper man, and eats a clove.

"What is the meaning of this general intoxication?" he then asks, quite severely. "Why does this mass-meeting, greatly under the influence of inferior liquor as it plainly is, intrude thus upon the last hours of a Ritualistic gentleman and a humorous publisher?"

"Because, Uncle Jack," returns Edwin Drood, holding his hands curiously behind him as he speaks, "this is a night of general rejoicing in Bumsteadville, in honor of my reappearance; and, directed by your landlord, Mr. Smythe, we have come out to make you join in our cheer. We are all heartily sorry for the great anguish you have endured in consequence of my unexplained absence. Let me tell you how it was, as I have already told all our friends here. You

know where you placed me while you were in your clove-
trance, and I was so unbecomingly asleep, on Christmas
night. Well, I was discovered there, in less than three
hours thereafter, by John McLaughlin, who carried me to
his own house, and there managed to awaken me. Recovering my senses, I was disgusted with myself, ashamed of what
had happened, and anxious to leave Bumsteadville. I swore
' Old Mortality ' to secrecy —— "

" — Which I have observed," explains McLaughlin, nodding.

" — And started immediately for Egypt, in Illinois," continues Mr. Drood. " There I went into railroading ; am engaged to a nice little girl there ; and came back two days
ago to explain myself all around. Returning here, I saw
John McLaughlin first, who told me that a certain Mr.
Clews was here to unravel the Mystery about me, and persuaded me to let Mr. Clews work you into another visit to
the cellar in the Pauper Burial Ground, and there appear to
you as my own ghost, before finally revealing myself as I
now do."

The glassy eyes of the Ritualistic organist are fixed upon
him in a most uncomfortable manner, but no comment
comes.

"And I, Mr. Bumstead," says the old lawyer, "must
apologize to you for having indulged a wrong suspicion.
Possibly you were rather rash in charging everybody else
with assassination and larceny, and offering to marry my

ward upon the strength of her dislike to you : but we'll say
no more of those things now. Miss Potts has consented
to become Mrs. Pendragon ; Miss Pendragon is the betrothed
of Rev. Mr. Simpson. —"

"— Miss Carowthers honors me with a matrimonial preference," interpolates Judge Sweeney, gallantly bowing to that
spinster. —

"— Breachy Mr. Blodgett !" sighs the lady to herself. —

"— And three weddings will help us to forget everything
but that which is bright and pleasant," concludes the lawyer.

Next steps to the front Mr. Tracey Clews, with his surprising head of hair, and archly remarks :

"I believe you take me for a literary man, Mr. Bumstead."

"What is that to me, sir ? *I've* no money to lend," returns the organist, with marked uneasiness.

"To tell you the truth," proceeds the author of "The
Amateur Detective," — "to tell you the whole truth, I have
been playing the detective with you by order of Mr. Dibble,
and hope you will excuse my practice upon you."

"He is my clerk," explains Mr. Dibble.

Whereupon Mr. Tracey Clews dexterously whips off his
brush of red hair, and stands revealed as Mr. Bladams.*

Merely waiting to granulate one more clove, Mr. Bum-

---

* In the original, the conversation of *Mr. Grewgious* and *Rosa*, in Chapter XX.,
concerning the mysteriously absent *Bazzard*, the old lawyer's clerk, justifies this
identity in the Adaptation.

stead settles the rope about his neck anew, squints around under the wet towel in a curiously ghastly manner, and thus addresses the meeting : —

"Ladies and gen'le'men — I've listened to y'r impudence with patience, and on any other 'casion would be happy to see y'all safe home. At present, however, Mr. Bentham and I desire to be left alone, if 'ts all th' same t' you. You can come for the bodies in th' morning."

"Bentham! Bentham!" calls the Gospeller, "I can't see you acting in that way, old friend. Come home with me to-night, and we'll talk of starting a Religious Weekly together. That's your only successful American Comic Paper."

"By Jove! so it is!" bawls Jeremy Bentham, like one possessed. "I never thought of that before! I'm with you, my boy." And, hastily slipping the rope from his neck, he hurries to his friend's side.

"And you, Uncle Jack — look at this!" exclaims Mr. E. Drood, bringing from behind his back and presenting to the melancholy organist a thing that looks, at first glance, like an incredibly slim little black girl, headless, with no waist at all, and balanced on one leg.

Mr. Bumstead reaches for it mechanically; a look of intelligence comes into his glassy eyes; then they fairly flame.

"Allie!" he cries, dancing ecstatically.

It is the Umbrella — old familiar bone-handle, brass fer-rule — in a bran-new dress of alpaca!

All gaze at him with unspeakable emotion, as, with the rope cast from him, he pats his dear old friend, opens her half way, shuts her again, and the while smiles with ineffable tenderness.

Suddenly a shriek — the voice of Flora — breaks the si-lence : —

"It rains! — oh, my complexion!"

"Rains?" thunders the regenerated Bumstead, in a tone of inconceivable triumph. "So it does. Now then, Allie, do your duty!" and with a softly wooing, hospitable air, he opens the umbrella and holds it high over his head.

By a common instinct they all swarm in upon him, cram-ing their heads far over each other's shoulders to secure a share of the Providential shelter. The glare of the great bonfire falls upon the scene; the rain pours down in tor-rents : they crowd in upon him on all sides, until what was once a stately Ritualistic man resembles some tremendous monster with seventeen wriggling bodies, thirty-four legs, and an alpaca canopy above all!

THE END.